A CHATTO & WINDUS PAPERBACK
CWP 29

THE CAPTIVE

PART TWO

Marcel Proust's continuous novel *À la Recherche du Temps Perdu* (REMEMBRANCE OF THINGS PAST) was originally published in eight parts, the titles and dates of which were: I. *Du Coté de Chez Swann* (1913); II. *À l'Ombre des Jeunes Filles en Fleurs* (1918), awarded the Prix Goncourt in 1919; III. *Le Coté de Guermantes I* (1920); IV. *Le Coté de Guermantes II, Sodome et Gomorrhe I* (1921); V. *Sodome et Gomorrhe II* (1922); VI. *La Prisonnière* (1923); VII. *Albertine Disparue* (1925); VIII. *Le Temps Retrouvé* (1927).

Du Coté de Chez Swann has been published in English as SWANN'S WAY: *À l'Ombre des Jeunes Filles en Fleurs* as WITHIN A BUDDING GROVE: *Le Coté de Guermantes* as THE GUERMANTES WAY: *Sodome et Gomorrhe* as CITIES OF THE PLAIN: *La Prisonnière* as THE CAPTIVE: *Albertine Disparue* as THE SWEET CHEAT GONE: and *Le Temps Retrouvé* as TIME REGAINED. The first seven parts were translated by C. K. Scott Moncrieff; the eighth by Stephen Hudson.

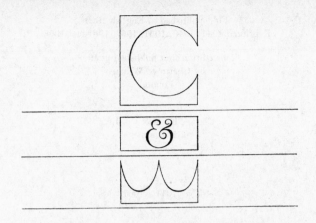

THE CAPTIVE

PART TWO

MARCEL PROUST

Translated by
C. K. Scott Moncrieff

CHATTO & WINDUS

LONDON

First published in English 1929
Reprinted 1941, 1949, 1951, 1957, 1961 and 1968

This edition first published in 1968
by Chatto & Windus
London

*

Clarke, Irwin & Co. Ltd.
Toronto

SBN   7011   1067   8

The drawing on the cover is from
an etching by Philippe Jullian

Printed in Great Britain by R. & R. Clark, Ltd., Edinburgh

CONTENTS

*

Part 2

THE CAPTIVE

CHAPTER II (*continued*)

The Verdurins quarrel with M. de Charlus

BRICHOT'S coarse pleasantries, in the early days of his friendship with the Baron, had given place, as soon as it was a question, not of uttering commonplaces, but of understanding, to an awkward feeling which concealed a certain merriment. He reassured himself by recalling pages of Plato, lines of Virgil, because, being mentally as well as physically blind, he did not understand that in those days to fall in love with a young man was like, in our day (Socrates's jokes reveal this more clearly than Plato's theories), keeping a dancing girl before one marries and settles down. M. de Charlus himself would not have understood, he who confused his mania with friendship, which does not resemble it in the least, and the athletes of Praxiteles with obliging boxers. He refused to see that for the last nineteen hundred years (" a pious courtier under a pious prince would have been an atheist under an atheist prince," as La Bruyère reminds us) all conventional homosexuality—that of Plato's young friends as well as that of Virgil's shepherds—has disappeared, that what survives and increases is only the involuntary, the neurotic kind, which we conceal from other people and disguise to ourself. And M. de Charlus would have been wrong in not denying frankly the pagan genealogy. In exchange for a little plastic beauty, how vast the moral superiority! The shepherd in Theocritus who sighs for love of a boy, later on will have no reason to be less hard of heart, less dull of wit than the other shepherd whose flute sounds for Amaryllis. For the former is not suffering from a malady, he is conforming to the customs of his time. It is the homosexuality that survives in spite of obstacles, a thing of scorn and loathing, that is the only true form, the only form that can be found conjoined in a person with an enhancement of his moral qualities. We are appalled at the apparently close relation between these and our bodily attributes, when we think of the slight dislocation of a purely physical taste, the slight blemish in one of the senses, which explain why the world of poets and musicians, so firmly barred against the Duc de Guermantes, opens its portals to M. de Charlus. That the latter should shew taste in the furnishing of his home, which is that of an eclectic housewife, need not surprise us; but the narrow loophole that opens upon Beethoven and Veronese! This does not exempt the sane from a feeling of alarm when a madman who has composed a sublime poem, after explaining to them in the most logical fashion that he has been shut up by mistake, through his wife's machinations, imploring them to intercede for him with the governor of the asylum, complaining of the promiscuous company that is forced upon him, concludes as follows: "You see that man who is waiting to speak to me on the lawn, whom I am obliged to put up with; he thinks that he is Jesus Christ. That alone will shew you the sort of lunatics that I have to live among; he cannot be Christ, for I am Christ myself!" A moment earlier, you were on the point of going to assure the governor that a mistake had been made. At this final speech, even if you bear in mind the admirable poem at which this same man is working every day, you shrink from him, as Mme. de Surgis's sons shrank from M. de

Charlus, not that he would have done them any harm, but because of his ceaseless invitations, the ultimate purpose of which was to pinch their chins. The poet is to be pitied, who must, with no Virgil to guide him, pass through the circles of an inferno of sulphur and brimstone, to cast himself into the fire that falls from heaven, in order to rescue a few of the inhabitants of Sodom! No charm in his work; the same severity in his life as in those of the unfrocked priests who follow the strictest rule of celibacy so that no one may be able to ascribe to anything but loss of faith their discarding of the cassock.

Making a pretence of not seeing the seedy individual who was following in his wake (whenever the Baron ventured into the Boulevards or crossed the waiting-room in Saint-Lazare station, these followers might be counted by the dozen who, in the hope of " touching him for a dollar," never let him out of their sight), and afraid at the same time that the other might have the audacity to accost him, the Baron had devoutly lowered his darkened eyelids which, in contrast to his rice-powdered cheeks, gave him the appearance of a Grand Inquisitor painted by El Greco. But this priestly expression caused alarm, and he looked like an unfrocked **priest,** various compromises to which he had been driven by the need to apologise for his taste and to keep it secret having had the effect of bringing to the surface of his face precisely what the Baron sought to conceal, a debauched life indicated by moral decay. This last, indeed, whatever be its cause, is easily detected, for it is never slow in taking bodily form and proliferates upon a face, especially on the cheeks and round the eyes, as physically as the ochreous yellows accumulate there in a case of jaundice or repulsive reds in a case of skin disease. Nor was it merely in the cheeks, or rather the chaps of this painted face, in the mammiferous chest, the aggressive rump of this body allowed to deteriorate and invaded by obesity, upon which there now floated iridescent as a film of oil, the vice at one time so jealously confined by M. de Charlus in the most secret chamber of his heart. Now it overflowed in all his speech.

"So this is how you prowl the streets at night, Brichot, with a good-looking young man," he said as he joined us, while the disappointed ruffian made off. "A fine example. We must tell your young pupils at the Sorbonne that this is how you behave. But, I must say, the society of youth seems to be good for you, Monsieur le Professeur, you are as fresh as a rosebud. I have interrupted you, you looked as though you were enjoying yourselves like a pair of giddy girls, and had no need of an old Granny Killjoy like myself. I shan't take it to the confessional, since you are almost at your destination." The Baron's mood was all the more blithe since he knew nothing whatever about the scene that afternoon, Jupien having decided that it was better to protect his niece against a repetition of the onslaught than to inform M. de Charlus. And so the Baron was still looking forward to the marriage, and delighting in the thought of it. One would suppose that it is a consolation to these great solitaries to give their tragic celibacy the relief of a fictitious fatherhood. "But, upon my word, Brichot," he went on, turning with a laugh to gaze at us, "I feel quite awkward when I see you in such gallant company. You were like a pair of lovers. Going along arm in arm, I say, Brichot, you do go the pace!" Ought one to ascribe this speech to the senility of a particular state of mind, less capable than in the past of controlling its reflexes, which in moments of automatism lets out a secret that has been so carefully hidden for forty years? Or rather to that contempt for plebeian opinion which all the Guermantes felt in their hearts, and of which M. de Charlus's brother, the Duke, was displaying a variant form when, regardless of the fact that my mother could see him, he used to shave standing by his bedroom window in his unbuttoned nightshirt. Had M. de Charlus contracted, during the roasting journeys between Doncières and Douville, the dangerous habit of making himself at ease, and, just as he would push back his straw hat in order to cool his huge forehead, of unfastening—at first, for a few moments only—the mask that for too long had been rigorously imposed upon his true face? His conjugal attitude towards Morel might well have astonished anyone who had observed it in its full extent. But M. de Charlus had reached the stage when the monotony of the pleasures that his vice has to offer became wearying. He had sought instinctively for novel displays, and, growing tired of the strangers whom he picked up, had passed to the opposite pole, to what he used to imagine that he would always loathe, the imitation of family life, or of fatherhood. Sometimes even this did not suffice him, he required novelty, and would go and spend the night with a woman, just as a normal man may, once in his life, have wished to go to bed with a boy, from a curiosity similar though inverse, and in either case equally unhealthy. The Baron's existence as one of the "faithful," living, for Charlie's sake, entirely among the little clan, had had, in stultifying the efforts that he had been making for years to keep up lying appearances, the same influence that a voyage of exploration or residence in the colonies has upon certain Europeans who discard the ruling principles by which they were guided at home. And yet, the internal revolution of a mind, ignorant at first of the anomaly contained in its body, then appalled at it after the discovery, and finally growing so used to it as to fail to perceive that it is not safe to confess to other people what the sinner has come in time to confess without shame to himself, had been even more effective in liberating M. de Charlus from the last vestiges of social constraint than the time that he spent at the Verdurins'. No banishment, indeed, to the South Pole, or to the summit of Mont Blanc, can separate us so entirely from our fellow creatures as a prolonged residence in the seclusion of a secret vice, that is to say of a state of mind that is different from theirs. A vice (so M. de Charlus used at one time to style it) to which the Baron now gave the genial aspect of a mere failing, extremely common, attractive on the whole and almost amusing, like laziness, absent-mindedness or greed. Conscious of the curiosity that his own striking personality aroused, M. de Charlus derived a certain pleasure from satisfying, whetting, sustaining it. Just as a Jewish journalist will come forward day after day as the champion of Catholicism, not, probably, with any hope of being taken seriously, but simply in order not to disappoint the good-natured amusement of his readers, M. de Charlus would genially denounce evil habits among the little clan, as he would have mimicked a person speaking English or imitated Mounet-Sully, without waiting to be asked, so as to pay his scot with a good grace, by displaying an amateur talent in society; so that M. de Charlus now threatened Brichot that he would report to the Sorbonne that he was in the habit of walking about with young men, exactly as the circumcised scribe keeps referring in and out of season to the "Eldest Daughter of the Church" and the "Sacred Heart of Jesus," that is to say without the least trace of hypocrisy, but with a distinctly histrionic effect. It was not only the change in the words themselves, so different from those that he allowed himself to use in the past, that seemed to require some explanation, there was also the change that had occurred in his intonations, his gestures, all of which now singularly resembled the type M. de Charlus used most fiercely to castigate; he would now utter unconsciously almost the same little cries (unconscious in him, and all the more deep-rooted) as are uttered consciously by the inverts who refer to one another as "she"; as though this deliberate "camping", against which M. de Charlus had for so long set his face, were after all merely a brilliant and faithful imitation of the manner that men of the Charlus type, whatever they may say, are compelled to adopt when they have reached a certain stage in their malady, just as sufferers from general paralysis or locomotor ataxia inevitably end by displaying certain symptoms. As a matter of fact—and this is what this purely unconscious "camping" revealed—the difference between the stern Charlus, dressed all in black, with his stiffly brushed hair, whom I had known, and the painted young men, loaded with rings, was no more than the purely imaginary difference that exists between an excited person who talks fast, keeps moving all the time, and a neurotic who talks slowly, preserves a perpetual phlegm, but is tainted with the same neurasthenia in the eyes of the physician who knows that each of the two is devoured by the same anguish and marred by the same defects. At the same time one could tell that M. de Charlus had aged from wholly different signs, such as the extraordinary frequency in his conversation of certain expressions that had taken root in it and used now to crop up at every moment (for instance: "the chain of circumstances") upon which the Baron's speech leaned in sentence after sentence as upon a necessary prop. "Is Charlie here yet?" Brichot asked M. de Charlus as we came in sight of the door. "Oh, I don't know," said the Baron, raising his arms and half-shutting his eyes with the air of a person who does not wish anyone to accuse him of being indiscreet, all the more so as he had probably been reproached by Morel for things which he had said and which the other, as timorous as he was vain, and as ready to deny M. de Charlus as he was to boast of his friendship, had considered serious albeit they were quite unimportant. "You know, he never tells me what he's going to do." If the conversations of two people bound by a tie of intimacy are full of falsehood, this occurs no less spontaneously in the conversations that a third person holds with a lover on the subject of the person with whom the latter is in love, whatever be the sex of that person.

"Have you seen him lately?" I asked M. de Charlus, with the object of seeming at once not to be afraid of mentioning Morel to him and not to believe that they were actually living together. "He came in, as it happened, for five minutes this morning while I was still half asleep, and sat down on the side of my bed, as though he

wanted to ravish me." I guessed at once that M. de
Charlus had seen Charlie within the last hour, for if we
ask a woman when she last saw the man whom we know
to be—and whom she may perhaps suppose that we
suspect of being—her lover, if she has just taken tea with
him, she replies: "I saw him for an instant before lun-
cheon." Between these two incidents the only difference
is that one is false and the other true, but both are
equally innocent, or, if you prefer it, equally culpable.
And so we should be unable to understand why the mistress (in this case, M. de Charlus) always chooses the
false version, did we not know that such replies are determined, unknown to the person who utters them, by a
number of factors which appear so out of proportion to
the triviality of the incident that we do not take the
trouble to consider them. But to a physicist the space
occupied by the tiniest ball of pith is explained by the
harmony of action, the conflict or equilibrium, of laws of
attraction or repulsion which govern far greater worlds.
Just as many different laws acting in opposite directions
dictate the more general responses with regard to the
innocence, the "platonism," or on the contrary the carnal
reality of the relations that one has with the person whom
one says one saw in the morning when one has seen him
or her in the evening. Here we need merely record,
without pausing to consider them, the desire to appear
natural and fearless, the instinctive impulse to conceal a
secret assignation, a blend of modesty and ostentation,
the need to confess what one finds so delightful and to
shew that one is loved, a divination of what the other
person knows or guesses—but does not say—a divination
which, exceeding or falling short of the other person's,

makes one now exaggerate, now under-estimate it, the spontaneous longing to play with fire and the determination to rescue something from the blaze. At the same time, speaking generally, let us say that M. de Charlus, notwithstanding the aggravation of his malady which perpetually urged him to reveal, to insinuate, sometimes boldly to invent compromising details, did intend, during this period in his life, to make it known that Charlie was not a man of the same sort as himself and that they were friends and nothing more. This did not prevent him (even though it may quite possibly have been true) from contradicting himself at times (as with regard to the hour at which they had last met), whether he forgot himself at such moments and told the truth, or invented a lie, boastingly or from a sentimental affectation or because he thought it amusing to baffle his questioner. "You know that he is to me," the Baron went on, "the best of comrades, for whom I have the greatest affection, as I am certain" (was he uncertain of it, then, that he felt the need to say that he was certain?) "he has for me, but there is nothing at all between us, nothing of that sort, you understand, nothing of that sort," said the Baron, as naturally as though he had been speaking of a woman. "Yes, he came in this morning to pull me out of bed. Though he knows that I hate anybody to see me in bed. You don't mind? Oh, it's horrible, it's so disturbing, one looks so perfectly hideous, of course I'm no longer five-and-twenty, they won't choose me to be Queen of the May, still one does like to feel that one is looking one's best."

It is possible that the Baron was in earnest when he spoke of Morel as a good comrade, and that he was being even more truthful than he supposed when he said: "I never know what he's doing; he tells me nothing about his life."

Indeed we may mention (interrupting for a few moments our narrative, which shall be resumed immediately after the closure of this parenthesis which opens at the moment when M. de Charlus, Brichot and myself are arriving at Mme. Verdurin's front door), we may mention that shortly before this evening the Baron had been plunged in grief and stupefaction by a letter which he had opened by mistake and which was addressed to Morel. This letter, which by a repercussion was to cause intense misery to myself also, was written by the actress Léa, notorious for her exclusive interest in women. And yet her letter to Morel (whom M. de Charlus had never suspected of knowing her, even) was written in the most impassioned tone. Its indelicacy prevents us from reproducing it here, but we may mention that Léa addressed him throughout in the feminine gender, with such expressions as: "Go on, you bad woman!" or "Of course you are so, my pretty, you know you are." And in this letter reference was made to various other women who seemed to be no less Morel's friends than Léa's. On the other hand, Morel's sarcasm at the Baron's expense and Léa's at that of an officer who was keeping her, and of whom she said: "He keeps writing me letters begging me to be careful! What do you say to that, my little white puss," revealed to M. de Charlus a state of things no less unsuspected by him than were Morel's peculiar and intimate relations with Léa. What most disturbed the Baron was the word "so." Ignorant at first of its application, he had eventually, at a time already remote in the past, learned that he himself was " so." And now the notion that he had acquired of this word was again put to the challenge. When he had discovered that he was " so," he had supposed this to mean that his tastes, as Saint-Simon says, did not lie in the direction of women. And here was this word " so " applied to Morel with an extension of meaning of which M. de Charlus was unaware, so much so that Morel gave proof, according to this letter, of his being " so " by having the same taste as certain women for other women. From that moment the Baron's jealousy had no longer any reason to confine itself to the men of Morel's acquaintance, but began to extend to the women also. So that the people who were " so " were not merely those that he had supposed to be " so," but a whole and vast section of the inhabitants of the planet, consisting of women as well as of men, loving not merely men but women also, and the Baron, in the face of this novel meaning of a word that was so familiar to him, felt himself tormented by an anxiety of the mind as well as of the heart, born of this twofold mystery which combined an extension of the field of his jealousy with the sudden inadequacy of a definition.

M. de Charlus had never in his life been anything but an amateur. That is to say, incidents of this sort could never be of any use to him. He worked off the painful impression that they might make upon him in violent scenes in which he was a past-master of eloquence, or in crafty intrigues. But to a person endowed with the qualities of a Bergotte, for instance, they might have been of inestimable value. This may indeed explain, to a certain extent (since we have to grope blindfold, but choose, like the lower animals, the herb that is good for us), why men like Bergotte have generally lived in the company of persons who were ordinary, false and malicious. Their beauty is sufficient for the writer's imagination, enhances his generosity, but does not in any way alter the nature of his companion, whose life, situated thousands of feet below the level of his own, her incredible stories, her lies carried farther, and, what is more, in another direction than what might have been expected, appear in occasional flashes. The lie, the perfect lie, about people whom we know, about the relations that we have had with them, about our motive for some action, a motive which we express in totally different terms, the lie as to what we are, whom we love, what we feel with regard to the person who loves us and believes that she has fashioned us in her own image because she keeps on kissing us morning, noon and night, that lie is one of the only things in the world that can open a window for us upon what is novel, unknown, that can awaken in us sleeping senses to the contemplation of universes that otherwise we should never have known. We are bound to say, in so far as M. de Charlus is concerned, that, if he was stupefied to learn with regard to Morel a certain number of things which the latter had carefully concealed from him, he was not justified in concluding from this that it was a mistake to associate too closely with the lower orders. We shall indeed see, in the concluding section of this work, M. de Charlus himself engaged in doing things which would have stupefied the members of his family and his friends far more than he could possibly have been stupefied by the revelations of Léa. (The revelation that he had found most painful had been that of a tour which Morel had made with Léa, whereas at the time he had assured M. de Charlus that he was studying music in Germany. He had found support for this falsehood in obliging friends in Germany to whom he had sent his letters, to be forwarded from there to M. de Charlus, who, as it happened, was so positive that Morel was there that he had not even looked at the postmark.) But it is time to rejoin the Baron as he advances with Brichot and myself towards the Verdurins' door.

"And what," he went on, turning to myself, "has become of your young Hebrew friend, whom we met at Douville? It occurred to me that, if you liked, one might perhaps invite him to the house one evening." For M. de Charlus, who did not shrink from employing a private detective to spy upon every word and action of Morel, for all the world like a husband or a lover, had not ceased to pay attention to other young men. The vigilance which he made one of his old servants maintain, through an agency, upon Morel, was so indiscreet that his footmen thought they were being watched, and one of the housemaids could not endure the suspense, never ventured into the street, always expecting to find a policeman at her heels. "She can do whatever she likes! It would be a waste of time and money to follow her! As if her goings on mattered to us!" the old servant ironically exclaimed, for he was so passionately devoted to his master that, albeit he in no way shared the Baron's tastes, he had come in time, with such ardour did he employ himself in their service, to speak of them as though they were his own. "He is the very best of good fellows," M. de Charlus would say of this old servant, for we never appreciate anyone so much as those who combine with

other great virtues that of placing themselves uncon-
ditionally at the disposal of our vices. It was moreover
of men alone that M. de Charlus was capable of feeling
any jealousy so far as Morel was concerned. Women
inspired in him no jealousy whatever. This is indeed an
almost universal rule with the Charlus type. The love
of the man with whom they are in love for a woman is
something different, which occurs in another animal species (a lion does not interfere with tigers); does not distress them; if anything, reassures them. Sometimes, it
is true, in the case of those who exalt their inversion to
the level of a priesthood, this love creates disgust. These
men resent their friends' having succumbed to it, not as
a betrayal but as a lapse from virtue. A Charlus, of a
different variety from the Baron, would have been as
indignant at the discovery of Morel's relations with a
woman as upon reading in a newspaper that he, the
interpreter of Bach and Händel, was going to play Puc-
cini. It is, by the way, for this reason that the young
men who, with an eye to their own personal advantage,
condescend to the love of men like Charlus assure them
that women inspire them only with disgust, just as they
would tell a doctor that they never touch alcohol, and
care only for spring water. But M. de Charlus, in this
respect, departed to some extent from the general rule.
Since he admired everything about Morel, the latter's
successes with women caused him no annoyance, gave him
the same joy as his successes on the platform, or at
écarté. "But do you know, my dear fellow, he has
women," he would say, with an air of disclosure, of
scandal, possibly of envy, above all of admiration. "He
is extraordinary," he would continue; "Everywhere, the

most famous whores can look at nobody but him. They stare at him everywhere, whether it's on the underground or in the theatre. It's becoming a nuisance! I can't go out with him to a restaurant without the waiter bringing him notes from at least three women. And always pretty women too. Not that there's anything surprising in that. I was watching him yesterday, I can quite understand it, he has become so beautiful, he looks just like a Bronzino, he is really marvellous." But M. de Charlus liked to shew that he was in love with Morel, to persuade other people, possibly to persuade himself, that Morel was in love with him. He applied to the purpose of having Morel always with him (notwithstanding the harm that the young fellow might do to the Baron's social position) a sort of self-esteem. For (and this is frequent among men of good position, who are snobs, and, in their vanity, sever all their social ties in order to be seen everywhere with a mistress, a person of doubtful or a lady of tarnished reputation, whom nobody will invite, and with whom nevertheless it seems to them flattering to be associated) he had arrived at that stage at which self-esteem devotes all its energy to destroying the goals to which it has attained, whether because, under the influence of love, a man finds a prestige which he is alone in perceiving in ostentatious relations with the beloved object, or because, by the waning of social ambitions that have been gratified, and the rising of a tide of subsidiary curiosities all the more absorbing the more platonic they are, the latter have not only reached but have passed the level at which the former found it difficult to remain.

As for young men in general, M. de Charlus found that to his fondness for them Morel's existence was not an obstacle, and that indeed his brilliant reputation as a violinist or his growing fame as a composer and journalist might in certain instances prove an attraction. Did anyone introduce to the Baron a young composer of an agreeable type, it was in Morel's talents that he sought an opportunity of doing the stranger a favour. "You must," he would tell him, "bring me some of your work so that Morel can play it at a concert or on tour. There is hardly any decent music written, now, for the violin. It is a godsend to find anything new. And abroad they appreciate that sort of thing enormously. Even in the provinces there are little musical societies where they love music with a fervour and intelligence that are quite admirable." Without any greater sincerity (for all this could serve only as a bait and it was seldom that Morel condescended to fulfil these promises), Bloch having confessed that he was something of a poet (when he was "in the mood", he had added with the sarcastic laugh with which he would accompany a platitude, when he could think of nothing original), M. de Charlus said to me: "You must tell your young Israelite, since he writes verses, that he must really bring me some for Morel. For a composer, that is always the stumbling block, to find something decent to set to music. One might even consider a libretto. It would not be without interest, and would acquire a certain value from the distinction of the poet, from my patronage, from a whole chain of auxiliary circumstances, among which Morel's talent would take the chief place, for he is composing a lot just now, and writing too, and very pleasantly, I must talk to you about it. As for his talent as a performer (there, as you know, he is already a past-master), you shall see this evening how well the lad plays Vinteuil's music; he over-whelms me; at his age, to have such an understanding while he is still such a boy, such a kid! Oh, this evening is only to be a little rehearsal. The big affair is to come off in two or three days. But it will be much more dis-tinguished this evening. And so we are delighted that you have come," he went on, employing the plural pro-noun doubtless because a King says: "It is our wish." "The programme is so magnificent that I have advised Mme. Verdurin to give two parties. One in a few days' time, at which she will have all her own friends, the other to-night at which the hostess is, to use a legal expression, 'disseized.' It is I who have issued the invitations, and I have collected a few people from another sphere, who may be useful to Charlie, and whom it will be nice for the Verdurins to meet. Don't you agree, it is all very well to have the finest music played by the greatest artists, the effect of the performance remains muffled in cotton-wool, if the audience is composed of the milliner from across the way and the grocer from round the corner. You know what I think of the intellectual level of people in society, still they can play certain quite important parts, among others that which in public events devolves upon the press, and which is that of being an organ of publicity. You know what I mean; I have for instance invited my sister-in-law Oriane; it is not certain that she will come, but it is on the other hand certain that, if she does come, she will understand absolutely nothing. But one does not ask her to understand, which is beyond her capacity, but to talk, a task which is admirably suited to her, and which she never fails to perform. What is the result? To-morrow as ever is, instead of the silence of

the milliner and the grocer, an animated conversation at
the Mortemarts' with Oriane telling everyone that she
has heard the most marvellous music, that a certain
Morel, and so forth; unspeakable rage of the people not
invited, who will say: 'Palamède thought, no doubt, that
we were unworthy; anyhow, who are these people who
were giving the party?' a counterblast quite as useful as
Oriane's praises, because Morel's name keeps cropping up
all the time and is finally engraved in the memory like a
lesson that one has read over a dozen times. All this
forms a chain of circumstances which may be of value
to the artist, to the hostess, may serve as a sort of megaphone for a performance which will thus be made audible
to a remote public. Really, it is worth the trouble; you
shall see what progress Charlie has made. And what is
more, we have discovered a new talent in him, my dear
fellow, he writes like an angel. Like an angel, I tell
you." M. de Charlus omitted to say that for some time
past he had been employing Morel, like those great
noblemen of the seventeenth century who scorned to sign
and even to write their own slanderous attacks, to compose certain vilely calumnious little paragraphs at the
expense of Comtesse Molé. Their insolence apparent
even to those who merely glanced at them, how much
more cruel were they to the young woman herself, who
found in them, so skilfully introduced that nobody but
herself saw the point, certain passages from her own correspondence, textually quoted, but interpreted in a sense
which made them as deadly as the cruellest revenge.
They killed the lady. But there is edited every day in
Paris, Balzac would tell us, a sort of spoken newspaper,
more terrible than its printed rivals. We shall see later

on that this verbal press reduced to nothing the power of a Charlus who had fallen out of fashion, and exalted far above him a Morel who was not worth the millionth part of his former patron. Is this intellectual fashion really so simple, and does it sincerely believe in the nullity of a Charlus of genius, in the incontestable authority of a crass Morel? The Baron was not so innocent in his implacable vengeance. Whence, no doubt, that bitter venom on his tongue, the spreading of which seemed to dye his cheeks with jaundice when he was in a rage. "You who knew Bergotte," M. de Charlus went on, "I thought at one time that you might, perhaps, by refreshing his memory with regard to the youngster's writings, collaborate in short with myself, help me to assist a two-fold talent, that of a musician and a writer, which may one day acquire the prestige of that of Berlioz. As you know, the Illustrious have often other things to think about, they are smothered in flattery, they take little interest except in themselves. But Bergotte, who was genuinely unpretentious and obliging, promised me that he would get into the *Gaulois,* or some such paper, those little articles, a blend of the humourist and the musician, which he really does quite charmingly now, and I am really very glad that Charlie should combine with his violin this little stroke of Ingres's pen. I know that I am prone to exaggeration, when he is concerned, like all the old fairy godmothers of the Conservatoire. What, my dear fellow, didn't you know that? You have never observed my little weakness. I pace up and down for hours on end outside the examination hall. I'm as happy as a queen. As for Charlie's prose, Bergotte assured me that it was really very good indeed."

M. de Charlus, who had long been acquainted with Bergotte through Swann, had indeed gone to see him a few days before his death, to ask him to find an opening for Morel in some newspaper for a sort of commentary, half humorous, upon the music of the day. In doing so, M. de Charlus had felt some remorse, for, himself a great admirer of Bergotte, he was conscious that he never went to see him for his own sake, but in order, thanks to the respect, partly intellectual, partly social, that Bergotte felt for him, to be able to do a great service to Morel, or to some other of his friends. That he no longer made use of people in society for any other purpose did not shock M. de Charlus, but to treat Bergotte thus had appeared to him more offensive, for he felt that Bergotte had not the calculating nature of people in society, and deserved better treatment. Only, his was a busy life, and he could never find time for anything except when he was greatly interested in something, when, for instance, it affected Morel. What was more, as he was himself extremely intelligent, the conversation of an intelligent man left him comparatively cold, especially that of Bergotte who was too much the man of letters for his liking and belonged to another clan, did not share his point of view. As for Bergotte, he had observed the calculated motive of M. de Charlus's visits, but had felt no resentment, for he had been incapable, throughout his life, of any consecutive generosity, but anxious to give pleasure, broadminded, insensitive to the pleasure of administering a rebuke. As for M. de Charlus's vice, he had never partaken of it to the smallest extent, but had found in it rather an element of colour in the person affected, *fas et nefas*, for an artist, consisting not in moral examples but in memories of Plato or of Sodom. "But you, fair youth, we never see you at Quai Conti. You don't abuse their hospitality!" I explained that I went out as a rule with my cousin. "Do you hear that! He goes out with his cousin! What a most particularly pure young man!" said M. de Charlus to Brichot. Then, turning again to myself: "But we are not asking you to give an account of your life, my boy. You are free to do anything that amuses you. We merely regret that we have no share in it. Besides, you shew very good taste, your cousin is charming, ask Brichot, she quite turned his head at Douville. We shall regret her absence this evening. But you did just as well, perhaps, not to bring her with you. Vinteuil's music is delightful. But I have heard that we are to meet the composer's daughter and her friend, who have a terrible reputation. That sort of thing is always awkward for a girl. They are sure to be there, unless the ladies have been detained in the country, for they were to have been present without fail all afternoon at a rehearsal which Mme. Verdurin was giving to-day, to which she had invited only the bores, her family, the people whom she could not very well have this evening. But a moment ago, before dinner, Charlie told us that the sisters Vinteuil, as we call them, for whom they were all waiting, never came." Notwithstanding the intense pain that I had felt at the sudden association with its effect, of which alone I had been aware, of the cause, at length discovered, of Albertine's anxiety to be there that afternoon, the presence publicly announced (but of which I had been ignorant) of Mlle. Vinteuil and her friend, my mind was still sufficiently detached to remark that M. de Charlus, who had told us, a few minutes earlier, that he had not seen Charlie since the morning, was now brazenly admitting that he had seen him before dinner. My pain became visible. "Why, what is the matter with you?" said the Baron, "You are quite green; come, let us go in, you will catch cold, you don't look at all well." It was not any doubt as to Albertine's virtue that M. de Charlus's words had awakened in me. Many other doubts had penetrated my mind already; at each fresh doubt we feel that the measure is heaped full, that we cannot cope with it, then we manage to find room for it all the same, and once it is introduced into our vital essence it enters into competition there with so many longings to believe, so many reasons to forget, that we speedily become accustomed to it, and end by ceasing to pay it any attention. There remains only, like a partly healed pain, the menace of possible suffering, which, the counterpart of desire, a feeling of the same order, and like it become the centre of our thoughts, radiates through them to an infinite circumference a wistful melancholy, as desire radiates pleasures whose origin we fail to perceive, wherever anything may suggest the idea of the person with whom we are in love. But pain revives as soon as a fresh doubt enters our mind complete; even if we assure ourself almost immediately: "I shall deal with this, there must be some method by which I need not suffer, it cannot be true," nevertheless there has been a first moment in which we suffered as though we believed it. If we had merely members, such as legs and arms, life would be endurable; unfortunately we carry inside us that little organ which we call the heart, which is subject to certain maladies in the course of which it is infinitely impressionable by everything that concerns the life of a certain person, so that a lie—that most harmless of things, in the midst of which we live so unconcernedly, if the lie be told by ourself or by strangers—coming from that person, causes the little heart, which surgeons ought really to be able to excise from us, intolerable anguish. Let us not speak of the brain, for our mind may go on reasoning interminably in the course of this anguish, it does no more to mitigate it than by taking thought can we soothe an aching tooth. It is true that this person is to blame for having lied to us, for she had sworn to us that she would always tell us the truth. But we know from our own shortcomings, towards other people, how little an oath is worth. And we have deliberately believed them when they came from her, the very person to whose interest it has always been to lie to us, and whom, more-over, we did not select for her virtues. It is true that, later on, she would almost cease to have any need to lie to us—at the moment when our heart will have grown indifferent to her falsehood—because then we shall not feel any interest in her life. We know this, and, notwith-standing, we deliberately sacrifice our own life, either by killing ourself for her sake, or by letting ourself be sen-tenced to death for having murdered her, or simply by spending, in the course of a few evenings, our whole for-tune upon her, which will oblige us presently to commit suicide because we have not a penny in the world. Be-sides, however calm we may imagine ourself when we are in love, we always have love in our heart in a state of unstable equilibrium. A trifle is sufficient to exalt it to the position of happiness, we radiate happiness, we smother in our affection not her whom we love, but those who have given us merit in her eyes, who have protected her from every evil temptation; we think that our mind is at ease, and a word is sufficient: " Gilberte is not coming," " Mademoiselle Vinteuil is expected," to make all the pre-conceived happiness towards which we were rising collapse, to make the sun hide his face, to open the bag of the winds and let loose the internal tempest which one day we shall be incapable of resisting. That day, the day upon which the heart has become so frail, our friends who respect us are pained that such trifles, that certain persons, can so affect us, can bring us to death's door. But what are they to do? If a poet is dying of septic pneumonia, can one imagine his friends explaining to the pneumococcus that the poet is a man of talent and that it ought to let him recover? My doubt, in so far as it referred to Mlle. Vinteuil, was not entirely novel. But to a certain extent, my jealousy of the afternoon, inspired by Léa and her friends, had abolished it. Once that peril of the Trocadéro was removed, I had felt that I had recaptured for all time complete peace of mind. But what was entirely novel to me was a certain excursion as to which Andrée had told me: " We went to this place and that, we didn't meet any-one," and during which, on the contrary, Mlle. Vinteuil had evidently arranged to meet Albertine at Mme. Verdurin's. At this moment I would gladly have allowed Albertine to go out by herself, to go wherever she might choose, pro-vided that I might lock up Mlle. Vinteuil and her friend somewhere and be certain that Albertine would not meet them. The fact is that jealousy is, as a rule, partial, of intermittent application, whether because it is the painful extension of an anxiety which is provoked now by one person, now by another with whom our mistress may be in love, or because of the exiguity of our thought which is able to realise only what it can represent to itself and leaves everything else in an obscurity which can cause us only a proportionately modified anguish.

Just as we were about to ring the bell we were overtaken by Saniette who informed us that Princess Sherbatoff had died at six o'clock, and added that he had not at first recognised us. "I envisaged you, however, for some time," he told us in a breathless voice. "Is it aught but curious that I should have hesitated?" To say "Is it not curious" would have seemed to him wrong, and he had acquired a familiarity with obsolete forms of speech that was becoming exasperating. "Not but what you are people whom one may acknowledge as friends." His grey complexion seemed to be illuminated by the livid glow of a storm. His breathlessness, which had been noticeable, as recently as last summer, only when M. Verdurin "jumped down his throat," was now continuous. "I understand that an unknown work of Vinteuil is to be performed by excellent artists, and singularly by Morel." "Why singularly?" inquired the Baron who detected a criticism in the adverb. "Our friend Saniette," Brichot made haste to exclaim, acting as interpreter, "is prone to speak, like the excellent scholar that he is, the language of an age in which 'singularly' was equivalent to our 'especially.'"

As we entered the Verdurins' hall, M. de Charlus asked me whether I was engaged upon any work and as I told him that I was not, but that I was greatly interested at the moment in old dinner-services of plate and porcelain, he assured me that I could not see any finer than those that the Verdurins had; that moreover I might have seen them at la Raspelière, since, on the pretext that one's possessions are also one's friends, they were so silly as to cart everything down there with them; it would be less convenient to bring everything out for my benefit on the evening of a party; still, he would tell them to shew me anything that I wished to see. I begged him not to do anything of the sort. M. de Charlus unbuttoned his greatcoat, took off his hat, and I saw that the top of his head had now turned silver in patches. But like a precious shrub which is not only coloured with autumn tints but certain leaves of which are protected by bandages of wadding or incrustations of plaster, M. de Charlus received from these few white hairs at his crest only a further variegation added to those of his face. And yet, even beneath the layers of different expressions, paint and hypocrisy which formed such a bad "make-up," his face continued to hide from almost everyone the secret that it seemed to me to be crying aloud. I was almost put to shame by his eyes in which I was afraid of his surprising me in the act of reading it, as from an open book, by his voice which seemed to me to be repeating it in every tone, with an untiring indecency. But secrets are well kept by such people, for everyone who comes in contact with them is deaf and blind. The people who learned the truth from some one else, from the Verdurins for instance, believed it, but only for so long as they had not met M. de Charlus. His face, so far from spreading, dissipated every scandalous rumour. For we form so extravagant an idea of certain characters that we would be incapable of identifying one of them with the familiar features of a person of our acquaintance. And we find it difficult to believe in such a person's vices, just as we can never believe in the genius of a person with whom we went to the Opera last night.

M. de Charlus was engaged in handing over his great-coat with the instructions of a familiar guest. But the footman to whom he was handing it was a newcomer, and quite young. Now M. de Charlus had by this time begun, as people say, to "lose his bearings" and did not always remember what might and what might not be done. The praiseworthy desire that he had felt at Balbec to shew that certain topics did not alarm him, that he was not afraid to declare with regard to some one or other: "He is a nice-looking boy," to utter, in short, the same words as might have been uttered by somebody who was not like himself, this desire he had now begun to express by saying on the contrary things which nobody could ever have said who was not like him, things upon which his mind was so constantly fixed that he forgot that they do not form part of the habitual preoccupation of people in general. And so, as he gazed at the new footman, he raised his forefinger in the air in a menacing fashion and, thinking that he was making an excellent joke: "You are not to make eyes at me like that, do you hear?" said the Baron, and, turning to Brichot: "He has a quaint little face, that boy, his nose is rather fun," and, completing his joke, or yielding to a desire, he lowered his forefinger horizontally, hesitated for an instant, then, unable to control himself any longer, thrust it irresistibly forwards at the footman and touched the tip of his nose, saying "Pif!" "That's a rum card," the footman said to himself, and inquired of his companions whether it was a joke or what it was. "It is just a way he has," said the butler (who regarded the Baron as slightly

" touched," " a bit balmy "), " but he is one of Madame's friends for whom I have always had the greatest respect, he has a good heart."

" Are you coming back this year to Incarville? " Brichot asked me. " I believe that our hostess has taken la Raspelière again, for all that she has had a crow to pick with her landlords. But that is nothing, it is a cloud that passes," he added in the optimistic tone of the newspapers that say: " Mistakes have been made, it is true, but who does not make mistakes at times? " But I remembered the state of anguish in which I had left Balbec, and felt no desire to return there. I kept putting off to the morrow my plans for Albertine. " Why, of course he is coming back, we need him, he is indispensable to us," declared M. de Charlus with the authoritative and uncomprehending egoism of friendliness.

At this moment M. Verdurin appeared to welcome us. When we expressed our sympathy over Princess Sherbatoff, he said: " Yes, I believe she is rather ill." " No, no, she died at six o'clock," exclaimed Saniette. " Oh, you exaggerate everything," was M. Verdurin's brutal retort, for, since he had not cancelled his party, he preferred the hypothesis of illness, imitating unconsciously the Duc de Guermantes. Saniette, not without fear of catching cold, for the outer door was continually being opened, stood waiting resignedly for some one to take his hat and coat. " What are you hanging about there for, like a whipped dog? " M. Verdurin asked him. " I am waiting until one of the persons who are charged with the cloakroom can take my coat and give me a number." " What is that you say? " demanded M. Verdurin with a stern expression. " ' Charged with the cloakroom? '

Are you going off your head? 'In charge of the cloak-room,' is what we say, if we've got to teach you to speak your own language, like a man who has had a stroke." "Charged with a thing is the correct form," murmured Saniette in a stifled tone; "the abbé Le Batteux. . . ." "You make me tired, you do," cried M. Verdurin in a voice of thunder. "How you do wheeze! Have you been running upstairs to an attic?" The effect of M. Verdurin's rudeness was that the servants in the cloakroom allowed other guests to take precedence of Saniette and, when he tried to hand over his things, replied: "Wait for your turn, Sir, don't be in such a hurry." "There's system for you, competent fellows, that's right, my lads," said M. Verdurin with an approving smile, in order to encourage them in their tendency to keep Saniette waiting till the end. "Come along," he said to us, "the creature wants us all to catch our death hanging about in his be-loved draught. Come and get warm in the drawing-room. 'Charged with the cloakroom,' indeed, what an idiot!" "He is inclined to be a little precious, but he's not a bad fellow," said Brichot. "I never said that he was a bad fellow, I said that he was an idiot," was M. Verdurin's harsh retort.

Meanwhile Mme. Verdurin was busily engaged with Cottard and Ski. Morel had just declined (because M. de Charlus could not be present) an invitation from some friends of hers to whom she had promised the services of the violinist. The reason for Morel's refusal to per-form at the party which the Verdurins' friends were giv-ing, a reason which we shall presently see reinforced by others of a far more serious kind, might have found its justification in a habit common to the leisured classes in general but specially distinctive of the little nucleus. To be sure, if Mme. Verdurin intercepted between a newcomer and one of the faithful a whispered speech which might let it be supposed that they were already acquainted, or wished to become more intimate (" On Friday, then, at So-and-so's," or " Come to the studio any day you like; I am always there until five o'clock, I shall look forward to seeing you "), agitated, supposing the newcomer to occupy a "position" which would make him a brilliant recruit to the little clan, the Mistress, while pretending not to have heard anything, and preserving in her fine eyes, shadowed by the habit of listening to Debussy more than they would have been by that of sniffing cocaine, the extenuated expression that they derived from musical intoxication alone, revolved nevertheless behind her splendid brow, inflated by all those quartets and the headaches that were their consequence, thoughts which were not exclusively polyphonic, and unable to contain herself any longer, unable to postpone the injection for another instant, flung herself upon the speakers, drew them apart, and said to the newcomer, pointing to the "faithful" one: "You wouldn't care to come and dine to meet *him,* next Saturday, shall we say, or any day you like, with some really nice people! Don't speak too loud, as I don't want to invite all this mob " (a word used to denote for five minutes the little nucleus, disdained for the moment in favour of the newcomer in whom so many hopes were placed).

But this infatuated impulse, this need to make friendly overtures, had its counterpart. Assiduous attendance at their Wednesdays aroused in the Verdurins an opposite tendency. This was the desire to quarrel, to hold aloof.

It had been strengthened, had almost been wrought to a frenzy during the months spent at la Raspelière, where they were all together morning, noon and night. M. Verdurin went out of his way to prove one of his guests in the wrong, to spin webs in which he might hand over to his comrade spider some innocent fly. Failing a grievance, he would invent some absurdity. As soon as one of the faithful had been out of the house for half an hour, they would make fun of him in front of the others, would feign surprise that their guests had not noticed how his teeth were never clean, or how on the contrary he had a mania for brushing them twenty times a day. If any one took the liberty of opening a window, this want of breeding would cause a glance of disgust to pass between host and hostess. A moment later Mme. Verdurin would ask for a shawl, which gave M. Verdurin an excuse for saying in a tone of fury: "No, I shall close the window, I wonder who had the impertinence to open it," in the hearing of the guilty wretch who blushed to the roots of his hair. You were rebuked indirectly for the quantity of wine that you had drunk. "It won't do you any harm. Navvies thrive on it!" If two of the faithful went out together without first obtaining permission from the Mistress, their excursions led to endless comments, however innocent they might be. Those of M. de Charlus with Morel were not innocent. It was only the fact that M. de Charlus was not staying at la Raspelière (because Morel was obliged to live near his barracks) that retarded the hour of satiety, disgust, retching. That hour was, however, about to strike.

Mme. Verdurin was furious and determined to "enlighten" Morel as to the ridiculous and detestable part that M. de Charlus was making him play. "I must add," she went on (Mme. Verdurin, when she felt that she owed anyone a debt of gratitude which would be a burden to him, and was unable to rid herself of it by killing him, would discover a serious defect in him which would honourably dispense her from shewing her gratitude), "I must add that he gives himself airs in my house which I do not at all like." The truth was that Mme. Verdurin had another more serious reason than Morel's refusal to play at her friends' party for picking a quarrel with M. de Charlus. The latter, overcome by the honour he was doing the Mistress in bringing to Quai Conti people who after all would never have come there for her sake, had, on hearing the first names that Mme. Verdurin had suggested as those of people who ought to be invited, pronounced the most categorical ban upon them in a peremptory tone which blended the rancorous pride of a crotchetty nobleman with the dogmatism of the expert artist in questions of entertainment who would cancel his programme and withhold his collaboration sooner than agree to concessions which, in his opinion, would endanger the success of the whole. M. de Charlus had given his approval, hedging it round with reservations, to Saintine alone, with whom, in order not to be bothered with his wife, Mme. de Guermantes had passed, from a daily intimacy, to a complete severance of relations, but whom M. de Charlus, finding him intelligent, continued to see. True, it was among a middle-class set, with a cross-breeding of the minor nobility, where people are merely very rich and connected with an aristocracy whom the true aristocracy does not know, that Saintine, at one time the flower of the Guermantes set, had gone to seek his fortune and, he imagined, a social foothold. But Mme. Verdurin, knowing the blue-blooded pretensions of the wife's circle, and failing to take into account the husband's position (for it is what is immediately over our head that gives us the impression of altitude and not what is almost invisible to us, so far is it lost in the clouds), felt that she ought to justify an invitation of Saintine by pointing out that he knew a great many people, " having married Mlle. ——." The ignorance which this assertion, the direct opposite of the truth, revealed in Mme. Verdurin caused the Baron's painted lips to part in a smile of indulgent scorn and wide comprehension. He disdained a direct answer, but as he was always ready to express in social examples theories which shewed the fertility of his mind and the arrogance of his pride, with the inherited frivolity of his occupations: " Saintine ought to have come to me before marrying," he said, " there is such a thing as social as well as physiological eugenics, and I am perhaps the only specialist in existence. Saintine's case aroused no discussion, it was clear that, in making the marriage that he made, he was tying a stone to his neck, and hiding his light under a bushel. His social career was at an end. I should have explained this to him, and he would have understood me, for he is quite intelligent. On the other hand, there was a person who had everything that he required to make his position exalted, predominant, world-wide, only a terrible cable bound him to the earth. I helped him, partly by pressure, partly by force, to break his bonds and now he has won, with a triumphant joy, the freedom, the omnipotence that he owes to me; it required, perhaps, a little determination on his part, but what a reward!

Thus a man can himself, when he has the sense to listen to me, become the midwife of his destiny." It was only too clear that M. de Charlus had not been able to influence his own; action is a different thing from speech, even eloquent speech, and from thought, even the thoughts of genius. "But, so far as I am concerned, I live the life of a philosopher who looks on with interest at the social reactions which I have foretold, but who does not assist them. And so I have continued to visit Saintine, who has always received me with the whole-hearted deference which is my due. I have even dined with him in his new abode, where one is as heavily bored, in the midst of the most sumptuous splendour, as one used to be amused in the old days when, living from hand to mouth, he used to assemble the best society in a wretched attic. Him, then, you may invite, I give you leave, but I rule out with my veto all the other names that you have mentioned. And you will thank me for it, for, if I am an expert in arranging marriages, I am no less an expert in arranging parties. I know the rising people who give tone to a gathering, make it go; and I know also the names that will bring it down to the ground, make it fall flat." These exclusions were not always founded upon the Baron's personal resentments nor upon his artistic refinements, but upon his skill as an actor. When he had perfected, at the expense of somebody or something, an entirely successful epigram, he was anxious to let it be heard by the largest possible audience, but took care not to admit to the second performance the audience of the first who could have borne witness that the novelty was not novel. He would then rearrange his drawing-room, simply because he did not alter his programme, and, when he had scored a success in conversation, would, if need be, have organised a tour, and given exhibitions in the provinces. Whatever may have been the various motives for these exclusions, they did not merely annoy Mme. Verdurin, who felt her authority as a hostess impaired, they also did her great damage socially, and for two reasons. The first was that M. de Charlus, even more susceptible than Jupien, used to quarrel, without anyone's ever knowing why, with the people who were most suited to be his friends. Naturally, one of the first punishments that he could inflict upon them was that of not allowing them to be invited to a party which he was giving at the Verdurins'. Now these pariahs were often people who are in the habit of ruling the roast, as the saying is, but who in M. de Charlus's eyes had ceased to rule it from the day on which he had quarrelled with them. For his imagination, in addition to finding people in the wrong in order to quarrel with them, was no less ingenious in stripping them of all importance as soon as they ceased to be his friends. If, for instance, the guilty person came of an extremely old family, whose dukedom, however, dates only from the nineteenth century, such a family as the Montesquiou, from that moment all that counted for M. de Charlus was the precedence of the dukedom, the family becoming nothing. " They are not even Dukes," he would exclaim. " It is the title of the abbé de Montesquiou which passed most irregularly to a collateral, less than eighty years ago. The present Duke, if Duke he can be called, is the third. You may talk to me if you like of people like the Uzès, the la Trémoïlle, the Luynes, who are tenth or fourteenth Dukes, or my brother who is twelfth Duc de Guermantes and seventeenth Prince of Cordova. The

Montesquiou are descended from an old family, what would that prove, supposing that it were proved? They have descended so far that they have reached the four-teenth storey below stairs." Had he on the contrary quarrelled with a gentleman who possessed an ancient dukedom, who boasted the most magnificent connexions, was related to ruling princes, but to whose line this distinc-tion had come quite suddenly without any length of pedi-gree, a Luynes for instance, the case was altered, pedigree alone counted. " I ask you;—M. Alberti, who does not emerge from the mire until Louis XIII. What can it matter to us that favouritism at court allowed them to pick up dukedoms to which they have no right? " What was more, with M. de Charlus, the fall came immediately after the exaltation because of that tendency peculiar to the Guermantes to expect from conversation, from friend-ship, something that these are incapable of giving, as well as the symptomatic fear of becoming the objects of slander. And the fall was all the greater, the higher the exaltation had been. Now nobody had ever found such favour with the Baron as he had markedly shewn for Comtesse Molé. By what sign of indifference did she reveal, one fine day, that she had been unworthy of it? The Comtesse always maintained that she had never been able to solve the problem. The fact remains that the mere sound of her name aroused in the Baron the most violent rage, provoked the most eloquent but the most terrible philippics. Mme. Verdurin, to whom Mme. Molé had been very kind, and who was founding, as we shall see, great hopes upon her and had rejoiced in anticipation at the thought that the Comtesse would meet in her house all the noblest names, as the Mistress said, " of France and Navarre," at once proposed to invite "Madame de Molé." "Oh, my God! Everyone has his own taste," M. de Charlus had replied, "and if you, Madame, feel a desire to converse with Mme. Pipelet, Mme. Gibout and Mme. Joseph Prudhomme, I ask nothing better, but let it be on an evening when I am not present. I could see as soon as you opened your mouth that we do not speak the same language, since I was mentioning the names of the nobility, and you retort with the most obscure names of professional and tradespeople, dirty scandalmongering little bounders, little women who imagine themselves patronesses of the arts because they repeat, an octave lower, the manners of my Guermantes sister-in-law, like a jay that thinks it is imitating a peacock. I must add that it would be positively indecent to admit to a party which I am pleased to give at Mme. Verdurin's a person whom I have with good reason excluded from my society, a sheep devoid of birth, loyalty, intelligence, who is so idiotic as to suppose that she is capable of playing the Duchesse de Guermantes and the Princesse de Guermantes, a combination which is in itself idiotic, since the Duchesse de Guermantes and the Princesse de Guermantes are poles apart. It is as though a person should pretend to be at once Reichenberg and Sarah Bernhardt. In any case, even if it were not impossible, it would be extremely ridiculous. Even though I may, myself, smile at times at the exaggeration of one and regret the limitations of the other, that is my right. But that up-start little frog trying to blow herself out to the magnitude of two great ladies who, at all events, always reveal the incomparable distinction of blood, it is enough, as the saying is, to make a cat laugh. The Molé! That is a name which must not be uttered in my hearing, or else I must simply withdraw," he concluded with a smile, in the tone of a doctor, who, thinking of his patient's interests in spite of that same patient's opposition, lets it be understood that he will not tolerate the collaboration of a homoeopath. On the other hand, certain persons whom M. de Charlus regarded as negligible might indeed be so for him but not for Mme. Verdurin. M. de Charlus, with his exalted birth, could afford to dispense with people in the height of fashion, the assemblage of whom would have made Mme. Verdurin's drawing-room one of the first in Paris. She, at the same time, was beginning to feel that she had already on more than one occasion missed the coach, not to mention the enormous retardation that the social error of the Dreyfus case had inflicted upon her, not without doing her a service all the same. I forget whether I have mentioned the disapproval with which the Duchesse de Guermantes had observed certain persons of her world who, subordinating everything else to the Case, excluded fashionable women from their drawing-rooms and admitted others who were not fashionable, because they were for or against the fresh trial, and had then been criticised in her turn by those same ladies, as lukewarm, unsound in her views, and guilty of placing social distinctions above the national interests; may I appeal to the reader, as to a friend with regard to whom one completely forgets, at the end of a conversation, whether one has remembered, or had an opportunity to tell him something important? Whether I have done so or not, the attitude of the Duchesse de Guermantes can easily be imagined, and indeed if we look at it in the light of subsequent history may appear, from the social point of view, perfectly correct. M. de Cambremer regarded the Dreyfus case as a foreign machination intended to destroy the Intelligence Service, to undermine discipline, to weaken the army, to divide the French people, to pave the way for invasion. Literature being, apart from a few of La Fontaine's fables, a sealed book to the Marquis, he left it to his wife to prove that the cruelly introspective writers of the day had, by creating a spirit of irreverence, arrived by a parallel course at a similar result. "M. Reinach and M. Hervieu are in the plot," she would say. Nobody will accuse the Dreyfus case of having premeditated such dark designs upon society. But there it certainly has broken down the hedges. The social leaders who refuse to allow politics into society are as foreseeing as the soldiers who refuse to allow politics to permeate the army. Society is like the sexual appetite; one does not know at what forms of perversion it may not arrive, once we have allowed our choice to be dictated by aesthetic considerations. The reason that they were Nationalists gave the Faubourg Saint-Germain the habit of entertaining ladies from another class of society; the reason vanished with Nationalism, the habit remained. Mme. Verdurin, by the bond of Dreyfusism, had attracted to her house certain writers of distinction who for the moment were of no advantage to her socially, because they were Dreyfusards. But political passions are like all the rest, they do not last. Fresh generations arise which are incapable of understanding them. Even the generation that felt them changes, feels political passions which, not being modelled exactly upon their predecessors, make it rehabilitate some of the excluded, the reason for exclusion having altered. Monarchists no longer cared, at the time of the Dreyfus case, whether a man had been a Republican, that is to say a Radical, that is to say Anti-clerical, provided that he was an Antisemite and a Nationalist. Should a war ever come, patriotism would assume another form and if a writer was chauvinistic nobody would stop to think whether he had or had not been a Dreyfusard. It was thus that, at each political crisis, at each artistic revival, Mme. Verdurin had collected one by one, like a bird building its nest, the several items, useless for the moment, of what would one day be her Salon. The Dreyfus case had passed, Anatole France remained. Mme. Verdurin's strength lay in her genuine love of art, the trouble that she used to take for her faithful, the marvellous dinners that she gave for them alone, without inviting anyone from the world of fashion. Each of the faithful was treated at her table as Bergotte had been treated at Mme. Swann's. When a boon companion of this sort had turned into an illustrious man whom everybody was longing to meet, his presence at Mme. Verdurin's had none of the artificial, composite effect of a dish at an official or farewell banquet, cooked by Potel or Chabot, but was merely a delicious "ordinary" which you would have found there in the same perfection on a day when there was no party at all. At Mme. Verdurin's the cast was trained to perfection, the repertory most select, all that was lacking was an audience. And now that the public taste had begun to turn from the rational and French art of a Bergotte, and to go in, above all things, for exotic forms of music, Mme. Verdurin, a sort of official representative in Paris of all foreign artists, was not long in making her appearance, by the side of the exquisite Princess Yourbelietef, an aged

Fairy Godmother, grim but all-powerful, to the Russian dancers. This charming invasion, against whose seductions only the stupidest of critics protested, infected Paris, as we know, with a fever of curiosity less burning, more purely aesthetic, but quite as intense perhaps as that aroused by the Dreyfus case. There again Mme. Verdurin, but with a very different result socially, was to take her place in the front row. Just as she had been seen by the side of Mme. Zola, immediately under the bench, during the trial in the Assize Court, so when the new generation of humanity, in their enthusiasm for the Russian ballet, thronged to the Opéra, crowned with the latest novelty in aigrettes, they invariably saw in a stage box Mme. Verdurin by the side of Princess Yourbeletief. And just as, after the emotions of the law courts, people used to go in the evening to Mme. Verdurin's, to meet Picquart or Labori in the flesh and what was more to hear the latest news of the Case, to learn what hopes might be placed in Zurlinden, Loubet, Colonel Jouaust, the Regulations, so now, little inclined for sleep after the enthusiasm aroused by *Sheherazade* or *Prince Igor,* they repaired to Mme. Verdurin's, where under the auspices of Princess Yourbeletief and their hostess an exquisite supper brought together every night the dancers themselves, who had abstained from dinner so as to be more resilient, their director, their designers, the great composers Igor Stravinski and Richard Strauss, a permanent little nucleus, around which, as round the supper-table of M. and Mme. Helvétius, the greatest ladies in Paris and foreign Royalties were not too proud to gather. Even those people in society who professed to be endowed with taste and drew unnecessary distinctions between the various Russian ballets, regarding the setting of the *Sylphides* as somehow " purer " than that of *Sheherazade,* which they were almost prepared to attribute to negro inspiration, were enchanted to meet face to face the great revivers of theatrical taste, who in an art that is perhaps a little more artificial than that of the easel had created a revolution as profound as Impressionism itself.

To revert to M. de Charlus, Mme. Verdurin would not have minded so much if he had placed on his Index only Comtesse Molé and Mme. Bontemps, whom she had picked out at Odette's on the strength of her love of the fine arts, and who during the Dreyfus case had come to dinner occasionally bringing her husband, whom Mme. Verdurin called " lukewarm," because he was not making any move for a fresh trial, but who, being extremely intelligent, and glad to form relations in every camp, was delighted to shew his independence by dining at the same table as Labori, to whom he listened without uttering a word that might compromise himself, but managed to slip in at the right moment a tribute to the loyalty, recognised by all parties, of Jaurès. But the Baron had similarly proscribed several ladies of the aristocracy whose acquaintance Mme. Verdurin, on the occasion of some musical festivity or a collection for charity, had recently formed and who, whatever M. de Charlus might think of them, would have been, far more than himself, essential to the formation of a fresh nucleus at Mme. Verdurin's, this time aristocratic. Mme. Verdurin had indeed been reckoning upon this party, to which M. de Charlus would be bringing her women of the same set, to mix her new friends with them, and had been relishing in anticipation the surprise that the latter would feel upon meeting at Quai Conti their own friends or relatives invited there by the Baron. She was disappointed and furious at his veto. It remained to be seen whether the evening, in these conditions, would result in profit or loss to herself. The loss would not be too serious if only M. de Charlus's guests came with so friendly a feeling for Mme. Verdurin that they would become her friends in the future. In this case the mischief would be only half done, these two sections of the fashionable world, which the Baron had insisted upon keeping apart, would be united later on, he himself being excluded, of course, when the time came. And so Mme. Verdurin was awaiting the Baron's guests with a certain emotion. She would not be slow in discovering the state of mind in which they came, and the degree of intimacy to which she might hope to attain. While she waited, Mme. Verdurin took counsel with the faithful, but, upon seeing M. de Charlus enter the room with Brichot and myself, stopped short. Greatly to our astonishment, when Brichot told her how sorry he was to learn that her dear friend was so seriously ill, Mme. Verdurin replied: " Listen, I am obliged to confess that I am not at all sorry. It is useless to pretend to feel what one does not feel." No doubt she spoke thus from want of energy, because she shrank from the idea of wearing a long face throughout her party, from pride, in order not to appear to be seeking excuses for not having cancelled her invitations, from self-respect also and social aptitude, because the absence of grief which she displayed was more honourable if it could be attributed to a peculiar antipathy, suddenly revealed, to the Princess, rather than to a universal insensibility, and because her hearers could not fail to be disarmed by a

sincerity as to which there could be no doubt. If Mme.
Verdurin had not been genuinely unaffected by the death
of the Princess, would she have gone on to excuse herself
for giving the party, by accusing herself of a far more
serious fault? Besides, one was apt to forget that Mme.
Verdurin **would thus** have admitted, while confessing her
grief, that she had not had the strength of mind to forego
a pleasure; whereas the indifference of the friend was
something more shocking, more immoral, but less humili-
ating, and consequently easier to confess than the frivolity
of the hostess. In matters of crime, where the culprit
is in danger, it is his material interest that prompts the
confession. Where the fault incurs no penalty, it is self-
esteem. Whether it was that, doubtless feeling the pretext to be too hackneyed of the people who, so as not to
allow a bereavement to interrupt their life of pleasure, go
about saying that it seems to them useless to display the
outward signs of a grief which they feel in their hearts,
Mme. Verdurin preferred to imitate those intelligent
culprits who àre revolted by the commonplaces of innocence and whose defence—a partial admission, though
they do not know it—consists in saying that they would
see no harm in doing what they are accused of doing,
although, as it happens, they have had no occasion to do
it; or that, having adopted, to explain her conduct, the
theory of indifference, she found, once she had started
upon the downward slope of her unnatural feeling, that
it was distinctly original to have felt it, that she displayed
a rare perspicacity in having managed to diagnose her
own symptoms, and a certain "nerve" in proclaiming
them; anyhow, Mme. Verdurin kept dwelling upon her
want of grief, not without a certain proud satisfaction, as

of a paradoxical psychologist and daring dramatist. "Yes, it is very funny," she said, "I hardly felt it. Of course, I don't mean to say that I wouldn't rather she were still alive, she was not a bad person." "Yes, she was," put in M. Verdurin. "Ah! He doesn't approve of her because he thought that I was doing myself harm by having her here, but he is quite pig-headed about that." "Do me the justice to admit," said M. Verdurin, "that I never approved of your having her. I always told you that she had a bad reputation." "But I have never heard a thing against her," protested Saniette. "What!" exclaimed Mme. Verdurin, "everybody knew; bad isn't the word, it was scandalous, appalling. No, it has nothing to do with that. I couldn't explain, myself, what I felt; I didn't dislike her, but I took so little interest in her that, when we heard that she was seriously ill, my husband himself was quite surprised, and said: 'Anyone would think that you didn't mind.' Why, this evening, he offered to put off the party, and I insisted upon having it, because I should have thought it a farce to shew a grief which I do not feel." She said this because she felt that it had a curious smack of the "independent theatre," and was at the same time singularly convenient; for an admitted insensibility or immorality simplifies life as much as does easy virtue; it converts reproachable actions, for which one no longer need seek any excuse, into a duty imposed by sincerity. And the faithful listened to Mme. Verdurin's speech with the blend of admiration and misgiving which certain cruelly realistic plays, that shewed a profound observation, used at one time to cause, and, while they marvelled to see their beloved Mistress display a novel aspect of her rectitude and independence, more than one of them, albeit he assured himself that after all it would not be the same thing, thought of his own death, and asked himself whether, on the day when death came to him, they would draw the blinds or give a party at Quai Conti. "I am very glad that the party has not been put off, for my guests' sake," said M. de Charlus, not realising that in expressing himself thus he was offending Mme. Verdurin. Meanwhile I was struck, as was everybody who approached Mme. Verdurin that evening, by a far from pleasant odour of rhino-gomenol. The reason was as follows. We know that Mme. Verdurin never expressed her artistic feelings in a moral, but always in a physical fashion, so that they might appear more inevitable and more profound. So, if one spoke to her of Vinteuil's music, her favourite, she remained unmoved, as though she expected to derive no emotion from it. But after a few minutes of a fixed, almost abstracted gaze, in a sharp, matter of fact, scarcely civil tone (as though she had said to you: "I don't in the least mind your smoking, it's because of the carpet; it's a very fine one (not that that matters either), but it's highly inflammable, I'm dreadfully afraid of fire, and I shouldn't like to see you all roasted because some one had carelessly dropped a cigarette end on it"), she replied: "I have no fault to find with Vinteuil; to my mind, he is the greatest composer of the age, only I can never listen to that sort of stuff without weeping all the time" (she did not apply any pathos to the word "weeping," she would have used precisely the same tone for "sleeping"; certain slander-mongers used indeed to insist that the latter verb would have been more applicable, though no one could ever be certain, for she listened to the music with her face buried in her hands, and certain snoring sounds might after all have been sobs). "I don't mind weeping, not in the least; only I get the most appalling colds afterwards. It stuffs up my mucous membrane, and the day after I look like nothing on earth. I have to inhale for days on end before I can utter. However, one of Cottard's pupils, a charming person, has been treating me for it. He goes by quite an original rule: 'Prevention is better than cure.' And he greases my nose before the music begins. It is radical. I can weep like all the mothers who ever lost a child, not a trace of a cold. Sometimes a little conjunctivitis, that's all. It is absolutely efficacious. Otherwise I could never have gone on listening to Vinteuil. I was just going from one bronchitis to another." I could not refrain from alluding to Mlle. Vinteuil. "Isn't the composer's daughter to be here," I asked Mme. Verdurin, "with one of her friends?" "No, I have just had a telegram," Mme. Verdurin said evasively, "they have been obliged to remain in the country." I felt a momentary hope that there might never have been any question of their leaving it and that Mme. Verdurin had announced the presence of these representatives of the composer only in order to make a favourable impression upon the performers and their audience. "What, didn't they come, then, to the rehearsal this afternoon?" came with a feigned curiosity from the Baron who was anxious to let it appear that he had not seen Charlie. The latter came up to greet me. I whispered a question in his ear about Mlle. Vinteuil; he seemed to me to know little or nothing about her. I signalled to him not to let himself be heard and told him that we should discuss the question later on. He bowed, and assured me that he would be delighted to place himself entirely at my disposal. I observed that he was far more polite, more respectful, than he had been in the past. I spoke warmly of him —who might perhaps be able to help me to clear up my suspicions—to M. de Charlus who replied: "He only does what is natural, there would be no point in his living among respectable people if he didn't learn good manners." These, according to M. de Charlus, were the old manners of France, untainted by any British bluntness. Thus when Charlie, returning from a tour in the provinces or abroad, arrived in his travelling suit at the Baron's, the latter, if there were not too many people present, would kiss him without ceremony upon both cheeks, perhaps a little in order to banish by so ostentatious a display of his affection any idea of its being criminal, perhaps because he could not deny himself a pleasure, but still more, doubtless, from a literary sense, as upholding and illustrating the traditional manners of France, and, just as he would have countered the Munich or modern style of furniture by keeping in his rooms old armchairs that had come to him from a great-grandmother, countering the British phlegm with the affection of a warm-hearted father of the eighteenth century, unable to conceal his joy at beholding his son once more. Was there indeed a trace of incest in this paternal affection? It is more probable that the way in which M. de Charlus habitually appeased his vicious cravings, as to which we shall learn something in due course, was not sufficient for the need of affection, which had remained unsatisfied since the death of his wife; the fact remains that after having thought more than once of a second marriage, he was now devoured by a maniacal desire to adopt an heir. People said that he was going to adopt Morel, and there was nothing extraordinary in that. The invert who has been unable to feed his passion save on a literature written for women-loving men, who used to think of men when he read Musset's *Nuits,* feels the need to partake, nevertheless, in all the social activities of the man who is not an invert, to keep a lover, as the old frequenter of the Opera keeps ballet-girls, to settle down, to marry or form a permanent tie, to become a father.

M. de Charlus took Morel aside on the pretext of making him tell him what was going to be played, but above all finding a great consolation, while Charlie shewed him his music, in displaying thus publicly their secret intimacy. In the mean time I myself felt a certain charm. For albeit the little clan included few girls, on the other hand girls were abundantly invited on the big evenings. There were a number present, and very pretty girls too, whom I knew. They wafted smiles of greeting to me across the room. The air was thus decorated at every moment with the charming smile of some girl. That is the manifold, occasional ornament of evening parties, as it is of days. We remember an atmosphere because girls were smiling in it.

Many people might have been greatly surprised had they overheard the furtive remarks which M. de Charlus exchanged with a number of important gentlemen at this party. These were two Dukes, a distinguished General, a great writer, a great physician, a great barrister. And the remarks in question were: "By the way, did you notice the footman, I mean the little fellow they take on the carriage? At our cousin Guermantes', you don't know of anyone?" "At the moment, no." "I say, though, outside the door, where the carriages stop, there used to be a fair little person, in breeches, who seemed to me most attractive. She called my carriage most charmingly, I would gladly have prolonged the conversation." "Yes, but I believe she's altogether against it, besides, she puts on airs, you like to get to business at once, you would loathe her. Anyhow, I know there's nothing doing, a friend of mine tried." "That is a pity, I thought the profile very fine, and the hair superb." "Really, as much as that? I think, if you had seen a little more of her, you would have been disillusioned. No, in the supper-room, only two months ago you would have seen a real marvel, a great fellow six foot six, a perfect skin, and loves it, too. But he's gone off to Poland." "Ah, that is rather a long way." "You never know, he may come back, perhaps. One always meets again somewhere." There is no great social function that does not, if, in taking a section of it, we contrive to cut sufficiently deep, resemble those parties to which doctors invite their patients, who utter the most intelligent remarks, have perfect manners, and would never shew that they were mad did they not whisper in our ear, pointing to some old gentleman who goes past: "That's Joan of Arc."

"I feel that it is our duty to enlighten him," Mme. Verdurin said to Brichot. "Not that I have anything against Charlus, far from it. He is a pleasant fellow and as for his reputation, I don't mind saying that it is not of a sort that can do me any harm! As far as I'm concerned, in our little clan, in our table-talk, as I detest flirts, the men who talk nonsense to a woman in a corner instead of discussing interesting topics, I've never had any fear with Charlus of what happened to me with

Swann, and Elstir, and lots of them. With him I was quite safe, he would come to my dinners, all the women in the world might be there, you could be certain that the general conversation would not be disturbed by flirtations and whisperings. Charlus is in a class of his own, one doesn't worry, he might be a priest. Only, he must not be allowed to take it upon himself to order about the young men who come to the house and make a nuisance of himself in our little nucleus, or he'll be worse than a man who runs after women." And Mme. Verdurin was sincere in thus proclaiming her indulgence towards Charlism. Like every ecclesiastical power she regarded human frailties as less dangerous than anything that might undermine the principle of authority, impair the orthodoxy, modify the ancient creed of her little Church. "If he does, then I shall bare my teeth. What do you say to a gentleman who tried to prevent Charlie from coming to a rehearsal because he himself was not invited? So he's going to be taught a lesson, I hope he'll profit by it, otherwise he can simply take his hat and go. He keeps the boy under lock and key, upon my word he does." And, using exactly the same expressions that almost anyone else might have used, for there are certain not in common currency which some particular subject, some given circumstance recalls almost inevitably to the mind of the speaker, who imagines that he is giving free expression to his thought when he is merely repeating mechanically the universal lesson, she went on: "It's impossible to see Morel nowadays without that great lout hanging round him, like an armed escort." M. Verdurin offered to take Charlie out of the room for a minute to explain things to him, on the pretext of asking him a question. Mme. Verdurin was afraid that this might upset him, and that he would play badly in consequence. It would be better to postpone this performance until after the other. Perhaps even until a later occasion. For however Mme. Verdurin might look forward to the delicious emotion that she would feel when she knew that her husband was engaged in enlightening Charlie in the next room, she was afraid, if the shot missed fire, that he would lose his temper and would fail to reappear on the sixteenth.

What ruined M. de Charlus that evening was the ill-breeding—so common in their class—of the people whom he had invited and who were now beginning to arrive. Having come there partly out of friendship for M. de Charlus and also out of curiosity to explore these novel surroundings, each Duchess made straight for the Baron as though it were he who was giving the party and said, within a yard of the Verdurins, who could hear every word: "Shew me which is mother Verdurin; do you think I really need speak to her? I do hope, at least, that she won't put my name in the paper to-morrow, nobody would ever speak to me again. What! That woman with the white hair, but she looks quite presentable." Hearing some mention of Mlle. Vinteuil, who, however, was not in the room, more than one of them said: "Ah! The sonata-man's daughter? Shew me her" and, each finding a number of her friends, they formed a group by themselves, watched, sparkling with ironical curiosity, the arrival of the faithful, able at the most to point a finger at the odd way in which a person had done her hair, who, a few years later, was to make this the fashion in the very best society, and, in short, regretted that they did not find this house as different from the houses that they knew, as they had hoped to find it, feeling the disappointment of people in society who, having gone to the Boîte à Bruant in the hope that the singer would make a butt of them, find themselves greeted on their arrival with a polite bow instead of the expected:

> Ah! voyez c'te gueule, c'te binette.
> Ah! voyez c'te gueule qu'elle a.

M. de Charlus had, at Balbec, given me a perspicacious criticism of Mme. de Vaugoubert who, notwithstanding her keen intellect, had brought about, after his unexpected prosperity, the irremediable disgrace of her husband. The rulers to whose Court M. de Vaugoubert was accredited, King Theodosius and Queen Eudoxia, having returned to Paris, but this time for a prolonged visit, daily festivities had been held in their honour, in the course of which the Queen, on the friendliest terms with Mme. de Vaugoubert, whom she had seen for the last ten years in her own capital, and knowing neither the wife of the President of the Republic nor those of his Ministers, had neglected these ladies and kept entirely aloof with the Ambassadress. This lady, believing her own position to be unassailable—M. de Vaugoubert having been responsible for the alliance between King Theodosius and France—had derived from the preference that the Queen shewed for her society a proud satisfaction but no anxiety at the peril that threatened her, which took shape a few months later in the fact, wrongly considered impossible by the too confident couple, of the brutal dismissal from the Service of M. de Vaugoubert. M. de Charlus, remarking in the " crawler " upon the downfall of his lifelong friend, expressed his astonishment that an intelligent woman had not, in such circumstances, brought all her influence with the King and Queen to bear, so as to secure that she might not seem to possess any influence, and to make them transfer to the wives of the President and his Ministers a civility by which those ladies would have been all the more flattered, that is to say which would have made them more inclined, in their satisfaction, to be grateful to the Vaugouberts, inasmuch as they would have supposed that civility to be spontaneous, and not dictated by them. But the man who can see the mistakes of others need only be exhilarated by circumstances in order to succumb to them himself. And M. de Charlus, while his guests fought their way towards him, to come and congratulate him, thank him, as though he were the master of the house, never thought of asking them to say a few words to Mme. Verdurin. Only the Queen of Naples, in whom survived the same noble blood that had flowed in the veins of her sisters the Empress Elisabeth and the Duchesse d'Alençon, made a point of talking to Mme. Verdurin as though she had come for the pleasure of meeting her rather than for the music and for M. de Charlus, made endless pretty speeches to her hostess, could not cease from telling her for how long she had been wishing to make her acquaintance, expressed her admiration for the house and spoke to her of all manner of subjects as though she were paying a call. She would so much have liked to bring her niece Elisabeth, she said (the niece who shortly afterwards was to marry Prince Albert of Belgium), who would be so sorry. She stopped talking when she saw the musicians mount the platform, asking which of them was Morel. She can scarcely have been under any illusion as to the motives that led M. de Charlus to desire that the young virtuoso should be surrounded with so much glory. But the venerable wisdom of a sovereign in whose veins flowed the blood of one of the noblest races in history, one of the richest in experience, scepticism and pride, made her merely regard the inevitable defects of the people whom she loved best, such as her cousin Charlus (whose mother had been, like herself, a "Duchess in Bavaria"), as misfortunes that rendered more precious to them the support that they might find in herself and consequently made it even more pleasant to her to provide that support. She knew that M. de Charlus would be doubly touched by her having taken the trouble to come, in the circumstances. Only, being as good as she had long ago shewn herself brave, this heroic woman who, a soldier-queen, had herself fired her musket from the ramparts of Gaeta, always ready to take her place chivalrously by the weaker side, seeing Mme. Verdurin alone and abandoned, and unaware (for that matter) that she ought not to leave the Queen, had sought to pretend that for her, the Queen of Naples, the centre of this party, the lodestone that had made her come was Mme. Verdurin. She expressed her regret that she would not be able to remain until the end, as she had, although she never went anywhere, to go on to another party, and begged that on no account, when she had to go, should any fuss be made for her, thus discharging Mme. Verdurin of the honours which the latter did not even know that she ought to render.

One must, however, do M. de Charlus the justice of saying that, if he entirely forgot Mme. Verdurin and allowed her to be ignored, to a scandalous extent, by the

people "of his own world" whom he had invited, he did,
on the other hand, realise that he must not allow these
people to display, during the "symphonic recital" itself,
the bad manners which they were exhibiting towards the
Mistress. Morel had already mounted the platform, the
musicians were assembling, and one could still hear conversations, not to say laughter, speeches such as "it
appears, one has to be initiated to understand it." Immediately M. de Charlus, drawing himself erect, as though
he had entered a different body from that which I had
seen, not an hour ago, crawling towards Mme. Verdurin's
door, assumed a prophetic expression and regarded the
assembly with an earnestness which indicated that this
was not the moment for laughter, whereupon one saw a
rapid blush tinge the cheeks of more than one lady thus
publicly rebuked, like a schoolgirl scolded by her teacher
in front of the whole class. To my mind, M. de Charlus's attitude, noble as it was, was somehow slightly
comic; for at one moment he pulverised his guests with
a flaming glare, at another, in order to indicate to them
as with a *vade mecum* the religious silence that ought to
be observed, the detachment from every worldly consideration, he furnished in himself, as he raised to his fine
brow his white-gloved hands, a model (to which they
must conform) of gravity, already almost of ecstasy,
without acknowledging the greetings of late-comers so
indelicate as not to understand that it was now the time
for High Art. They were all hypnotised; no one dared
utter a sound, move a chair; respect for music—by virtue
of Palamède's prestige—had been instantaneously in-
culcated in a crowd as ill-bred as it was exclusive.

When I saw appear on the little platform, not only

Morel and a pianist, but performers upon other instruments as well, I supposed that the programme was to begin with works of composers other than Vinteuil. For I imagined that the only work of his in existence was his sonata for piano and violin.

Mme. Verdurin sat in a place apart, the twin hemispheres of her pale, slightly roseate brow magnificently curved, her hair drawn back, partly in imitation of an eighteenth century portrait, partly from the desire for coolness of a fever-stricken patient whom modesty forbids to reveal her condition, aloof, a deity presiding over musical rites, patron saint of Wagnerism and sick-headaches, a sort of almost tragic Norn, evoked by the spell of genius in the midst of all these bores, in whose presence she would more than ordinarily scorn to express her feelings upon hearing a piece of music which she knew better than they. The concert began, I did not know what they were playing, I found myself in a strange land. Where was I to locate it? Into what composer's country had I come? I should have been glad to know, and, seeing nobody near me whom I might question, I should have liked to be a character in those *Arabian Nights* which I never tired of reading and in which, in moments of uncertainty, there arose a genie or a maiden of ravishing beauty, invisible to everyone else but not to the embarrassed hero to whom she reveals exactly what he wishes to learn. Well, at this very moment I was favoured with precisely such a magical apparition. As, in a stretch of country which we suppose to be strange to us and which as a matter of fact we have approached from a new angle, when after turning out of one road we find ourself emerging suddenly upon another every inch of which is familiar only we have not been in the habit of entering it from that end, we say to ourself immediately: "Why, this is the lane that leads to the garden gate of my friends the X——; I shall be there in a minute," and there, indeed, is their daughter at the gate, come out to greet us as we pass; so, all of a sudden, I found myself, in the midst of this music that was novel to me, right in the heart of Vinteuil's sonata; and, more marvellous than any maiden, the little phrase, enveloped, harnessed in silver, glittering with brilliant effects of sound, as light and soft as silken scarves, came towards me, recognisable in this new guise. My joy at having found it again was enhanced by the accent, so friendlily familiar, which it adopted in addressing me, so persuasive, so simple, albeit without dimming the shimmering beauty with which it was resplendent. Its intention, however, was, this time, merely to shew me the way, which was not the way of the sonata, for this was an unpublished work of Vinteuil in which he had merely amused himself, by an allusion which was explained at this point by a sentence in the programme which one ought to have been reading simultaneously, in making the little phrase reappear for a moment. No sooner was it thus recalled than it vanished, and I found myself once more in an unknown world, but I knew now, and everything that followed only confirmed my knowledge, that this world was one of those which I had never even been capable of imagining that Vinteuil could have created, for when, weary of the sonata which was to me a universe thoroughly explored, I tried to imagine others equally beautiful but different, I was merely doing what those poets do who fill their artificial paradise with meadows, flowers and streams which duplicate those existing already upon Earth. What was now before me made me feel as keen a joy as the sonata would have given me if I had not already known it, and consequently, while no less beautiful, was different. Whereas the sonata opened upon a dawn of lilied meadows, parting its slender whiteness to suspend itself over the frail and yet consistent mingling of a rustic bower of honeysuckle with white geraniums, it was upon continuous, level surfaces like those of the sea that, in the midst of a stormy morning beneath an already lurid sky, there began, in an eery silence, in an infinite void, this new masterpiece, and it was into a roseate dawn that, in order to construct itself progressively before me, this unknown universe was drawn from silence and from night. This so novel redness, so absent from the tender, rustic, pale sonata, tinged all the sky, as dawn does, with a mysterious hope. And a song already thrilled the air, a song on seven notes, but the strangest, the most different from any that I had ever imagined, from any that I could ever have been able to imagine, at once ineffable and piercing, no longer the cooing of a dove as in the sonata, but rending the air, as vivid as the scarlet tinge in which the opening bars had been bathed, something like the mystical crow of a cock, an ineffable but overshrill appeal of the eternal morning. The cold atmosphere, soaked in rain, electric—of a quality so different, feeling wholly other pressures, in a world so remote from that, virginal and endowed only with vegetable life, of the sonata—changed at every moment, obliterating the empurpled promise of the Dawn. At noon, however, beneath a scorching though transitory sun, it seemed to fulfil itself in a dull, almost rustic bliss in which the peal of clanging, racing bells (like those which kindled the blaze of the square outside the church of Combray, which Vinteuil, who must often have heard them, had perhaps discovered at that moment in his memory like a colour which the painter's hand has conveyed to his palette) seemed to materialise the coarsest joy. To be honest, from the aesthetic point of view, this joyous motive did not appeal to me, I found it almost ugly, its rhythm dragged so laboriously along the ground that one might have succeeded in imitating almost everything that was essential to it by merely making a noise, sounds, by the tapping of drumsticks upon a table. It seemed to me that Vinteuil had been lacking, here, in inspiration, and consequently I was a little lacking also in the power of attention.

I looked at the Mistress, whose sullen immobility seemed to be protesting against the noddings—in time with the music—of the empty heads of the ladies of the Faubourg. She did not say: "You understand that I know something about this music, and more than a little! If I had to express all that I feel, you would never hear the end of it!" She did not say this. But her upright, motionless body, her expressionless eyes, her straying locks said it for her. They spoke also of her courage, said that the musicians might go on, need not spare her nerves, that she would not flinch at the andante, would not cry out at the allegro. I looked at the musicians. The violoncellist dominated the instrument which he clutched between his knees, bowing his head to which its coarse features gave, in moments of mannerism, an involuntary expression of disgust; he leaned over it, fingered it with the same domestic patience with which he might have plucked a cabbage, while by his side the harpist (a mere girl) in a short skirt, bounded on either side by the lines of her golden quadrilateral like those which, in the magic chamber of a Sibyl, would arbitrarily denote the ether, according to the consecrated rules, seemed to be going in quest, here and there, at the point required, of an exquisite sound, just as though, a little allegorical deity, placed in front of the golden trellis of the heavenly vault, she were gathering, one by one, its stars. As for Morel, a lock, hitherto invisible and lost in the rest of his hair, had fallen loose and formed a curl upon his brow. I turned my head slightly towards the audience to discover what M. de Charlus might be feeling at the sight of this curl. But my eyes encountered only the face, or rather the hands of Mme. Verdurin, for the former was entirely buried in the latter.

But very soon, the triumphant motive of the bells having been banished, dispersed by others, I succumbed once again to the music; and I began to realise that if, in the body of this septet, different elements presented themselves in turn, to combine at the close, so also Vinteuil's sonata, and, as I was to find later on, his other works as well, had been no more than timid essays, exquisite but very slight, towards the triumphant and complete masterpiece which was revealed to me at this moment. And so too, I could not help recalling how I had thought of the other worlds which Vinteuil might have created as of so many universes as hermetically sealed as each of my own love-affairs, whereas in reality I was obliged to admit that in the volume of my latest love—that is to say, my love for Albertine—my first inklings of love for her (at Balbec at the very beginning, then after the game of ferret, then on the night when she slept at the hotel, then in Paris on the foggy afternoon, then on the night of the Guermantes' party, then at Balbec again, and finally in Paris where my life was now closely linked to her own) had been nothing more than experiments; indeed, if I were to consider, not my love for Albertine, but my life as a whole, my earlier love-affairs had themselves been but slight and timid essays, experiments, which paved the way to this vaster love: my love for Albertine. And I ceased to follow the music, in order to ask myself once again whether Albertine had or had not seen Mlle. Vinteuil during the last few days, as we interrogate afresh an internal pain, from which we have been distracted for a moment. For it was in myself that Albertine's possible actions were performed. Of each of the people whom we know we possess a double, but it is generally situated on the horizon of our imagination, of our memory; it remains more or less external to ourself, and what it has done or may have done has no greater capacity to cause us pain than an object situated at a certain distance, which provides us with only the painless sensations of vision. The things that affect these people we perceive in a contemplative fashion, we are able to deplore them in appropriate language which gives other people a sense of our kindness of heart, we do not feel them; but since the wound inflicted on me at Balbec, it was in my heart, at a great depth, difficult to extract, that Albertine's double was lodged. What I saw of her hurt me, as a sick man would be hurt whose senses were so seriously deranged that the sight of a colour would be felt by him internally like a knife-thrust in his living flesh. It was fortunate that I had not already yielded to the temptation to break with

Albertine; the boring thought that I should have to see
her again presently, when I went home, was a trifling
matter compared with the anxiety that I should have felt
if the separation had been permanent at this moment
when I felt a doubt about her before she had had time
to become immaterial to me. At the moment when I
pictured her thus to myself waiting for me at home, like
a beloved wife who found the time of waiting long, and
had perhaps fallen asleep for a moment in her room, I
was caressed by the passage of a tender phrase, homely
and domestic, of the septet. Perhaps—everything is so
interwoven and superimposed in our inward life—it had
been inspired in Vinteuil by his daughter's sleep—his
daughter, the cause to-day of all my troubles—when it
enveloped in its quiet, on peaceful evenings, the work of
the composer, this phrase which calmed me so, by the
same soft background of silence which pacifies certain of
Schumann's reveries, during which, even when " the Poet
is speaking," one can tell that " the child is asleep."
Asleep, awake, I should find her again this evening, when
I chose to return home, Albertine, my little child. And
yet, I said to myself, something more mysterious than Albertine's love seemed to be promised at the outset of this
work, in those first cries of dawn. I endeavoured to
banish the thought of my mistress, so as to think only
of the composer. Indeed, he seemed to be present. One
would have said that, reincarnate, the composer lived for
all time in his music; one could feel the joy with which
he was choosing the colour of some sound, harmonising
it with the rest. For with other and more profound
gifts Vinteuil combined that which few composers, and
indeed few painters have possessed, of using colours not

merely so lasting but so personal that, just as time has been powerless to fade them, so the disciples who imitate him who discovered them, and even the masters who surpass him do not pale their originality. The revolution that their apparition has effected does not live to see its results merge unacknowledged in the work of subsequent generations; it is liberated, it breaks out again, and alone, whenever the innovator's works are performed in all time to come. · Each note underlined itself in a colour which all the rules in the world could not have taught the most learned composers to imitate, with the result that Vinteuil, albeit he had appeared at his hour and was fixed in his place in the evolution of music, would always leave that place to stand in the forefront, whenever any of his compositions was performed, which would owe its appearance of having blossomed after the works of other more recent composers to this quality, apparently paradoxical and actually deceiving, of permanent novelty. A page of symphonic music by Vinteuil, familiar already on the piano, when one heard it rendered by an orchestra, like a ray of summer sunlight which the prism of the window disintegrates before it enters a dark dining-room, revealed like an unsuspected, myriad-hued treasure all the jewels of the *Arabian Nights*. But how can one compare to that motionless brilliance of light what was life, perpetual and blissful motion? This Vinteuil, whom I had known so timid and sad, had been capable—when he had to select a tone, to blend another with it—of audacities, had enjoyed a good fortune, in the full sense of the word, as to which the hearing of any of his works left one in no doubt. The joy that such chords had aroused in him, the increase of strength that it had given him wherewith to discover others led the listener on also from one discovery to another, or rather it was the composer himself who guided him, deriving from the colours that he had invented a wild joy which gave him the strength to discover, to fling himself upon the others which they seemed to evoke, enraptured, quivering, as though from the shock of an electric spark, when the sublime came spontaneously to life at the clang of the brass, panting, drunken, maddened, dizzy, while he painted his great musical fresco, like Michelangelo strapped to his scaffold and dashing, from his supine position, tumultuous brush-strokes upon the ceiling of the Sistine chapel. Vinteuil had been dead for many years; but in the sound of these instruments which he had animated, it had been given him to prolong, for an unlimited time, a part at least of his life. Of his life as a man merely? If art was indeed but a prolongation of life, was it worth while to sacrifice anything to it, was it not as unreal as life itself? If I was to listen properly to this septet, I could not pause to consider the question. No doubt the glowing septet differed singularly from the candid sonata; the timid question to which the little phrase replied, from the breathless supplication to find the fulfilment of the strange promise that had resounded, so harsh, so supernatural, so brief, setting athrob the still inert crimson of the morning sky, above the sea. And yet these so widely different phrases were composed of the same elements, for just as there was a certain universe, perceptible by us in those fragments scattered here and there, in private houses, in public galleries, which were Elstir's universe, the universe which he saw, in which he lived, so too the music of Vinteuil extended, note by

note, key by key, the unknown colourings of an inestimable, unsuspected universe, made fragmentary by the
gaps that occurred between the different occasions of
hearing his work performed; those two so dissimilar
questions which commanded the so different movements
of the sonata and the septet, the former breaking into
short appeals a line continuous and pure, the latter weld-
ing together into an indivisible structure a medley of
scattered fragments, were nevertheless, one so calm and
timid, almost detached and as though philosophic, the
other so anxious, pressing, imploring, were nevertheless
the same prayer, poured forth before different risings of
the inward sun and merely refracted through the different
mediums of other thoughts, of artistic researches carried
on through the years in which he had tried to create
something new. A prayer, a hope which was at heart
the same, distinguishable beneath these disguises in the
various works of Vinteuil, and on the other hand not to
be found elsewhere than in his works. For these phrases
historians of music might indeed find affinities, a
pedigree in the works of other great composers, but
merely for subordinate reasons, from external resemblances, from analogies which were ingeniously discovered
by reasoning rather than felt by a direct impression.
The impression that these phrases of Vinteuil imparted
was different from any other, as though, notwithstanding
the conclusions to which science seems to point, the individual did really exist. And it was precisely when he
was seeking vigorously to be something new that one
recognised beneath the apparent differences the profound
similarities; and the deliberate resemblances that existed
in the body of a work, when Vinteuil repeated once and

again a single phrase, diversified it, amused himself by altering its rhythm, by making it reappear in its original form, these deliberate resemblances, the work of the intellect, inevitably superficial, never succeeded in being as striking as those resemblances, concealed, involuntary, which broke out in different colours, between the two separate masterpieces; for then Vinteuil, seeking to do something new, questioned himself, with all the force of his creative effort, reached his own essential nature at those depths, where, whatever be the question asked, it is in the same accent, that is to say its own, that it replies. Such an accent, the accent of Vinteuil, is separated from the accents of other composers by a difference far greater than that which we perceive between the voices of two people, even between the cries of two species of animal: by the difference that exists between the thoughts of those other composers and the eternal investigations of Vinteuil, the question that he put to himself in so many forms, his habitual speculation, but as free from analytical formulas of reasoning as if it were being carried out in the world of the angels, so that we can measure its depth, but without being any more able to translate it into human speech than are disincarnate spirits when, evoked by a medium, he questions them as to the mysteries of death. And even when I bore in mind the acquired originality which had struck me that afternoon, that kinship which musical critics might discover among them, it is indeed a unique accent to which rise, and return in spite of themselves those great singers that original composers are, which is a proof of the irreducibly individual existence of the soul. Though Vinteuil might try to make more solemn, more grand, or to make more sprightly and gay what he saw reflected in the mind of his audience, yet, in spite of himself, he submerged it all beneath an undercurrent which makes his song eternal and at once recognisable. This song, different from those of other singers, similar to all his own, where had Vinteuil learned, where had he heard it? Each artist seems thus to be the native of an unknown country, which he himself has forgotten, different from that from which will emerge, making for the earth, another great artist. When all is said, Vinteuil, in his latest works, seemed to have drawn nearer to that unknown country. The atmosphere was no longer the same as in the sonata, the questioning phrases became more pressing, more uneasy, the answers more mysterious; the clean-washed air of morning and evening seemed to influence even the instruments. Morel might be playing marvellously, the sounds that came from his violin seemed to me singularly piercing, almost blatant. This harshness was pleasing, and, as in certain voices, one felt in it a sort of moral virtue and intellectual superiority. But this might give offence. When his vision of the universe is modified, purified, becomes more adapted to his memory of the country of his heart, it is only natural that this should be expressed by a general alteration of sounds in the musician, as of colours in the painter. Anyhow, the more intelligent section of the public is not misled, since people declared later on that Vinteuil's last compositions were the most profound. Now no programme, no subject supplied any intellectual basis for judgment. One guessed therefore that it was a question of transposition, an increasing profundity of sound.

This lost country composers do not actually remember,

but each of them remains all his life somehow attuned to it; he is wild with joy when he is singing the airs of his native land, betrays it at times in his thirst for fame, but then, in seeking fame, turns his back upon it, and it is only when he despises it that he finds it when he utters, whatever the subject with which he is dealing, that peculiar strain the monotony of which—for whatever its subject it remains identical in itself—proves the permanence of the elements that compose his soul. But is it not the fact then that from those elements, all the real residuum which we are obliged to keep to ourself, which cannot be transmitted in talk, even by friend to friend, by master to disciple, by lover to mistress, that ineffable something which makes a difference in quality between what each of us has felt and what he is obliged to leave behind at the threshold of the phrases in which he can communicate with his fellows only by limiting himself to external points common to us all and of no interest, art, the art of a Vinteuil like that of an Elstir, makes the man himself apparent, rendering externally visible in the colours of the spectrum the intimate com- position of those worlds which we call individual persons and which, without the aid of art, we should never know? A pair of wings, a different mode of breathing, which would enable us to traverse infinite space, would in no way help us, for, if we visited Mars or Venus keeping the same senses, they would clothe in the same aspect as the things of the earth everything that we should be capable of seeing. The only true voyage of discovery, the only fountain of Eternal Youth, would be not to visit strange lands but to possess other eyes, to behold the universe through the eyes of another, of a hundred others, to behold the hundred universes that each of them beholds, that each of them is; and this we can contrive with an Elstir, with a Vinteuil; with men like these we do really fly from star to star. The andante had just ended upon a phrase filled with a tenderness to which I had entirely abandoned myself; there followed, before the next movement, a short interval during which the performers laid down their instruments and the audience exchanged impressions. A Duke, in order to shew that he knew what he was talking about, declared: "It is a difficult thing to play well." Other more entertaining people conversed for a moment with myself. But what were their words, which like every human and external word, left me so indifferent, compared with the heavenly phrase of music with which I had just been engaged? I was indeed like an angel who, fallen from the inebriating bliss of paradise, subsides into the most humdrum reality. And, just as certain creatures are the last surviving testimony to a form of life which nature has discarded, I asked myself if music were not the unique example of what might have been—if there had not come the invention of language, the formation of words, the analysis of ideas—the means of communication between one spirit and another. It is like a possibility which has ended in nothing; humanity has developed along other lines, those of spoken and written language. But this return to the unanalysed was so inebriating, that on emerging from that paradise, contact with people who were more or less intelligent seemed to me of an extraordinary insignificance. People—I had been able during the music to remember them, to blend them with it; or rather I had blended with the music little more than the memory of one person only, which was

Albertine. And the phrase that ended the andante seemed to me so sublime that I said to myself that it was a pity that Albertine did not know it, and, had she known it, would not have understood what an honour it was to be blended with anything so great as this phrase which brought us together, and the pathetic voice of which she seemed to have borrowed. But, once the music was interrupted, the people who were present seemed utterly lifeless. Refreshments were handed round. M. de Charlus accosted a footman now and then with: "How are you? Did you get my note? Can you come?" No doubt there was in these remarks the freedom of the great nobleman who thinks he is flattering his hearer and is himself more one of the people than a man of the middle classes; there was also the cunning of the criminal who imagines that anything which he volunteers is on that account regarded as innocent. And he added, in the Guermantes tone of Mme. de Villeparisis: "He's a good young fellow, such a good sort, I often employ him at home." But his adroitness turned against the Baron, for people thought his intimate conversation and correspondence with footmen extraordinary. The footmen themselves were not so much flattered as embarrassed, in the presence of their comrades. Meanwhile the septet had begun again and was moving towards its close; again and again one phrase or another from the sonata recurred, but always changed, its rhythm and harmony different, the same and yet something else, as things recur in life; and they were phrases of the sort which, without our being able to understand what affinity assigns to them as their sole and necessary home the past life of a certain composer, are to be found only in his work, and appear constantly in it, where they are the fairies, the dryads, the household gods; I had at the start distinguished in the septet two or three which reminded me of the sonata. Presently—bathed in the violet mist which rose particularly in Vinteuil's later work, so much so that, even when he introduced a dance measure, it remained captive in the heart of an opal—I caught the sound of another phrase from the sonata, still hovering so remote that I barely recognised it; hesitating, it approached, vanished as though in alarm, then returned, joined hands with others, come, as I learned later on, from other works, summoned yet others which became in their turn attractive and persuasive, as soon as they were tamed, and took their places in the ring, a ring divine but permanently invisible to the bulk of the audience, who, having before their eyes only a thick veil through which they saw nothing, punctuated arbitrarily with admiring exclamations a continuous boredom which was becoming deadly. Then they withdrew, save one which I saw reappear five times or six, without being able to distinguish its features, but so caressing, so different—as was no doubt the little phrase in Swann's sonata—from anything that any woman had ever made me desire, that this phrase which offered me in so sweet a voice a happiness which would really have been worth the struggle to obtain it, is perhaps—this invisible creature whose language I did not know and whom I understood so well—the only Stranger that it has ever been my good fortune to meet. Then this phrase broke up, was transformed, like the little phrase in the sonata, and became the mysterious appeal of the start. A phrase of a plaintive kind rose in opposition to it, but so profound, so vague, so internal, almost so organic and visceral that one could not tell at each of its repetitions whether they were those of a theme or of an attack of neuralgia. Presently these two motives were wrestling together in a close fight in which now one disappeared entirely, and now the listener could catch only a fragment of the other. A wrestling match of energies only, to tell the truth; for if these creatures attacked one another, it was rid of their physical bodies, of their appearance, of their names, and finding in me an inward spectator, himself indifferent also to their names and to all details, interested only in their immaterial and dynamic combat and following with passion its sonorous changes. In the end the joyous motive was left triumphant; it was no longer an almost anxious appeal addressed to an empty sky, it was an ineffable joy which seemed to come from Paradise, a joy as different from that of the sonata as from a grave and gentle angel by Bellini, playing the theorbo, would be some archangel by Mantegna sounding a trump. I might be sure that this new tone of joy, this appeal to a super-terrestrial joy, was a thing that I would never forget. But should I be able, ever, to realise it? This question seemed to me all the more important, inasmuch as this phrase was what might have seemed most definitely to characterise —from its sharp contrast with all the rest of my life, with the visible world—those impressions which at remote intervals I recaptured in my life as starting-points, foundation-stones for the construction of a true life: the impression that I had felt at the sight of the steeples of Martinville, or of a line of trees near Balbec. In any case, to return to the particular accent of this phrase, how strange it was that the presentiment most different from

what life assigns to us on earth, the boldest approxima-
tion to the bliss of the world beyond should have been
materialised precisely in the melancholy, respectable little
old man whom we used to meet in the Month of Mary at
Combray; but, stranger still, how did it come about that
this revelation, the strangest that I had yet received, of
an unknown type of joy, should have come to me from
him, since, it was understood, when he died he left nothing
behind him but his sonata, all the rest being non-existent
in indecipherable scribblings. Indecipherable they may
have been, but they had nevertheless been in the end
deciphered, by dint of patience, intelligence and respect,
by the only person who had lived sufficiently in Vinteuil's
company to understand his method of working, to interpret his orchestral indications: Mlle. Vinteuil's friend.
Even in the lifetime of the great composer, she had
acquired from his daughter the reverence that the latter
felt for her father. It was because of this reverence that,
in those moments in which people run counter to their
natural inclinations, the two girls had been able to find
an insane pleasure in the profanations which have already been narrated. (Her adoration of her father was
the primary condition of his daughter's sacrilege. And
no doubt they ought to have foregone the delight of that
sacrilege, but it did not express the whole of their natures.) And, what is more, the profanations had become
rarefied until they disappeared altogether, in proportion
as their morbid carnal relations, that troubled, smoulder-
ing fire, had given place to the flame of a pure and lofty
friendship. Mlle. Vinteuil's friend was sometimes worried by the importunate thought that she had perhaps
hastened the death of Vinteuil. At any rate, by spending

years in poring over the cryptic scroll left by him, in establishing the correct reading of those illegible hieroglyphs, Mlle. Vinteuil's friend had the consolation of assuring the composer whose grey hairs she had sent in sorrow to the grave an immortal and compensating glory. Relations which are not consecrated by the laws establish bonds of kinship as manifold, as complex, even more solid than those which spring from marriage. Indeed, without pausing to consider relations of so special a nature, do we not find every day that adultery, when it is based upon genuine love, does not upset the family sentiment, the duties of kinship, but rather revivifies them. Adultery brings the spirit into what marriage would often have left a dead letter. A good-natured girl who merely from convention will wear mourning for her mother's second husband has not tears enough to shed for the man whom her mother has chosen out of all the world as her lover. Anyhow, Mlle. Vinteuil had acted only in a spirit of Sadism, which did not excuse her, but it gave me a certain consolation to think so later on. She must indeed have realised, I told myself, at the moment when she and her friend profaned her father's photograph, that what they were doing was merely morbidity, silliness, and not the true and joyous wickedness which she would have liked to feel. This idea that it was merely a pretence of wickedness spoiled her pleasure. But if this idea recurred to her mind later on, as it had spoiled her pleasure, so it must then have diminished her grief. " It was not I," she must have told herself, " I was out of my mind. I myself mean still to pray for my father's soul, not to despair of his forgiveness." Only it is possible that this idea, which had certainly presented itself to her in her pleasure, may not have presented itself in her grief. I would have liked to be able to put it into her mind. I am sure that I should have done her good and that I should have been able to reestablish between her and the memory of her father a pleasant channel of communication.

As in the illegible note-books in which a chemist of genius, who does not know that death is at hand, jots down discoveries which will perhaps remain forever unknown, Mlle. Vinteuil's friend had disentangled, from papers more illegible than strips of papyrus, dotted with a cuneiform script, the formula eternally true, forever fertile, of this unknown joy, the mystic hope of the crimson Angel of the dawn. And I to whom, albeit not so much perhaps as to Vinteuil, she had been also, she had been once more this very evening, by reviving afresh my jealousy of Albertine, she was above all in the future to be the cause of so many sufferings, it was thanks to her, in compensation, that there had been able to come to my ears the strange appeal which I should never for a moment cease to hear, as the promise and proof that there existed something other, realisable no doubt by art, than the nullity that I had found in all my pleasures and in love itself, and that if my life seemed to me so empty, at least there were still regions unexplored.

What she had enabled us, thanks to her labour, to know of Vinteuil was, to tell the truth, the whole of Vinteuil's work. Compared with this septet, certain phrases from the sonata which alone the public knew appeared so commonplace that one failed to understand how they could have aroused so much admiration. Similarly we are surprised that, for years past, pieces as trivial as the *Evening Star* or *Elisabeth's Prayer* can have aroused in the concert-hall fanatical worshippers who wore themselves out in applause and in crying *encore* at the end of what after all is poor and trite to us who know *Tristan,* the *Rheingold* and the *Meistersinger.* We are left to suppose that those featureless melodies contained already nevertheless in infinitesimal, and for that reason, perhaps, more easily assimilable quantities, something of the originality of the masterpieces which, in retrospect, are alone of importance to us, but which their very perfection may perhaps have prevented from being understood; they have been able to prepare the way for them in our hearts. Anyhow it is true that, if they gave a confused presentiment of the beauties to come, they left these in a state of complete obscurity. It was the same with Vinteuil; if at his death he had left behind him— excepting certain parts of the sonata—only what he had been able to complete, what we should have known of him would have been, in relation to his true greatness, as little as, in the case of, say, Victor Hugo, if he had died after the *Pas d'Armes du Roi Jean,* the *Fiancée du Timbalier* and *Sarah la Baigneuse,* without having written a line of the *Légende des Siècles* or the *Contemplations:* what is to us his real work would have remained purely potential, as unknown as those universes to which our perception does not attain, of which we shall never form any idea.

Anyhow, the apparent contrast, that profound union between genius (talent too and even virtue) and the sheath of vices in which, as had happened in the case of Vinteuil, it is so frequently contained, preserved, was legible, as in a popular allegory, in the mere assembly of the guests among whom I found myself once again when the music had come to an end. This assembly, albeit limited this time to Mme. Verdurin's drawing-room, resembled many others, the ingredients of which are unknown to the general public, and which philosophical journalists, if they are at all well-informed, call Parisian, or Panamist, or Dreyfusard, never suspecting that they may equally well be found in Petersburg, Berlin, Madrid, and at every epoch; if as a matter of fact the Under Secretary of State for Fine Arts, an artist to his fingertips, well-bred and smart, several Duchesses and three Ambassadors with their wives were present this evening at Mme. Verdurin's, the proximate, immediate cause of their presence lay in the relations that existed between M. de Charlus and Morel, relations which made the Baron anxious to give as wide a celebrity as possible to the artistic triumphs of his young idol, and to obtain for him the cross of the Legion of Honour; the remoter cause which had made this assembly possible was that a girl living with Mlle. Vinteuil in the same way as the Baron was living with Charlie had brought to light a whole series of works of genius which had been such a revelation that before long a subscription was to be opened under the patronage of the Minister of Education, with the object of erecting a statue of Vinteuil. Moreover, these works had been assisted, no less than by Mlle. Vinteuil's relations with her friend, by the Baron's relations with Charlie, a sort of cross-road, a short cut, thanks to which the world was enabled to overtake these works without the preliminary circuit, if not of a want of comprehension which would long persist, at least of a complete ignorance which might have lasted for years. Whenever an event occurs which is within the range of the vulgar mind of the moralising journalist, a political event as a rule, the moralising journalists are convinced that there has been some great change in France, that we shall never see such evenings again, that no one will ever again admire Ibsen, Renan, Dostoievski, D'Annunzio, Tolstoi, Wagner, Strauss. For moralising journalists take their text from the equivocal undercurrents of these official manifestations, in order to find something decadent in the art which is there celebrated and which as often as not is more austere than any other. But there is no name among those most revered by these moralising journalists which has not quite naturally given rise to some such strange gathering, although its strangeness may have been less flagrant and better concealed. In the case of this gathering, the impure elements that associated themselves with it struck me from another aspect; to be sure, I was as well able as anyone to dissociate them, having learned to know them separately, but anyhow it came to pass that some of them, those which concerned Mlle. Vinteuil and her friend, speaking to me of Combray, spoke to me also of Albertine, that is to say of Balbec, since it was because I had long ago seen Mlle. Vinteuil at Montjouvain and had learned of her friend's intimacy with Albertine, that I was presently, when I returned home, to find, instead of solitude, Albertine awaiting me, and that the others, those which concerned Morel and M. de Charlus, speaking to me of Balbec, where I had seen, on the platform at Doncières, their intimacy begin, spoke to me of Combray and of its two " ways," for M. de Charlus was one of those Guermantes, Counts of Combray, inhabiting Combray without having any dwelling there, between earth and heaven, like Gilbert the Bad in his window: while, after all, Morel was the son of that old valet who had enabled me to know the lady in pink, and had permitted me, years after, to identify her with Mme. Swann.

M. de Charlus repeated, when, the music at an end, his guests came to say good-bye to him, the same error that he had made when they arrived. He did not ask them to shake hands with their hostess, to include her and her husband in the gratitude that was being showered on himself. There was a long queue waiting, but a queue that led to the Baron alone, a fact of which he must have been conscious, for as he said to me a little later: "The form of the artistic celebration ended in a ' few-words-in-the-vestry' touch that was quite amusing." The guests even prolonged their expressions of gratitude with indiscriminate remarks which enabled them to remain for a moment longer in the Baron's presence, while those who had not yet congratulated him on the success of his party hung wearily in the rear. A stray husband or two may have announced his intention of going; but his wife, a snob as well as a Duchess, protested: "No, no, even if we are kept waiting an hour, we cannot go away without thanking Palamède, who has taken so much trouble. There is nobody else left now who can give entertainments like this." Nobody would have thought of asking to be introduced to Mme. Verdurin any more than to the attendant in a theatre to which some great lady has for one evening brought the whole aristocracy. "Were you at Eliane de Montmorency's yesterday, cousin?" asked Mme. de Mortemart, seeking an excuse to prolong their conversation. "Good gracious, no; I like Eliane, but I never can understand her invitations. I must be very stupid, I'm afraid," he went on, parting his lips in a broad smile, while Mme. de Mortemart realised that she was to be made the first recipient of " one of Palamède's " as she had often been of " one of Oriane's." " I did indeed receive a card a fortnight ago from the charming Eliane. Above the questionably authentic name of ' Montmorency ' was the following kind invitation: 'My dear cousin, will you please remember me next Friday at half-past nine.' Beneath were written two less gratifying words: ' Czech Quartet.' These seemed to me incomprehensible, and in any case to have no more connexion with the sentence above than the words 'My dear ——,' which you find on the back of a letter, with nothing else after them, when the writer has already begun again on the other side, and has not taken a fresh sheet, either from carelessness or in order to save paper. I am fond of Eliane: and so I felt no annoyance, I merely ignored the strange and inappropriate allusion to a Czech Quartet, and, as I am a methodical man, I placed on my chimneypiece the invitation to remember Madame de Montmorency on Friday at half-past nine. Although renowned for my obedient, punctual and meek nature, as Buffon says of the camel "—at this, laughter seemed to radiate from M. de Charlus who knew that on the contrary he was regarded as the most impossible person to live with—" I was a few minutes late (it took me a few minutes to change my clothes), and without any undue remorse, thinking that half-past nine meant ten, at the stroke of ten in a comfortable dressing-gown, with warm slippers on my feet, I sat down in my chimney corner to remember Eliane as she had asked me and with a concentration which began to relax only at half-past ten. Tell her please that I complied strictly with her audacious request. I am sure she will be gratified." Mme. de Mortemart was helpless with laughter, in which M. de Charlus joined. "And to-morrow," she went on, forgetting that she had already long exceeded the time that might be allotted to her, "are you going to our La Rochefoucauld cousins?" "Oh, that, now, is quite impossible, they have invited me, and you too, I see, to a thing it is utterly impossible to imagine, which is called, if I am to believe their card of invitation, a 'dancing tea.' I used to be considered pretty nimble when I was young, but I doubt whether I could ever decently have drunk a cup of tea while I was dancing. No, I have never cared for eating or drinking in unnatural positions. You will remind me that my dancing days are done. But even sitting down comfortably to drink my tea—of the quality of which I am suspicious since it is called 'dancing'—I should be afraid lest other guests younger than myself, and less nimble possibly than I was at their age, might spill their cups over my clothes which would interfere with my pleasure in draining my own." Nor indeed was M. de Charlus content with leaving Mme. Verdurin out of the conversation while he spoke of all manner of subjects which he seemed to be taking pleasure in developing and varying, that cruel pleasure which he had always enjoyed of keeping indefinitely on their feet the friends who were waiting with an excruciating patience for their turn to come; he even criticised all that part of the entertainment for which Mme. Verdurin was responsible. "But, talking about cups, what in the world are those strange little bowls which remind me of the vessels in which, when I was a young man, people used to get sorbets from Poiré Blanche. Somebody said to me just now that they were for 'iced coffee.' But if it comes to that, I have seen neither coffee nor ice. What curious little objects—so very ambiguous." In saying this M. de Charlus had placed his white-gloved hands vertically over his lips and had modestly circumscribed his indicative stare as though he were afraid of being heard, or even seen by his host and hostess. But this was a mere feint, for in a few minutes he would be offering the same criticisms to the Mistress herself, and a little later would be insolently enjoining: "No more iced-coffee cups, remember! Give them to one of your friends whose house you wish to disfigure. But warn her not to have them in the drawing-room, or people might think that they had come into the wrong room, the things are so exactly like chamberpots." "But, cousin," said the guest, lowering her own voice also, and casting a questioning glance at M. de Charlus, for she was afraid of offending not Mme. Verdurin but him, "perhaps she doesn't quite know yet. . . ." "She shall be taught." "Oh!" laughed the guest, "she couldn't have a better teacher! She *is* lucky! If you are in charge, one can be sure there won't be a false note." "There wasn't one, if it comes to that, in the music." "Oh! It was sublime. One of those pleasures which can never be forgotten. Talking of that marvellous violinist," she went on, imagining in her innocence that M. de Charlus was interested in the violin "pure and simple," "do you happen to know one whom I heard the other day playing too wonderfully a sonata by Fauré, his name is Frank. . . ." "Oh, he's a horror," replied M. de Charlus, overlooking the rudeness of a contradiction which implied that his cousin was lacking in taste. "As far as violinists are concerned, I advise you to confine yourself to mine." This paved the way to a fresh exchange of glances, at once furtive and scrutinous, between M. de Charlus and his cousin, for, blushing and seeking by her zeal to atone for her blunder, Mme. de Mortemart went on to suggest to M. de Charlus that she might give a party, to hear Morel play. Now, so far as she was concerned, this party had not the object of bringing an unknown talent into prominence, an object which she would, however, pretend to have in mind, and which was indeed that of M. de Charlus. She regarded it only as an opportunity for giving a particularly smart party and was calculating already whom she would invite and whom she would reject. This business of selection, the chief preoccupation of people who give parties (even the people whom "society" journalists are so impudent or so foolish as to call "the élite"), alters at once the expression—and the handwriting—of a hostess more profoundly than any hypnotic suggestion. Before she had even thought of what Morel was to play (which she regarded, and rightly, as a secondary consideration, for even if everybody this evening, from fear of M. de Charlus, had observed a polite silence during the music, it would never have occurred to anyone to listen to it), Mme. de Mortemart, having decided that Mme. de Valcourt was not to be one of the elect, had automatically assumed that air of conspiracy, of a secret plotting which so degrades even those women in society who can most easily afford to ignore what "people will say." "Wouldn't it be possible for me to give a party, for people to hear your friend play?" murmured Mme. de Mortemart, who, while addressing herself exclusively to M. de Charlus, could not refrain, as though under a fascination, from casting a glance at Mme. de Valcourt (the rejected) in order to make certain that the other was too far away to hear her. "No she cannot possibly hear what I am saying," Mme. de Mortemart concluded inwardly, re-assured by her own glance which as a matter of fact had had a totally different effect upon Mme. de Valcourt from that intended: "Why," Mme. de Valcourt had said to herself when she caught this glance, "Marie-Thérèse is planning something with Palamède which I am not to be told." "You mean my protégé," M. de Charlus corrected, as merciless to his cousin's choice of words as he was to her musical endowments. Then without paying the slightest attention to her silent prayers, as she made a smiling apology: "Why, yes . . ." he said in a loud tone, audible throughout the room, "although there is always a risk in that sort of exportation of a fascinating personality into surroundings that must inevitably diminish his transcendent gifts and would in any case have to be adapted to them." Madame de Mortemart told herself that the aside, the pianissimo of her question had been a waste of trouble, after the megaphone through which the answer had issued. She was mistaken. Mme. de Valcourt heard nothing, for the simple reason that she did not understand a single word. Her anxiety diminished and would rapidly have been extinguished had not Mme. de Mortemart, afraid that she might have been given away and afraid of having to invite Mme. de Valcourt, with whom she was on too intimate terms to be able to leave her out if the other knew about her party beforehand, raised her eyelids once again in Edith's direction, as though not to lose sight of a threatening peril, lowering them again briskly so as not to commit herself. She intended, on the morning after the party, to write her one of those letters, the complement of the revealing glance, letters which people suppose to be subtle and which are tantamount to a full and signed confession. For instance: "Dear Edith, I am so sorry about you, I did not really expect you last night" ("How could she have expected me," Edith would ask herself, "since she never invited me?") "as I know that you are not very fond of parties of that sort, which rather bore you. We should have been greatly honoured, all the same, by your company" (never did Mme. de Mortemart employ the word "honoured," except in the letters in which she attempted to cloak a lie in the semblance of truth). "You know that you are always at home in our house. however, you were quite right, as it was a complete failure, like everything that is got up at a moment's notice." But already the second furtive glance darted at her had enabled Edith to grasp everything that was concealed by the complicated language of M. de Charlus. This glance was indeed so violent that, after it had struck Mme. de Valcourt, the obvious secrecy and mischievous intention that it embodied rebounded upon a young Peruvian whom Mme. de Mortemart intended, on the contrary, to invite. But being of a suspicious nature, seeing all too plainly the mystery that was being made without realising that it was not intended to mystify him, he at once conceived a violent hatred of Mme. de Mortemart and determined to play all sorts of tricks upon her, such as ordering fifty iced coffees to be sent to her house on a day when she was not giving a party, or, when she was, inserting a paragraph in the newspapers announcing that the party was postponed, and publishing false reports of her other parties, in which would figure the notorious names of all the people whom, for various reasons, a hostess does not invite or even allow to be introduced to her. Mme. de Mortemart need not have bothered herself about Mme. de Valcourt. M. de Charlus was about to spoil, far more effectively than the other's presence could spoil it, the projected party. "But, my dear cousin," she said in response to the expression "adapting the surroundings," the meaning of which her momentary state of hyperaesthesia had enabled her to discern, "we shall save you all the trouble. I undertake to ask Gilbert to arrange everything." "Not on any account, all the more as he must not be invited to it. Nothing can be arranged except by myself. The first thing is to exclude all the people who have ears and hear not." M. de Charlus's cousin, who had been reckoning upon Morel as an attraction in order to give a party at which she could say that, unlike so many of her kinswomen, she had "had Palamède," carried her thoughts abruptly, from this prestige of M. de Charlus, to all sorts of people with whom he would get her into trouble if he began interfering with the list of her guests. The thought that the Prince de Guermantes (on whose account, partly, she was anxious to exclude Mme. de Valcourt, whom he declined to meet) was not to be invited, alarmed her. Her eyes assumed an uneasy expression. "Is the light, which is rather too strong, hurting you?" inquired M. de Charlus with an apparent seriousness the underlying irony of which she failed to perceive. "No, not at all, I was thinking of the difficulty, not for myself of course, but for my family, if Gilbert were to hear that I had given a party without inviting him, when he never has a cat on his housetop without. . . ." "Why of course, we must begin by eliminating the cat on the housetop, which could only miaow; I suppose that the din of talk has prevented you from realising that it was a question not of doing the civilities of a hostess but of proceeding to the rites customary at every true celebration." Then, deciding, not that the next person had been kept waiting too long, but that it did not do to exaggerate the favours shewn to one who had in mind not so much Morel as her own visiting-list, M. de Charlus, like a physician who cuts short a consultation when he considers that it has lasted long enough, gave his cousin a signal to withdraw, not by bidding her good night but by turning to the person immediately behind her. "Good evening, Madame de Montesquiou, marvellous, wasn't it? I have not seen Hélène, tell her that every general abstention, even the most noble, that is to say her own, must include exceptions, if they are brilliant, as has been the case to-night. To shew that one is rare is all very well, but to subordinate one's rarity, which is only negative, to what is precious is better still. In your sister's case, and I value more than anyone her systematic *absence* from places where what is in store for her is not worthy of her, here to-night, on the contrary, her presence at so memorable an exhibition as this would have been a *presidence*, and would have given your sister, already so distinguished, an additional distinction." Then he turned to a third person, M. d'Argencourt. I was greatly astonished to see in this room, as friendly and flattering towards M. de Charlus as he was severe with him elsewhere, insisting upon Morel's being introduced to him and telling him that he hoped he would come and see him, M. d'Argencourt, that terrible scourge of men such as M. de Charlus. At the moment he was living in the thick of them. It was certainly not because he had in any sense become one of them himself. But for some time past he had practically deserted his wife for a young woman in society whom he adored. Being intelligent herself, she made him share her taste for intelligent people, and was most anxious to have M. de Charlus in her house. But above all M. d'Argencourt, extremely jealous and not unduly potent, feeling that he was failing to satisfy his captive and anxious at once to introduce her to people and to keep her amused, could do so without risk to himself only by surrounding her with innocuous men, whom he thus cast for the part of guardians of his seraglio. These men found that he had become quite pleasant and declared that he was a great deal more intelligent than they had supposed, a discovery that delighted him and his mistress.

The remainder of M. de Charlus's guests drifted away fairly rapidly. Several of them said: "I don't want to call at the vestry" (the little room in which the Baron, with Charlie by his side, was receiving congratulations, and to which he himself had given the name), "but I must let Palamède see me so that he shall know that I stayed to the end." Nobody paid the slightest attention to Mme. Verdurin. Some pretended not to know which was she and said good night by mistake to Mme. Cottard, appealing to me for confirmation with a "That *is* Mme. Verdurin, ain't it?" Mme. d'Arpajon asked me, in the hearing of our hostess: "Tell me, has there ever been a Monsieur Verdurin?" The Duchesses, finding none of the oddities that they expected in this place which they had hoped to find more different from anything that they already knew, made the best of a bad job by going into fits of laughter in front of Elstir's paintings; for all the rest of the entertainment, which they found more in keeping than they had expected with the style with which they were familiar, they gave the credit to M. de Charlus, saying: "How clever Palamède is at arranging things; if he were to stage an opera in a stable or a bathroom, it would still be perfectly charming." The most noble ladies were those who shewed most fervour in congratulating M. de Charlus upon the success of a party, of the secret motive of which some of them were by no means unaware, without, however, being embarrassed by the knowledge, this class of society—remembering perhaps certain epochs in history when their own family had already arrived at an identical stage of brazenly conscious effrontery—carrying their contempt for scruples almost as far as their respect for etiquette. Several of them engaged Charlie on the spot for different evenings on which he was to come and play them Vinteuil's septet, but it never occurred to any of them to invite Mme. Verdurin. This last was already blind with fury when M. de Charlus who, his head in the clouds, was incapable of perceiving her condition, decided that it would be only decent to invite the Mistress to share his joy. And it was perhaps yielding to his literary preciosity rather than to an overflow of pride that this specialist in artistic entertainments said to Mme. Verdurin: "Well, are you satisfied? I think you have reason to be; you see that when I set to work to give a party there are no half-measures. I do not know whether your heraldic knowledge enables you to gauge the precise importance of the display, the weight that I have lifted, the volume of air that I have displaced for you. You have had the Queen of Naples, the brother of the King of Bavaria, the three premier peers. If Vinteuil is Mahomet, we may say that we have brought to him some of the least movable of mountains. Bear in mind that to attend your party the Queen of Naples has come up from Neuilly, which is a great deal more difficult for her than evacuating the Two Sicilies," he went on, with a deliberate sneer, notwithstanding his admiration for the Queen. "It is an historic event. Just think that it is perhaps the first time she has gone anywhere since the fall of Gaeta. It is probable that the dictionaries of dates will record as culminating points the day of the fall of Gaeta and that of the Verdurins' party. The fan that she laid down, the better to applaud Vinteuil, deserves to become more famous than the fan that Mme. de Metternich broke because the audience hissed Wagner." "Why, she has left it here," said Mme. Verdurin, momentarily appeased by the memory of the Queen's kindness to herself, and she shewed M. de Charlus the fan which was lying upon a chair. "Oh! What a touching spectacle!" exclaimed M. de Charlus, approaching the relic with veneration. "It is all the more touching, it is so hideous; poor little Violette is incredible!" And spasms of emotion and irony coursed through him alternately. "Oh dear, I don't know whether you feel this sort of thing as I do. Swann would positively have died of convulsions if he had seen it. I am sure, whatever price it fetches, I shall buy the fan at the Queen's sale. For she is bound to be sold up, she hasn't a penny," he went on, for he never ceased to intersperse the cruellest slanders with the most sincere veneration, albeit these sprang from two opposing natures, which, however, were combined in himself. They might even be brought to bear alternately upon the same incident. For M. de Charlus who in his comfortable state as a wealthy man ridiculed the poverty of the Queen was himself often to be heard extolling that poverty and, when anyone spoke of Princesse Murat, Queen of the Two Sicilies, would reply: "I do not know to whom you are alluding. There is only one Queen of Naples, who is a sublime person and does not keep a carriage. But from her omnibus she annihilates every vehicle on the street and one could kneel down in the dust on seeing her drive past." "I shall bequeath it to a museum. In the meantime, it must be sent back to her, so that she need not hire a cab to come and fetch it. The wisest thing, in view of the historical interest of such an object, would be to steal the fan. But that would be awkward for her—since it is probable that she does not possess another!" he added, with a shout of laughter. "Anyhow, you see that for my sake she came. And that is not the only miracle that I have performed. I do not believe that anyone at the present day has the power to move the people whom I have brought here. However, everyone must be given his due. Charlie and the rest of the musicians played divinely. And, my dear Mistress," he added condescendingly, "you yourself have played your part on this occasion. Your name will not be unrecorded. History has preserved that of the page who armed Joan of Arc when she set out for battle; indeed you have served as a connecting link, you have made possible the fusion between Vinteuil's music and its inspired interpreter, you have had the intelligence to appreciate the capital importance of the whole chain of circumstances which would enable the interpreter to benefit by the whole weight of a considerable—if I were not referring to myself, I would say providential—personage, whom you were clever enough to ask to ensure the success of the gathering, to bring before Morel's violin the ears directly attached to the tongues that have the widest hearing; no, no, it is not a small matter. There can be no small matter in so complete a realisation. Everything has its part. The Duras was marvellous. In fact, everything; that is why," he concluded, for he loved to administer a rebuke, " I set my face against your inviting those persons—divisors who, among the overwhelming people whom I brought you would have played the part of the decimal points in a sum, reducing the others to a merely fractional value. I have a very exact appreciation of that sort of thing. You understand, we must avoid blunders when we are giving a party which ought to be worthy of Vinteuil, of his inspired interpreter, of yourself, and, I venture to say, of me. You were prepared to invite the Molé, and everything would have been spoiled. It would have been the little contrary, neutralising drop which deprives a potion of its virtue. The electric lights would have fused, the pastry would not have come in time, the orangeade would have given everybody a stomach-ache. She was the one person not to invite. At the mere sound of her name, as in a fairy-tale, not a note would have issued from the brass; the flute and the hautboy would have been stricken with a sudden silence. Morel himself, even if he had succeeded in playing a few bars, would not have been in tune, and instead of Vinteuil's septet you would have had a parody of it by Beckmesser, ending amid catcalls. I, who believe strongly in personal influence, could feel quite plainly in the expansion of a certain largo, which opened itself right out like a flower, in the supreme satisfaction of the finale, which was not merely allegro but incomparably allegro, that the absence of the Molé was inspiring the musicians and was diffusing joy among the very instruments themselves. In any case, when one is at home to Queens one does not invite one's hall-portress." In calling her "the Molé" (as for that matter he said quite affectionately "the Duras") M. de Charlus was doing the lady justice. For all these women were the actresses of society and it is true also that, even regarding her from this point of view, Comtesse Molé did not justify the extraordinary reputation for intelligence that she had acquired, which made one think of those mediocre actors or novelists who, at certain periods, are hailed as men of genius, either because of the mediocrity of their competitors, among whom there is no artist capable of revealing what is meant by true talent, or because of the mediocrity of the public, which, did there exist an extraordinary individuality, would be incapable of understanding it. In Mme. Molé's case it is preferable, if not absolutely fair, to stop at the former explanation. The social world being the realm of nullity, there exist between the merits of women in society only insignificant degrees, which are at best capable of rousing to madness the rancours or the imagination of M. de Charlus. And certainly, if he spoke as he had just been speaking in this language which was a precious alloy of artistic and social elements, it was because his old-womanly anger and his culture as a man of the world furnished the genuine eloquence that he possessed with none but insignificant themes. Since the world of differences does not exist on the surface of the earth, among all the countries which our perception renders uniform, all the more reason why it should not exist in the social "world." Does it exist anywhere else? Vinteuil's septet had seemed to tell me that it did. But where? As M. de Charlus also enjoyed repeating what one person had said of another, seeking to stir up quarrels, to divide and reign, he added: "You have, by not inviting her, deprived Mme. Molé of the opportunity of saying: 'I can't think why this Mme. Verdurin should invite me. I can't imagine who these people are, I don't know them.' She was saying a year ago that you were boring her with your advances. She's a fool, never invite her again. After all, she's nothing so very wonderful. She can come to your house without making a fuss about it, seeing that I come here. In short," he concluded, "it seems to me that you have every reason to thank me, for, so far as it went, everything has been perfect. The Duchesse de Guermantes did not come, but one can't tell, it was better perhaps that she didn't. We shan't bear her any grudge, and we shall remember her all the same another time, not that one can help remembering her, her very eyes say to us 'Forget me not!', for they are a pair of myosotes" (here I thought to myself how strong the Guermantes spirit—the decision to go to one house and not to another —must be, to have outweighed in the Duchess's mind her fear of Palamède). "In the face of so complete a success, one is tempted like Bernardin de Saint-Pierre to see everywhere the hand of Providence. The Duchesse de Duras was enchanted. She even asked me to tell you so," added M. de Charlus, dwelling upon the words as though Mme. Verdurin must regard this as a sufficient honour. Sufficient and indeed barely credible, for he found it necessary, if he was to be believed, to add, completely carried away by the madness of those whom Jupiter has decided to ruin: " She has engaged Morel to come to her house, where the same programme will be repeated, and I even think of asking her for an invitation for M. Verdurin." This civility to the husband alone was, although no such idea even occurred to M. de Charlus, the most wounding outrage to the wife who, believing herself to possess, with regard to the violinist, by virtue of a sort of ukase which prevailed in the little clan, the right to forbid him to perform elsewhere without her express authorisation, was fully determined to forbid his appearance at Mme. de Duras's party.

The Baron's volubility was in itself an irritation to Mme. Verdurin who did not like people to form independent groups within their little clan. How often, even at la Raspelière, hearing M. de Charlus talking incessantly to Charlie instead of being content with taking his part in the so harmonious chorus of the clan, she had pointed to him and exclaimed: "What a rattle [1] he is! What a rattle! Oh, if it comes to rattles, he's a famous rattle!" But this time it was far worse. Inebriated with the sound of his own voice, M. de Charlus failed to realise that by cutting down the part assigned to Mme. Verdurin and confining it within narrow limits, he was calling forth that feeling of hatred which was in her only a special, social form of jealousy. Mme. Verdurin was genuinely fond of her regular visitors, the faithful of the little clan,

---

[1] Mme. Verdurin uses here the word *tapette,* being probably unaware of its popular meaning. C. K. S. M.

but wished them to be entirely devoted to their Mistress. Willing to make some sacrifice, like those jealous lovers who will tolerate a betrayal, but only under their own roof and even before their eyes, that is to say when there is no betrayal, she would allow the men to have mistresses, lovers, on condition that the affair had no social conse- quence outside her own house, that the tie was formed and perpetuated in the shelter of her Wednesdays. In the old days, every furtive peal of laughter that came from Odette when she conversed with Swann had gnawed her heartstrings, and so of late had every aside exchanged by Morel and the Baron; she found one consolation alone for her griefs which was to destroy the happiness of other people. She had not been able to endure for long that of the Baron. And here was this rash person precipitat- ing the catastrophe by appearing to be restricting the Mistress's place in her little clan. Already she could see Morel going into society, without her, under the Baron's aegis. There was but a single remedy, to make Morel choose between the Baron and herself, and, relying upon the ascendancy that she had acquired over Morel by the display that she made of an extraordinary perspicacity, thanks to reports which she collected, to falsehoods which she invented, all of which served to corroborate what he himself was led to believe, and what would in time be made plain to him, thanks to the pitfalls which she was preparing, into which her unsuspecting victims would fall, relying upon this ascendancy, to make him choose herself in preference to the Baron. As for the society ladies who had been present and had not even asked to be introduced to her, as soon as she grasped their hesita- tions or indifference, she had said: "Ah! I see what they are, the sort of old good-for-nothings that are not our style, it's the last time they shall set foot in this house." For she would have died rather than admit that anyone had been less friendly to her than she had hoped. "Ah! My dear General," M. de Charlus suddenly exclaimed, abandoning Mme. Verdurin, as he caught sight of General Deltour, Secretary to the President of the Republic, who might be of great value in securing Charlie his Cross, and who, after asking some question of Cottard, was rapidly withdrawing: "Good evening, my dear, delightful friend. So this is how you slip away without saying good-bye to me," said the Baron with a genial, self-satisfied smile, for he knew quite well that people were always glad to stay behind for a moment to talk to himself. And as, in his present state of excitement, he would answer his own questions in a shrill tone: "Well, did you enjoy it? Wasn't it really fine? The andante, what? It's the most touching thing that was ever written. I defy anyone to listen to the end without tears in his eyes. Charming of you to have come. Listen, I had the most perfect telegram this morning from Froberville, who tells me that as far as the Grand Chancery goes the difficulties have been smoothed away, as the saying is." M. de Charlus's voice continued to soar at this piercing pitch, as different from his normal voice as is that of a barrister making an emphatic plea from his ordinary utterance, a phenomenon of vocal amplification by over-excitement and nervous tension analogous to that which, at her own dinner-parties, raised to so high a diapason the voice and gaze alike of Mme. de Guermantes. "I intended to send you a note to-morrow by a messenger to tell you of my enthusiasm, until I could find an opportunity of speaking to you, but you have been so surrounded! Froberville's support is not to be despised, but for my own part, I have the Minister's promise," said the General. "Ah! Excellent. Besides, you have seen for yourself that it is only what such talent deserves. Hoyos was delighted, I didn't manage to see the Ambassadress, was she pleased? Who would not have been, except those that have ears and hear not, which does not matter so long as they have tongues and can speak." Taking advantage of the Baron's having withdrawn to speak to the general, Mme. Verdurin made a signal to Brichot. He, not knowing what Mme. Verdurin was going to say, sought to amuse her, and never suspecting the anguish that he was causing me, said to the Mistress: "The Baron is delighted that Mlle. Vinteuil and her friend did not come. They shock him terribly. He declares that their morals are appalling. You can't imagine how prudish and severe the Baron is on moral questions." Contrary to Brichot's expectation, Mme. Verdurin was not amused: "He is obscene," was her answer. "Take him out of the room to smoke a cigarette with you, so that my husband can get hold of his Dulcinea without his noticing it and warn him of the abyss that is yawning at his feet." Brichot seemed to hesitate. "I don't mind telling you," Mme. Verdurin went on, to remove his final scruples, "that I do not feel at all safe with a man like that in the house. I know, there are all sorts of horrible stories about him, and the police have him under supervision." And, as she possessed a certain talent of improvisation when inspired by malice, Mme. Verdurin did not stop at this: "It seems, he has been in prison. Yes, yes, I have been told by people who

knew all about it. I know, too, from a person who lives
in his street, that you can't imagine the ruffians that go
to his house." And as Brichot, who often went to the
Baron's, began to protest, Mme. Verdurin, growing animated, exclaimed: "But I can assure you! It is I who
am telling you," an expression with which she habitually
sought to give weight to an assertion flung out more or
less at random. "He will be found murdered in his bed
one of these days, as those people always are. He may
not go quite as far as that perhaps, because he is in the
clutches of that Jupien whom he had the impudence to
send to me, and who is an ex-convict, I know it, you
yourself know it, yes, for certain. He has a hold on him
because of some letters which are perfectly appalling, it
seems. I know it from somebody who has seen them, and
told me: 'You would be sick on the spot if you saw them.'
That is how Jupien makes him toe the line and gets all
the money he wants out of him. I would sooner die a
thousand times over than live in a state of terror like
Charlus. In any case, if Morel's family decides to bring
an action against him, I have no desire to be dragged in
as an accomplice. If he goes on, it will be at his own
risk, but I shall have done my duty. What is one to
do? It's no joke, I can tell you." And, agreeably
warmed already by the thought of her husband's impend-
ing conversation with the violinist, Mme. Verdurin said
to me: "Ask Brichot whether I am not a courageous
friend, and whether I am not capable of sacrificing myself
to save my comrades." (She was alluding to the circumstances in which she had, just in time, made him quarrel,
first of all with his laundress, and then with Mme. de
Cambremer, quarrels as a result of which Brichot had

become almost completely blind, and (people said) had taken to morphia.) "An incomparable friend, far-sighted and valiant," replied the Professor with an innocent emotion. "Mme. Verdurin prevented me from doing something extremely foolish," Brichot told me when she had left us. "She never hesitates to operate without anaesthetics. She is an interventionist, as our friend Cottard says. I admit, however, that the thought that the poor Baron is still unconscious of the blow that is going to fall upon him distresses me deeply. He is quite mad about that boy. If Mme. Verdurin should prove successful, there is a man who is going to be very miserable. However, it is not certain that she will not fail. I am afraid that she may only succeed in creating a misunderstanding between them, which, in the end, without parting them, will only make them quarrel with her." It was often thus with Mme. Verdurin and her faithful. But it was evident that in her the need to preserve their friendship was more and more dominated by the requirement that this friendship should never be challenged by that which they might feel for one another. Homosexuality did not disgust her so long as it did not tamper with orthodoxy, but like the Church she preferred any sacrifice rather than a concession of orthodoxy. I was beginning to be afraid lest her irritation with myself might be due to her having heard that I had prevented Albertine from going to her that afternoon, and that she might presently set to work, if she had not already begun, upon the same task of separating her from me which her husband, in the case of Charlus, was now going to attempt with the musician. "Come along, get hold of Charlus, find some excuse, there's no time to lose," said Mme. Verdurin, "and

whatever you do, don't let him come back here until I
send for you. Oh! What an evening," Mme. Verdurin
went on, revealing thus the true cause of her anger.
"Performing a masterpiece in front of those wooden
images. I don't include the Queen of Naples, she is intelligent, she is a nice woman" (which meant: "She has
been kind to me"). "But the others. Oh! It's enough
to drive anyone mad. What you can expect, I'm no
longer a girl. When I was young, people told me that
one must put up with boredom, I made an effort, but now,
oh no, it's too much for me, I am old enough to please myself, life is too short; bore myself, listen to idiots, smile,
pretend to think them intelligent. No, I can't do it.
Get along, Brichot, there's no time to lose." "I am going, Madame, I am going," said Brichot, as General
Deltour moved away. But first of all the Professor took
me aside for a moment: "Moral Duty," he said, "is less
clearly imperative than our Ethics teach us. Whatever
the Theosophical cafés and the Kantian beer-houses may
say, we are deplorably ignorant of the nature of Good.
I myself who, without wishing to boast, have lectured to
my pupils, in all innocence, upon the philosophy of the
said Immanuel Kant, I can see no precise ruling for the
case of social casuistry with which I am now confronted
in that Critique of Practical Reason in which the great
renegade of Protestantism platonised in the German
manner for a Germany prehistorically sentimental and
aulic, ringing all the changes of a Pomeranian mysticism.
It is still the Symposium, but held this time at Königs-
berg, in the local style, indigestible and reeking of sauer-
kraut, and without any good-looking boys. It is obvious
on the one hand that I cannot refuse our excellent hostess

the small service that she asks of me, in a fully orthodox conformity with traditional morals. One ought to avoid, above all things, for there are few that involve one in more foolish speeches, letting oneself be lured by words. But after all, let us not hesitate to admit that if the mothers of families were entitled to vote, the Baron would run the risk of being lamentably blackballed for the Chair of Virtue. It is unfortunately with the temperament of a rake that he pursues the vocation of a pedagogue; observe that I am not speaking evil of the Baron; that good man, who can carve a joint like nobody in the world, combines with a genius for anathema treasures of goodness. He can be most amusing as a superior sort of wag, whereas with a certain one of my colleagues, an Academician, if you please, I am bored, as Xenophon would say, at a hundred drachmae to the hour. But I am afraid that he is expending upon Morel rather more than a wholesome morality enjoins, and without knowing to what extent the young penitent shews himself docile or rebellious to the special exercises which his catechist imposes upon him by way of mortification, one need not be a learned clerk to be aware that we should be erring, as the other says, on the side of clemency with regard to this Rosicrucian who seems to have come down to us from Petronius, by way of Saint-Simon, if we granted him with our eyes shut, duly signed and sealed, permission to satanise. And yet, in keeping the man occupied while Mme. Verdurin, for the sinner's good and indeed rightly tempted by such a cure of souls, proceeds—by speaking to the young fool without any concealment—to remove from him all that he loves, to deal him perhaps a fatal blow, it seems to me that I am leading him into what one might call a man-trap, and I recoil as though from a base action." This said, he did not hesitate to commit it, but, taking him by the arm, began: "Come, Baron, let us go and smoke a cigarette, this young man has not yet seen all the marvels of the house." I made the excuse that I was obliged to go home. "Just wait a moment," said Brichot. "You remember, you are giving me a lift, and I have not forgotten your promise." "Wouldn't you like me, really, to make them bring out their plate, nothing could be simpler," said M. de Charlus. "You promised me, remember, not a word about Morel's decoration. I mean to give him the surprise of announcing it presently when people have begun to leave, although he says that it is of no importance to an artist, but that his uncle would like him to have it" (I blushed, for, I thought to myself, the Verdurins would know through my grandfather what Morel's uncle was). "Then you wouldn't like me to make them bring out the best pieces," said M. de Charlus. "Of course, you know them already, you have seen them a dozen times at la Raspelière." I dared not tell him that what might have interested me was not the mediocrity of even the most splendid plate in a middle-class household, but some specimen, were it only reproduced in a fine engraving, of Mme. Du Barry's. I was far too gravely preoccupied—even if I had not been by this revelation as to Mlle. Vinteuil's expected presence—always, in society, far too much distracted and agitated to fasten my attention upon objects that were more or less beautiful. It could have been arrested only by the appeal of some reality that addressed itself to my imagination, as might have been, this evening, a picture of that Venice of which I had thought so much

during the afternoon, or some general element, common
to several forms and more genuine than they, which, of
its own accord, never failed to arouse in me an inward
appreciation, normally lulled in slumber, the rising of
which to the surface of my consciousness filled me with
great joy. Well, as I emerged from the room known as
the concert-room, and crossed the other drawing-rooms
with Brichot and M. de Charlus, on discovering, transposed among others, certain pieces of furniture which I
had seen at la Raspelière and to which I had paid no
attention, I perceived, between the arrangement of the
town house and that of the country house, a certain
common air of family life, a permanent identity, and I
understood what Brichot meant when he said to me with
a smile: "There, look at this room, it may perhaps give
you an idea of what things were like in Rue Montalivet,
twenty-five years ago." From his smile, a tribute to the
defunct drawing-room which he saw with his mind's eye,
I understood that what Brichot, perhaps without realising
it, preferred in the old room, more than the large windows,
more than the gay youth of his hosts and their faithful,
was that unreal part (which I myself could discern from
some similarities between la Raspelière and Quai Conti)
of which, in a drawing-room as in everything else, the
external, actual part, liable to everyone's control, is but
the prolongation, was that part become purely imaginary,
of a colour which no longer existed save for my elderly
guide, which he was incapable of making me see, that
part which has detached itself from the outer world, to
take refuge in our soul, to which it gives a surplus value,
in which it is assimilated to its normal substance, trans-
forming itself—houses that have been pulled down, people

long dead, bowls of fruit at the suppers which we recall
—into that translucent alabaster of our memories, the
colour of which we are incapable of displaying, since we
alone see it, which enables us to say truthfully to other
people, speaking of things past, that they cannot form
any idea of them, that they do not resemble anything
that they have seen, while we are unable to think of them
ourself without a certain emotion, remembering that
it is upon the existence of our thoughts that there depends,
for a little time still, their survival, the brilliance of the
lamps that have been extinguished and the fragrance of
the arbours that will never bloom again. And possibly,
for this reason, the drawing-room in Rue Montalivert
disparaged, for Brichot, the Verdurins' present home.
But on the other hand it added to this home, in the
Professor's eyes, a beauty which it could not have in
those of a stranger. Those pieces of the original furniture that had been transported here, and sometimes arranged in the same groups, and which I myself remembered from la Raspelière, introduced into the new
drawing-room fragments of the old which, at certain
moments, recalled it so vividly as to create a hallucination
and then seemed themselves scarcely real from having
evoked in the midst of the surrounding reality fragments
of a vanished world which seemed to extend round about
them. A sofa that had risen up from dreamland between
a pair of new and thoroughly substantial armchairs,
smaller chairs upholstered in pink silk, the cloth surface
of a card-table raised to the dignity of a person since,
like a person, it had a past, a memory, retaining in the
chill and gloom of Quai Conti the tan of its roasting by
the sun through the windows of Rue Montalivet (where

it could tell the time of day as accurately as Mme. Verdurin herself) and through the glass doors at la Raspelière, where they had taken it and where it used to gaze out all day long over the flower-beds of the garden at the valley far below, until it was time for Cottard and the musician to sit down to their game; a posy of violets and pansies in pastel, the gift of a painter friend, now dead, the sole fragment that survived of a life that had vanished without leaving any trace, summarising a great talent and a long friendship, recalling his keen, gentle eyes, his shapely hand, plump and melancholy, while he was at work on it; the incoherent, charming disorder of the offerings of the faithful, which have followed the lady of the house on all her travels and have come in time to assume the fixity of a trait of character, of a line of destiny; a profusion of cut flowers, of chocolate-boxes which here as in the country systematised their growth in an identical mode of blossoming; the curious interpolation of those singular and superfluous objects which still appear to have been just taken from the box in which they were offered and remain for ever what they were at first, New Year's Day presents; all those things, in short, which one could not have isolated from the rest, but which for Brichot, an old frequenter of the Verdurin parties, had that patina, that velvety bloom of things to which, giving them a sort of profundity, an astral body has been added; all these things scattered before him, sounded in his ear like so many resonant keys which awakened cherished likenesses in his heart, confused reminiscences which, here in this drawing-room of the present day that was littered with them, cut out, defined, as on a fine day a shaft of sunlight cuts a section in the atmosphere, the furniture and carpets, and pursuing it from a cushion to a flower-stand, from a footstool to a lingering scent, from the lighting arrangements to the colour scheme, carved, evoked, spiritualised, called to life a form which might be called the ideal aspect, immanent in each of their successive homes, of the Verdurin drawing-room. "We must try," Brichot whispered in my ear, "to get the Baron upon his favourite topic. He is astounding." Now on the one hand I was glad of an opportunity to try to obtain from M. de Charlus information as to the coming of Mlle. Vinteuil and her friend. On the other hand, I did not wish to leave Albertine too long by herself, not that she could (being uncertain of the moment of my return, not to mention that, at so late an hour, she could not have received a visitor or left the house herself without arousing comment) make any evil use of my absence, but simply so that she might not find it too long. And so I told Brichot and M. de Charlus that I must shortly leave them. "Come with us all the same," said the Baron, whose social excitement was beginning to flag, but feeling that need to prolong, to spin out a conversation, which I had already observed in the Duchesse de Guermantes as well as in himself, and which, while distinctive of their family, extends in a more general fashion to all those people who, offering their minds no other realisation than talk, that is to say an imperfect realisation, remain unassuaged even after hours spent in one's company, and attach themselves more and more hungrily to their exhausted companion, from whom they mistakenly expect a satiety which social pleasures are incapable of giving. "Come, won't you," he repeated, "this is the pleasant moment at a party, the moment when all the guests have gone, the hour of Doña Sol; let us hope that it will end less tragically. Unfortunately you are in a hurry, in a hurry probably to go and do things which you would much better leave undone. People are always in a hurry and leave at the time when they ought to be arriving. We are here like Couture's philosophers, this is the moment in which to go over the events of the evening, to make what is called in military language a criticism of the operations. We might ask Mme. Verdurin to send us in a little supper to which we should take care not to invite her, and we might request Charlie —still *Hernani*—to play for ourselves alone the sublime adagio. Isn't it fine, that adagio? But where is the young violinist, I would like to congratulate him, this is the moment for tender words and embraces. Admit, Brichot, that they played like gods, Morel especially. Did you notice the moment when that lock of hair came loose? Ah, then, my dear fellow, you saw nothing at all. There was an F sharp at which Enesco, Capet and Thibaut might have died of jealousy; I may have appeared calm enough, I can tell you that at such a sound my heart was so wrung that I could barely control my tears. The whole room sat breathless; Brichot, my dear fellow," cried the Baron, gripping the other's arm which he shook violently, " it was sublime. Only young Charlie preserved a stony immobility, you could not even see him breathe, he looked like one of those objects of the inanimate world of which Théodore Rousseau speaks, which make us think, but do not think themselves. And then, all of a sudden," cried M. de Charlus with enthusiasm, making a pantomime gesture, " then . . . the Lock! And all the time, the charming little country-dance of the allegro vivace. You know, that lock was the symbol of the revelation, even to the most obtuse. The Princess of Taormina, deaf until then, for there are none so deaf as those that have ears and hear not, the Princess of Taormina, confronted by the message of the miraculous lock, realised that it was music that they were playing and not poker. Oh, that was indeed a solemn moment." "Excuse me, Sir, for interrupting you," I said to M. de Charlus, hoping to bring him to the subject in which I was interested, "you told me that the composer's daughter was to be present. I should have been most interested to meet her. Are you certain that she was expected?" "Oh, that I can't say." M. de Charlus thus complied, perhaps unconsciously, with that universal rule by which people withhold information from a jealous lover, whether in order to shew an absurd "comradeship," as a point of honour, and even if they detest her, with the woman who has excited his jealousy, or out of malice towards her, because they guess that jealousy can only intensify love, or from that need to be disagreeable to other people which consists in revealing the truth to the rest of the world but concealing it from the jealous, ignorance increasing their torment, or so at least the tormentors suppose, who, in their desire to hurt other people are guided by what they themselves believe, wrongly perhaps, to be most painful. "You know," he went on, "in this house they are a trifle prone to exaggerate, they are charming people, still they do like to catch celebrities of one sort or another. But you are not looking well, and you will catch cold in this damp room," he said, pushing a chair towards me. "Since you have not been well, you must take care of yourself, let me go and find you your coat. No, don't go for it yourself, you will lose your way and catch cold. How careless people are; you might be an infant in arms, you want an old nurse like me to look after you." "Don't trouble, Baron, let me go," said Brichot, and left us immediately; not being precisely aware perhaps of the very warm affection that M. de Charlus felt for me and of the charming lapses into simplicity and devotion that alternated with his delirious crises of grandeur and persecution, he was afraid that M. de Charlus, whom Mme. Verdurin had entrusted like a prisoner to his vigilance, might simply be seeking, under the pretext of asking for my greatcoat, to return to Morel and might thus upset the Mistress's plan.

Meanwhile Ski had sat down, uninvited, at the piano, and assuming—with a playful knitting of his brows, a remote gaze and a slight twist of his lips—what he imagined to be an artistic air, was insisting that Morel should play something by Bizet. "What, you don't like it, that boyish music of Bizet. Why, my dearr fellow," he said, with that rolling of the letter *r* which was one of his peculiarities, "it's rravishing." Morel, who did not like Bizet, said so in exaggerated terms and (as he had the reputation in the little clan of being, though it seems incredible, a wit) Ski, pretending to take the violinist's diatribes as paradoxes, bursts out laughing. His laugh was not, like M. Verdurin's, the stifled gasp of a smoker. Ski first of all assumed a subtle air, then allowed to escape, as though against his will, a single note of laughter, like the first clang from a belfry, followed by a silence in which the subtle gaze seemed to be making a competent examination of the absurdity of what had been said, then a second peal of laughter shook the air, followed presently by a merry angelus.

I expressed to M. de Charlus my regret that M. Brichot should be taking so much trouble. "Not at all, he is delighted, he is very fond of you, everyone is fond of you. Somebody was saying only the other day: 'We never see him now, he is isolating himself!' Besides, he is such a good fellow, is Brichot," M. de Charlus went on, never suspecting probably, in view of the affectionate, frank manner in which the Professor of Moral Philosophy conversed with him, that he had no hesitation in slandering him behind his back. "He is a man of great merit, immensely learned, and not a bit spoiled, his learning hasn't turned him into a bookworm, like so many of them who smell of ink. He has retained a breadth of outlook, a tolerance, rare in his kind. Sometimes, when one sees how well he understands life, with what a natural grace he renders everyone his due, one asks oneself where a humble little Sorbonne professor, an ex-schoolmaster, can have picked up such breeding. I am astonished at it myself." I was even more astonished when I saw the conversation of this Brichot, which the least refined of Mme. de Guermantes's friends would have found so dull, so heavy, please the most critical of them all, M. de Charlus. But to achieve this result there had collaborated, among other influences, themselves distinct also, those by virtue of which Swann, on the one hand, had so long found favour with the little clan, when he was in love with Odette, and on the other hand, after he married, found an attraction in Mme. Bontemps who, pretending to adore the Swann couple, came incessantly to call upon the wife and revelled in all the stories about the husband. Just as a writer gives the palm for intelligence, not to the most intelligent man, but to the worldling who utters a bold and tolerant comment upon the passion of a man for a woman, a comment which makes the writer's blue-stocking mistress agree with him in deciding that of all the people who come to her house the least stupid is after all this old beau who shews experience in the things of love, so M. de Charlus found more intelligent than the rest of his friends Brichot, who was not merely kind to Morel, but would cull from the Greek philosophers, the Latin poets, the authors of Oriental tales, appropriate texts which decorated the Baron's propensity with a strange and charming anthology. M. de Charlus had reached the age at which a Victor Hugo chooses to surround himself, above all, with Vacqueries and Meurices. He preferred to all others those men who tolerated his outlook upon life. " I see a great deal of him," he went on, in a balanced, sing-song tone, allowing no movement of his lips to stir his grave, powdered mask over which were purposely lowered his prelatical eyelids. " I attend his lectures, that atmosphere of the Latin Quarter refreshes me, there is a studious, thoughtful adolescence of young bourgeois, more intelligent, better read than were, in a different sphere, my own contemporaries. It is a different world, which you know probably better than I, they are young *bourgeois*," he said, detaching the last word to which he prefixed a string of *b*s, and emphasising it from a sort of habit of elocution, corresponding itself to a taste for fine distinctions in past history, which was peculiar to him, but perhaps also from inability to resist the pleasure of giving me a flick of his insolence. This did not in any way diminish the great and affectionate pity that was inspired in me by M. de Charlus (after Mme. Verdurin had revealed her plan in my hearing), it merely amused me, and indeed on any other occasion, when I should not have felt so kindly disposed towards him, would not have offended me. I derived from my grandmother such an absence of any self-importance that I might easily be found wanting in dignity. Doubtless, I was scarcely aware of this, and by dint of having seen and heard, from my schooldays onwards, my most esteemed companions take offence if anyone failed to keep an appointment, refuse to overlook any disloyal behaviour, I had come in time to exhibit in my speech and actions a second nature which was stamped with pride. It was indeed considered extremely proud, because, as I had never been timid, I had been easily led into duels, the moral prestige of which, however, I diminished by making little of them, which easily persuaded other people that they were absurd; but the true nature which we trample underfoot continues nevertheless to abide within us. Thus it is that at times, if we read the latest masterpiece of a man of genius, we are delighted to find in it all those of our own reflexions which we have always despised, joys and sorrows which we have repressed, a whole world of feelings scorned by us, the value of which the book in which we discover them afresh at once teaches us. I had come in time to learn from my experience of life that it was a mistake to smile a friendly smile when somebody made a fool of me, instead of feeling annoyed. But this want of self-importance and resentment, if I had so far ceased to express it as to have become almost entirely unaware that it existed in me, was nevertheless the primitive, vital element in which I was steeped. Anger and spite came to me only in a wholly different manner, in furious crises. What was more, the sense of justice was so far lacking in me as to amount to an entire want of moral sense. I was in my heart of hearts entirely won over to the side of the weaker party, and of anyone who was in trouble. I had no opinion as to the proportion in which good and evil might be blended in the relations between Morel and M. de Charlus, but the thought of the sufferings that were being prepared for M. de Charlus was intolerable to me. I would have liked to warn him, but did not know how to do it. "The spectacle of all that laborious little world is very pleasant to an old stick like myself. I do not know them," he went on, raising his hand with an air of reserve—so as not to appear to be boasting of his own conquests, to testify to his own purity and not to allow any suspicion to rest upon that of the students—"but they are most civil, they often go so far as to keep a place for me, since I am a very old gentleman. Yes indeed, my dear boy, do not protest, I am past forty," said the Baron, who was past sixty. "It is a trifle stuffy in the hall in which Brichot lectures, but it is always interesting." Albeit the Baron preferred to mingle with the youth of the schools, in other words to be jostled by them, sometimes, to save him a long wait in the lecture-room, Brichot took him in by his own door. Brichot might well be at home in the Sorbonne, at the moment when the janitor, loaded with chains of office, stepped out before him, and the master admired by his young pupils followed, he could not repress a certain timidity, and much as he desired to profit by that moment in which he felt himself so important to shew consideration for Charlus, he was neverthe-

less slightly embarrassed; so that the janitor should allow
him to pass, he said to him, in an artificial tone and with
a preoccupied air: "Follow me, Baron, they'll find a
place for you," then, without paying any more attention
to him, to make his own entry, he advanced by himself
briskly along the corridor. On either side, a double hedge
of young lecturers greeted him; Brichot, anxious not to
appear to be posing in the eyes of these young men to
whom he knew that he was a great pontiff, bestowed on
them a thousand glances, a thousand little nods of con-
nivence, to which his desire to remain martial, thoroughly
French, gave the effect of a sort of cordial encouragement
by an old soldier saying: "Damn it all, we can face the
foe." Then the applause of his pupils broke out. Brichot sometimes extracted from this attendance by M. de
Charlus at his lectures an opportunity for giving pleasure,
almost for returning hospitality. He would say to some
parent, or to one of his middle-class friends: "If it would
interest your wife or daughter, I may tell you that the
Baron de Charlus, Prince de Carency, a scion of the House
of Condé, attends my lectures. It is something to remember, having seen one of the last descendants of our
aristocracy who preserves the type. If they care to come,
they will know him because he will be sitting next to my
chair. Besides he will be alone there, a stout man, with
white hair and black moustaches, wearing the military
medal." "Oh, thank you," said the father. And, albeit
his wife had other engagements, so as not to disoblige
Brichot, he made her attend the lecture, while the daughter, troubled by the heat and the crowd, nevertheless
devoured eagerly with her eyes the descendant of Condé,
marvelling all the same that he was not crowned with

strawberry-leaves and looked just like anybody else of the present day. He meanwhile had no eyes for her, but more than one student, who did not know who he was, was amazed at his friendly glances, became self-conscious and stiff, and the Baron left the room full of dreams and melancholy. "Forgive me if I return to the subject," I said quickly to M. de Charlus, for I could hear Brichot returning, "but could you let me know by wire if you should hear that Mlle. Vinteuil or her friend is expected in Paris, letting me know exactly how long they will be staying and without telling anybody that I asked you." I had almost ceased to believe that she had been expected, but I wished to guard myself thus for the future. "Yes, I will do that for you, first of all because I owe you a great debt of gratitude. By not accepting what, long ago, I had offered you, you rendered me, to your own loss, an immense service, you left me my liberty. It is true that I have abdicated it in another fashion," he added in a melancholy tone beneath which was visible a desire to take me into his confidence; "that is what I continue to regard as the important fact, a whole combination of circumstances which you failed to turn to your own account, possibly because fate warned you at that precise minute not to cross my Path. For always man proposes and God disposes. Who knows whether if, on the day when we came away together from Mme. de Villeparisis's, you had accepted, perhaps many things that have since happened would never have occurred?" In some embarrassment, I turned the conversation, seizing hold of the name of Mme. de Villeparisis, and sought to find out from him, so admirably qualified in every respect, for what reasons Mme. de Villeparisis seemed to be held aloof by the aristocratic world. Not only did he not give me the solution of this little social problem, he did not even appear to me to be aware of its existence. I then realised that the position of Mme. de Villeparisis, if it was in later years to appear great to posterity, and even in the Marquise's lifetime to the ignorant rich, had appeared no less great at the opposite extremity of society, that which touched Mme. de Villeparisis, that of the Guermantes. She was their aunt; they saw first and foremost birth, connexions by marriage, the opportunity of impressing some sister-in-law with the importance of their own family. They regarded this less from the social than from the family point of view. Now this was more brilliant in the case of Mme. de Villeparisis than I had supposed. I had been impressed when I heard that the title Villeparisis was falsely assumed. But there are other examples of great ladies who have made degrading marriages and preserved a predominant position. M. de Charlus began by informing me that Mme. de Villeparisis was a niece of the famous Duchesse de ——, the most celebrated member of the great aristocracy during the July Monarchy, albeit she had refused to associate with the Citizen King and his family. I had so longed to hear stories about this Duchess! And Mme. de Villeparisis, the kind Mme. de Villeparisis, with those cheeks that to me had been the cheeks of an ordinary woman, Mme. de Villeparisis who sent me so many presents and whom I could so easily have seen every day, Mme. de Villeparisis was her niece brought up by her, in her home, at the Hôtel de ——. "She asked the Duc de Doudeauville," M. de Charlus told me, "speaking of the three sisters, 'Which of the sisters do you prefer?'

And when Doudeauville said: 'Madame de Villeparisis,' the Duchesse de —— replied 'Pig!' For the Duchess was extremely *witty*," said M. de Charlus, giving the word the importance and the special pronunciation in use among the Guermantes. That he should have thought the expression so "witty" did not, however, surprise me, for I had on many other occasions remarked the centrifugal, objective tendency which leads men to abdicate, when they are relishing the wit of others, the severity with which they would criticise their own, and to observe, to record faithfully, what they would have scorned to create. "But what on earth is he doing, that is my greatcoat he is bringing," he said, on seeing that Brichot had made so long a search to no better result. "I would have done better to go for it myself. However, you can put it on now. Are you aware that it is highly compromising, my dear boy, it is like drinking out of the same glass, I shall be able to read your thoughts. No, not like that, come, let me do it," and as he put me into his greatcoat, he pressed it down on my shoulders, fastened it round my throat, and brushed my chin with his hand, making the apology: "At his age, he doesn't know how to put on a coat, one has to titivate him, I have missed my vocation, Brichot, I was born to be a nursery-maid." I wanted to go home, but as M. de Charlus had expressed his intention of going in search of Morel, Brichot detained us both. Moreover, the certainty that when I went home I should find Albertine there, a certainty as absolute as that which I had felt in the afternoon that Albertine would return home from the Trocadéro, made me at this moment as little impatient to see her as I had been then when I was sitting at the piano, after Françoise had sent me her telephone message. And it was this calm that enabled me, whenever, in the course of this conversation, I attempted to rise, to obey Brichot's injunctions who was afraid that my departure might prevent Charlus from remaining with him until the moment when Mme. Verdurin was to come and fetch us. "Come," he said to the Baron, "stay a little here with us, you shall give him the accolade presently," Brichot added, fastening upon myself his almost sightless eyes to which the many operations that he had undergone had restored some degree of life, but which had not all the same the mobility necessary to the sidelong expression of malice. "The accolade, how absurd!" cried the Baron, in a shrill and rapturous tone. "My boy, I tell you, he imagines he is at a prize-giving, he is dreaming of his young pupils. I ask myself whether he don't sleep with them." "You wish to meet Mlle. Vinteuil," said Brichot, who had overheard the last words of our conversation. "I promise to let you know if she comes, I shall hear of it from Mme. Verdurin," for he doubtless foresaw that the Baron was in peril of an immediate exclusion from the little clan. "I see, so you think that I have less claim than yourself upon Mme. Verdurin," said M. de Charlus, "to be informed of the coming of these terribly disreputable persons. You know that they are quite notorious. Mme. Verdurin is wrong to allow them to come here, they are all very well for the fast set. They are friends with a terrible band of women. They meet in the most appalling places." At each of these words, my suffering was increased by the addition of a fresh suffering, changing in form. "Certainly not, I don't suppose that I have any better claim than yourself upon Mme. Verdurin," Brichot protested, punctuating his words, for he was afraid that he might have aroused the Baron's suspicions. And as he saw that I was determined to go, seeking to detain me with the bait of the promised entertainment: "There is one thing which the Baron seems to me not to have taken into account when he speaks of the reputation of these two ladies, namely that a person's reputation may be at the same time appalling and undeserved. Thus for instance, in the more notorious group which I shall call parallel, it is certain that the errors of justice are many and that history has registered convictions for sodomy against illustrious men who were wholly innocent of the charge. The recent discovery of Michelangelo's passionate love for a woman is a fresh fact which should entitle the friend of Leo X to the benefit of a posthumous retrial. The Michelangelo case seems to me clearly indicated to excite the snobs and mobilise the Villette, when another case in which anarchism reared its head and became the fashionable sin of our worthy dilettantes, but which must not even be mentioned now for fear of stirring up quarrels, shall have run its course." From the moment when Brichot began to speak of masculine reputations, M. de Charlus betrayed on every one of his features that special sort of impatience which one sees on the face of a medical or military expert when society people who know nothing about the subject begin to talk nonsense about points of therapeutics or strategy. "You know absolutely nothing about the matter," he said at length to Brichot. "Quote me a single reputation that is undeserved. Mention names. Oh yes, I know the whole story," was his brutal retort to a timid interruption by Brichot, "the people who tried it once long ago out of curiosity, or out of affection for a dead friend, and the man who, afraid he has gone too far, if you speak to him of the beauty of a man, replies that that is Chinese to him, that he can no more distinguish between a beautiful man and an ugly one than between the engines of two motor-cars, mechanics not being in his line. That's all stuff and nonsense. Mind you, I don't mean to say that a bad (or what is conventionally so called) and yet undeserved reputation is absolutely impossible. It is so exceptional, so rare, that for practical purposes it does not exist. At the same time I, who have a certain curiosity in ferreting things out, have known cases which were not mythical. Yes, in the course of my life, I have established (scientifically speaking, of course, you mustn't take me too literally) two unjustified reputations. They generally arise from a similarity of names, or from certain outward signs, a profusion of rings, for instance, which persons who are not qualified to judge imagine to be characteristic of what you were mentioning, just as they think that a peasant never utters a sentence without adding: ' Jarnignié,' or an Englishman: ' Goddam.' Dialogue for the boulevard theatres. What will surprise you is that the unjustified are those most firmly established in the eyes of the public. You yourself, Brichot, who would thrust your hand in the flames to answer for the virtue of some man or other who comes to this house and whom the enlightened know to be a wolf in sheep's clothing, you feel obliged to believe like every Tom, Dick and Harry in what is said about some man in the public eye who is the incarnation of those propensities to the common herd, when as a matter of fact, he doesn't care twopence for that sort of thing. I say twopence, because if we were to offer five-and-twenty louis, we should see the number of plaster saints dwindle down to nothing. As things are, the average rate of sanctity, if you see any sanctity in that sort of thing, is somewhere between thirty and forty per cent." If Brichot had transferred to the male sex the question of evil reputations, with me it was, inversely, to the female sex that, thinking of Albertine, I applied the Baron's words. I was appalled at his statistics, even when I bore in mind that he was probably enlarging his figures to reach the total that he would like to believe true, and had based them moreover upon the reports of persons who were scandalmongers and possibly liars, and had in any case been led astray by their own desire, which, coming in addition to that of M. de Charlus, doubtless falsified the Baron's calculations. "Thirty per cent!" exclaimed Brichot. "Why, even if the proportions were reversed I should still have to multiply the guilty a hundredfold. If it is as you say, Baron, and you are not mistaken, then we must confess that you are one of those rare visionaries who discern a truth which nobody round them has ever suspected. Just as Barrès made discoveries as to parliamentary corruption, the truth of which was afterwards established, like the existence of Leverrier's planet. Mme. Verdurin would prefer to cite men whom I would rather not name who detected in the Intelligence Bureau, in the General Staff, activities inspired, I am sure, by patriotic zeal, which I had never imagined. Upon free-masonry, German espionage, morphinomania, Léon Daudet builds up, day by day, a fantastic fairy-tale which turns out to be the barest truth. Thirty per cent!" Brichot repeated in stupefaction. It is only fair to say that M. de Charlus taxed the great majority of his contemporaries with inversion, always excepting those men with whom he himself had had relations, their case, provided that they had introduced the least trace of romance into those relations, appearing to him more complex. So it is that we see men of the world, who refuse to believe in women's honour, allow some remnants of honour only to the woman who has been their mistress, as to whom they protest sincerely and with an air of mystery: "No, you are mistaken, she is not that sort of girl." This unlooked-for tribute is dictated partly by their own self-respect which is flattered by the supposition that such favours have been reserved for them alone, partly by their simplicity which has easily swallowed everything that their mistress has given them to believe, partly from that sense of the complexity of life which brings it about that, as soon as we approach other people, other lives, ready-made labels and classifications appear unduly crude. "Thirty per cent! But have a care; less fortunate than the historians whose conclusions the future will justify, Baron, if you were to present to posterity the statistics that you offer us, it might find them erroneous. Posterity judges only from documentary evidence, and will insist on being assured of your facts. But as no document would be forthcoming to authenticate this sort of collective phenomena which the few persons who are enlightened are only too ready to leave in obscurity, the best minds would be moved to indignation, and you would be regarded as nothing more than a slanderer or a lunatic. After having, in the social examination, obtained top marks and the primacy upon this earth, you would taste the sorrows of a blackball beyond the grave. That is not worth powder and shot, to quote—may God forgive me—our friend Bossuet." " I am not interested in history," replied M. de Charlus, " this life is sufficient for me, it is quite interesting enough, as poor Swann used to say." "What, you knew Swann, Baron, I was not aware of that. Tell me, was he that way inclined? " Brichot inquired with an air of misgiving! "What a mind the man has! So you suppose that I only know men like that. No, I don't think so," said Charlus, looking to the ground and trying to weigh the pros and cons. And deciding that, since he was dealing with Swann whose hostility to that sort of thing had always been notorious, a half-admission could only be harmless to him who was its object and flattering to him who allowed it to escape in an insinuation: " I don't deny that long ago in our schooldays, once by accident," said the Baron, as though unwillingly and as though he were thinking aloud, then recovering himself: " But that was centuries ago, how do you expect me to remember, you are making a fool of me," he concluded with a laugh. " In any case, he was never what you'ld call a beauty! " said Brichot who, himself hideous, thought himself good-looking and was always ready to believe that other men were ugly. "Hold your tongue," said the Baron, "you don't know what you're talking about, in those days he had a peach-like complexion, and," he added, finding a fresh note for each syllable, " he was as beautiful as Cupid himself. Besides he was always charming. The women were madly in love with him." " But did you ever know his wife? " " Why, it was through me that he came to know her. I thought her charming in her disguise one evening when she played Miss Sacripant; I was with some fellows from the club, each of us took a woman home with him, and, although all that I wanted was to go to sleep, slanderous tongues alleged, for it is terrible how malicious people are, that I went to bed with Odette. Only she took advantage of the slanders to come and worry me, and I thought I might get rid of her by introducing her to Swann. From that moment she never let me go, she couldn't spell the simplest word, it was I who wrote all her letters for her. And it was I who, afterwards, had to take her out. That, my boy, is what comes of having a good reputation, you see. Though I only half deserved it. She forced me to help her to betray him, with five, with six other men." And the lovers whom Odette had had in succession (she had been with this man, then with that, those men not one of whose names had ever been guessed by poor Swann, blinded in turn by jealousy and by love, reckoning the chances and believing in oaths more affirmative than a contradiction which escapes from the culprit, a contradiction far more unseizable, and at the same time far more significant, of which the jealous lover might take advantage more logically than of the information which he falsely pretends to have received, in the hope of confusing his mistress), these lovers M. de Charlus began to enumerate with as absolute a certainty as if he had been repeating the list of the Kings of France. And indeed the jealous lover is, like the contemporaries of an historical event, too close, he knows nothing, and it is in the eyes of strangers that the comic aspect of adultery assumes the precision of history, and prolongs itself in lists of names which are, for that matter, unimportant and become painful only to another jealous lover, such as myself, who cannot help comparing his own case with that which he hears mentioned and asks himself whether the woman of whom he is suspicious cannot boast an equally illustrious list. But he can never know anything more, it is a sort of universal conspiracy, a " blindman's buff " in which everyone cruelly participates, and which consists, while his mistress flits from one to another, in holding over his eyes a bandage which he is perpetually attempting to tear off without success, for everyone keeps him blindfold, poor wretch, the kind out of kindness, the wicked out of malice, the coarse-minded out of their love of coarse jokes, the well-bred out of politeness and good-breeding, and all alike respecting one of those conventions which are called principles. " But did Swann never know that you had enjoyed her favours? " " What an idea! If you had suggested such a thing to Charles! It's enough to make one's hair stand up on end. Why, my dear fellow, he would have killed me on the spot, he was as jealous as a tiger. Any more than I ever confessed to Odette, not that she would have minded in the least, that . . . but you must not make my tongue run away with me. And the joke of it is that it was she who fired a revolver at him, and nearly hit me. Oh! I used to have a fine time with that couple; and naturally it was I who was obliged to act as his second against d'Osmond, who never forgave me. D'Osmond had carried off Odette and Swann, to console himself, had taken as his mistress, or make-be-lieve mistress, Odette's sister. But really you must not begin to make me tell you Swann's story, we should be here for ten years, don't you know, nobody knows more about him than I do. It was I who used to take Odette out when she did not wish to see Charles. It was all the

more awkward for me as I have a quite near relative who
bears the name Crécy, without of course having any manner of right to it, but still he was none too well pleased.
For she went by the name of Odette de Crécy, as she
very well might, being merely separated from a Crécy
whose wife she still was, and quite an authentic person,
a highly respectable gentleman out of whom she had
drained his last farthing. But why should I have to tell
you about this Crécy, I have seen you with him on the
crawler, you used to have him to dinner at Balbec. He
must have needed those dinners, poor fellow, he lived
upon a tiny allowance that Swann made him; I am greatly
afraid that, since my friend's death, that income must
have stopped altogether. What I do not understand,"
M. de Charlus said to me, " is that, since you used often
to go to Charles's, you did not ask me this evening to
present you to the Queen of Naples. In fact I can see
that you are less interested in *people* than in curiosities,
and that continues to surprise me in a person who knew
Swann, in whom that sort of interest was so far developed
that it is impossible to say whether it was I who initiated
him in these matters or he myself. It surprises me as
much as if I met a person who had known Whistler and
remained ignorant of what is meant by taste. By Jove,
it is Morel that ought really to have been presented to
her, he was passionately keen on it too, for he is the most
intelligent fellow you could imagine. It is a nuisance that
she has left. However, I shall effect the conjunction one
of these days. It is indispensable that he should know
her. The only possible obstacle would be if she were to
die in the night. Well, we may hope that it will not
happen." All of a sudden Brichot, who was still suffer-

ing from the shock of the proportion "thirty per cent." which M. de Charlus had revealed to him, Brichot who had continued all this time in the pursuit of his idea, with an abruptness which suggested that of an examining magistrate seeking to make a prisoner confess, but which was in reality the result of the Professor's desire to appear perspicacious and of the misgivings that he felt about launching so grave an accusation, spoke. "Isn't Ski like that?" he inquired of M. de Charlus with a sombre air. To make us admire his alleged power of intuition, he had chosen Ski, telling himself that since there were only three innocent men in every ten, he ran little risk of being mistaken if he named Ski who seemed to him a trifle odd, suffered from insomnia, scented himself, in short was not entirely normal. *"Nothing of the sort!"* exclaimed the Baron with a bitter, dogmatic, exasperated irony. "What you say is utterly false, absurd, fantastic. Ski is like that precisely to the people who know nothing about it; if he was, he would not look so like it, be it said without any intention to criticise, for he has a certain charm, indeed I find something very attractive about him." "But give us a few names, then," Brichot pursued with insistence. M. de Charlus drew himself up with a forbidding air. "Ah! my dear Sir, I, as you know, live in a world of abstraction, all that sort of thing interests me only from a transcendental point of view," he replied with the touchy susceptibility peculiar to men of his kind, and the affectation of grandiloquence that characterised his conversation. "To me, you understand, it is only general principles that are of any interest, I speak to you of this as I might of the law of gravitation." But these moments of irritable reaction in which the Baron sought to conceal his true life lasted but a short time compared with the hours of continual progression in which he allowed it to be guessed, displayed it with an irritating complacency, the need to confide being stronger in him than the fear of divulging his secret. "What I was trying to say," he went on, "is that for one evil reputation that is unjustified there are hundreds of good ones which are no less so. Obviously, the number of those who do not merit their reputations varies according to whether you rely upon what is said by men of their sort or by the others. And it is true that if the malevolence of the latter is limited by the extreme difficulty which they would find in believing that a vice as horrible to them as robbery or murder is being practised by men whom they know to be sensitive and sincere, the malevolence of the former is stimulated to excess by the desire to regard as—what shall I say?—accessible, men who appeal to them, upon the strength of information given them by people who have been led astray by a similar desire, in fact by the very aloofness with which they are generally regarded. I have heard a man, viewed with considerable disfavour on account of these tastes, say that he supposed that a certain man in society shared them. And his sole reason for believing it was that this other man had been polite to him! So many reasons for *optimism*," said the Baron artlessly, "in the computation of the number. But the true reason of the enormous difference that exists between the number calculated by the profane, and that calculated by the initiated, arises from the mystery with which the latter surround their actions, in order to conceal them from the rest, who, lacking any source of information, would be literally stupefied if they were to learn merely a quarter of the truth." "Then in our days, things are as they were among the Greeks," said Brichot. "What do you mean, among the Greeks? Do you suppose that it has not been going on ever since. Take the reign of Louis XIV, you have young Vermandois, Molière, Prince Louis of Baden, Brunswick, Charolais, Boufflers, the Great Condé, the Duc de Brissac." "Stop a moment, I knew about Monsieur, I knew about Brissac from Saint-Simon, Vendôme of course, and many others as well. But that old pest Saint-Simon often refers to the Great Condé and Prince Louis of Baden and never mentions it." "It seems a pity, I must say, that it should fall to me to teach a Professor of the Sorbonne his history. But, my dear Master, you are as ignorant as a carp." "You are harsh, Baron, but just. And, wait a moment, now this will please you, I remember now a song of the period composed in macaronic verse about a certain storm which surprised the Great Condé as he was going down the Rhône in the company of his friend, the Marquis de La Moussaye. Condé says:

> *Carus Amicus Mussaeus,*
> *Ah! Quod tempus, bonus Deus,*
> > *Landerirette*
> *Imbre sumus perituri.*

And La Moussaye reassures him with:

> *Securae sunt nostrae vitae*
> *Sumus enim Sodomitae*
> *Igne tantum perituri*
> > *Landeriri."*

"I take back what I said," said Charlus in a shrill and mannered tone, "you are a well of learning, you will write it down for me, won't you, I must preserve it in my family archives, since my great-great-great-grand-mother was a sister of M. le Prince." "Yes, but, Baron, with regard to Prince Louis of Baden I can think of nothing. However, at that period, I suppose that generally speaking the art of war. . . ." "What nonsense, Vendôme, Villars, Prince Eugène, the Prince de Conti, and if I were to tell you of all the heroes of Tonkin, Morocco, and I am thinking of men who are truly sublime, and pious, and 'new generation,' I should astonish you greatly. Ah! I should have something to teach the people who are making inquiries about the new generation which has rejected the futile complications of its elders, M. Bourget tells us! I have a young friend out there, who is highly spoken of, who has done great things, however, I am not going to tell tales out of school, let us return to the seventeenth century, you know that Saint-Simon says of the Maréchal d'Huxelles—one among many: 'Voluptuous in Grecian debaucheries which he made no attempt to conceal, he used to get hold of young officers whom he trained to his purpose, not to mention stalwart young valets, and this openly, in the army and at Strasbourg.' You have probably read Madame's *Letters*, all his men called him 'Putain.' She is quite outspoken about it." "And she was in a good position to know, with her husband." "Such an interesting character, Madame," said M. de Charlus. "One might base upon her the lyrical synthesis of 'Wives of Aunties.' First of all, the masculine type; generally the wife of an Auntie is a man, that is what makes it so easy for her to bear him children. Then Madame does not mention Monsieur's vices, but she does mention incessantly the same vice in other men, writing as a well-informed woman, from that tendency which makes us enjoy finding in other people's families the same defects as afflict us in our own, in order to prove to ourselves that there is nothing exceptional or degrading in them. I was saying that things have been much the same in every age. Nevertheless, our own is quite remarkable in that respect. And notwithstanding the instances that I have borrowed from the seventeenth century, if my great ancestor François C. de La Rochefoucauld were alive in these days, he might say of them with even more justification than of his own—come, Brichot, help me out: 'Vices are common to every age; but if certain persons whom everyone knows had appeared in the first centuries of our era, would anyone speak to-day of the prostitutions of Heliogabalus?' '*Whom everyone knows*' appeals to me immensely. I see that my sagacious kinsman understood the tricks of his most illustrious contemporaries as I understand those of my own. But men of that sort are not only far more frequent to-day. They have also special characteristics." I could see that M. de Charlus was about to tell us in what fashion these habits had evolved. The insistence with which M. de Charlus kept on reverting to this topic—into which, moreover, his intellect, constantly trained in the same direction, had acquired a certain penetration—was, in a complicated way, distinctly trying. He was as boring as a specialist who can see nothing outside his own subject, as irritating as a well-informed man whose vanity is flattered by the secrets which he possesses and is burning to divulge, as repellent as those people who, whenever their own defects are mentioned, spread themselves without noticing that they are giving offence, as obsessed as a maniac and as uncontrollably imprudent as a criminal. These characteristics which, at certain moments, became as obvious as those that stamp a madman or a criminal, brought me, as it happened, a certain consolation. For, making them undergo the necessary transposition in order to be able to draw from them deductions with regard to Albertine, and remembering her attitude towards Saint-Loup, and towards myself, I said to myself, painful as one of these memories and melancholy as the other was to me, I said to myself that they seemed to exclude the kind of deformity so plainly denounced, the kind of specialisation inevitably exclusive, it appeared, which was so vehemently apparent in the conversation as in the person of M. de Charlus. But he, as ill luck would have it, made haste to destroy these grounds for hope in the same way as he had furnished me with them, that is to say unconsciously. "Yes," he said, "I am no longer in my teens, and I have already seen many things change round about me, I no longer recognise either society, in which the barriers are broken down, in which a mob, devoid of elegance and decency, dance the tango even in my own family, or fashions, or politics, or the arts, or religion, or anything. But I must admit that the thing which has changed most of all is what the Germans call homosexuality. Good God, in my day, apart from the men who loathed women, and those who, caring only for women, did the other thing merely with an eye to profit, the homosexuals were sound family men and never kept mistresses except to screen themselves. If I had had a daughter to give away, it is among them that I should have looked for my son-in-law if I had wished to be certain that she would not

be unhappy. Alas! Things have changed entirely.
Nowadays they are recruited also from the men who are
the most insatiable with women. I thought I possessed
a certain instinct, and that when I said to myself: 'Certainly not,' I could not have been mistaken. Well, I give
it up. One of my friends, who is well-known for that
sort of thing, had a coachman whom my sister-in-law
Oriane found for him, a lad from Combray who was
something of a jack of all trades, but particularly in
trading with women, and who, I would have sworn, was
as hostile as possible to anything of that sort. He broke
his mistress's heart by betraying her with two women
whom he adored, not to mention the others, an actress
and a girl from a bar. My cousin the Prince de Guermantes, who has that irritating intelligence of people who
are too ready to believe anything, said to me one day:
'But why in the world does not X—— have his coachman? It might be a pleasure to Théodore' (which is
the coachman's name) 'and he may be annoyed at finding
that his master does not make advances to him.' I could
not help telling Gilbert to hold his tongue; I was overwrought both by that boasted perspicacity which, when
it is exercised indiscriminately, is a want of perspicacity,
and also by the silver-lined malice of my cousin who
would have liked X—— to risk taking the first steps so
that, if the going was good, he might follow." "Then the
Prince de Guermantes is like that, too?" asked Brichot
with a blend of astonishment and dismay. "Good God,"
replied M. de Charlus, highly delighted, "it is so notorious that I don't think I am guilty of an indiscretion if I
tell you that he is. Very well, the year after this, I
went to Balbec, where I heard from a sailor who used to

take me out fishing occasionally, that my Théodore, whose sister, I may mention, is the maid of a friend of Mme. Verdurin, Baroness Putbus, used to come down to the harbour to pick up now one sailor, now another, with the most infernal cheek, to go for a trip on the sea ' with extras.' " It was now my turn to inquire whether his employer, whom I had identified as the gentleman who at Balbec used to play cards all day long with his mistress, and who was the leader of the little group of four boon companions, was like the Prince de Guermantes. "Why, of course, everyone knows about him, he makes no attempt to conceal it." " But he had his mistress there with him." "Well, and what difference does that make? How innocent these children are," he said to me in a fatherly tone, little suspecting the grief that I extracted from his words when I thought of Albertine. " She is charming, his mistress." " But then his three friends are like himself." " Not at all," he cried, stopping his ears as though, in playing some instrument, I had struck a wrong note. " Now he has gone to the other extreme. So a man has no longer the right to have friends? Ah! Youth, youth; it gets everything wrong. We shall have to begin your education over again, my boy. Well," he went on, " I admit that this case, and I know of many others, however open a mind I may try to keep for every form of audacity, does embarrass me. I may be very old-fashioned, but I fail to understand," he said in the tone of an old Gallican speaking of some development of Ultramontanism, of a Liberal Royalist speaking of the *Action Française* or of a disciple of Claude Monet speaking of the Cubists. " I do not reproach these innovators, I envy them if anything, I try to understand them, but I do not succeed. If they are so passionately fond of woman, why, and especially in this workaday world where that sort of thing is so frowned upon, where they conceal themselves from a sense of shame, have they any need of what they call 'a bit of brown'? It is because it represents to them something else. What?" "What else can a woman represent to Albertine," I thought, and there indeed lay the cause of my anguish. "Decidedly, Baron," said Brichot, "should the Board of Studies ever think of founding a Chair of Homosexuality, I shall see that your name is the first to be submitted. Or rather, no; an Institute of Psycho-physiology would suit you better. And I can see you, best of all, provided with a Chair in the Collège de France, which would enable you to devote yourself to personal researches the results of which you would deliver, like the Professor of Tamil or Sanskrit, to the handful of people who are interested in them. You would have an audience of two, with your assistant, not that I mean to cast the slightest suspicion upon our corps of janitors, whom I believe to be above suspicion." "You know nothing about them," the Baron retorted in a harsh and cutting tone. "Besides you are wrong in thinking that so few people are interested in the subject. It is just the opposite." And without stopping to consider the incompatibility between the invariable trend of his own conversation and the reproach which he was about to heap upon other people: "It is, on the contrary, most alarming," said the Baron, with a scandalised and contrite air, "people are talking about nothing else. It is a scandal, but I am not exaggerating, my dear fellow! It appears that, the day before yesterday, at the Duchesse d'Agen's, they talked about nothing else for two hours on end; you can imagine, if women have taken to discussing that sort of thing, it is a positive scandal! What is vilest of all is that they get their information," he went on with an extraordinary fire and emphasis, " from pests, regular harlots like young Châtellerault, who has the worst reputation in the world, who tell them stories about other men. I have been told that he said more than enough to hang me, but I don't care, I am convinced that the mud and filth flung by an individual who barely escaped being turned out of the Jockey for cheating at cards can only fall back upon himself. I am sure that if I were Jane d'Agen, I should have sufficient respect for my drawing-room not to allow such subjects to be discussed in it, nor to allow my own flesh and blood to be dragged through the mire in my house. But there is no longer any society, any rules, any conventions, in conversation any more than in dress. Ah, my dear fellow, it is the end of the world. Everyone has become so malicious. The prize goes to the man who can speak most evil of his fellows. It is appalling."

As cowardly still as I had been long ago in my boyhood at Combray when I used to run away in order not to see my grandfather tempted with brandy and the vain efforts of my grandmother imploring him not to drink it, I had but one thought in my mind, which was to leave the Verdurins' house before the execution of M. de Charlus occurred. " I simply must go," I said to Brichot. " I am coming with you," he replied, " but we cannot slip away, English fashion. Come and say good-bye to Mme. Verdurin," the Professor concluded, as he made his way to the drawing-room with the air of a man who, in a guessing game, goes to find out whether he may "come back".

While we conversed, M. Verdurin, at a signal from his wife, had taken Morel aside. Indeed, had Mme. Verdurin decided, after considering the matter in all its aspects, that it was wiser to postpone Morel's enlightenment, she was powerless now to prevent it. There are certain desires, some of them confined to the mouth, which, as soon as we have allowed them to grow, insist upon being gratified, whatever the consequences may be; we are unable to resist the temptation to kiss a bare shoulder at which we have been gazing for too long and at which our lips strike like a serpent at a bird, to bury our sweet tooth in a cake that has fascinated and famished it, nor can we forego the delight of the amazement, anxiety, grief or mirth to which we can move another person by some unexpected communication. So, in a frenzy of melodrama, Mme. Verdurin had ordered her husband to take Morel out of the room and, at all costs, to explain matters to him. The violinist had begun by deploring the departure of the Queen of Naples before he had had a chance of being presented to her. M. de Charlus had told him so often that she was the sister of the Empress Elizabeth and of the Duchesse d'Alençon that Her Majesty had assumed an extraordinary importance in his eyes. But the Master explained to him that it was not to talk about the Queen of Naples that they had withdrawn from the rest, and then went straight to the root of the matter. "Listen," he had concluded after a long explanation: "listen; if you like, we can go and ask my wife what she thinks. I give you my word of honour, I've said nothing to her about it. We shall see how she looks at it. My advice is perhaps not the best, but you know how sound her judgment is; besides, she is extremely attached to yourself, let us go and submit the case to her." And while Mme. Verdurin, awaiting with impatience the emotions that she would presently be relishing as she talked to the musician, and again, after he had gone, when she made her husband give her a full report of their conversation, continued to repeat: "But what in the world can they be doing? I do hope that my husband, in keeping him all this time, has managed to give him his cue," M. Verdurin reappeared with Morel who seemed greatly moved. "He would like to ask your advice," M. Verdurin said to his wife, in the tone of a man who does not know whether his prayer will be heard. Instead of replying to M. Verdurin, it was to Morel that, in the heat of her passion, Mme. Verdurin addressed herself. "I agree entirely with my husband, I consider that you cannot tolerate this sort of thing for another instant," she exclaimed with violence, discarding as a useless fiction her agreement with her husband that she was supposed to know nothing of what he had been saying to the violinist. "How do you mean? Tolerate what?" stammered M. Verdurin, endeavouring to feign astonishment and seeking, with an awkwardness that was explained by his dismay, to defend his falsehood. "I guessed what you were saying to him," replied Mme. Verdurin, undisturbed by the improbability of this explanation, and caring little what, when he recalled this scene, the violinist might think of the Mistress's veracity. "No," Mme. Verdurin continued, "I feel that you ought not to endure any longer this degrading promiscuity with a tainted person whom nobody will have in her house," she went on, regardless of the fact that this was untrue and forgetting that she herself entertained him almost daily. "You are the talk of the Conservatoire," she added, feeling that this was the argument that carried most weight; "another month of this life and your artistic future is shattered, whereas, without Charlus, you ought to be making at least a hundred thousand francs a year." "But I have never heard anyone utter a word, I am astounded, I am very grateful to you," Morel murmured, the tears starting to his eyes. But, being obliged at once to feign astonishment and to conceal his shame, he had turned redder and was perspiring more abundantly than if he had played all Beethoven's sonatas in succession, and tears welled from his eyes which the Bonn Master would certainly not have drawn from him. "If you have never heard anything, you are unique in that respect. He is a gentleman with a vile reputation and the most shocking stories are told about him. I know that the police are watching him and that is perhaps the best thing for him if he is not to end like all those men, murdered by hooligans," she went on, for as she thought of Charlus the memory of Mme. de Duras recurred to her, and in her frenzy of rage she sought to aggravate still further the wounds that she was inflicting on the unfortunate Charlie, and to avenge herself for those that she had received in the course of the evening. "Anyhow, even financially, he can be of no use to you, he is completely ruined since he has become the prey of people who are blackmailing him, and who can't even make him fork out the price of the tune they call, still less can he pay you for your playing, for it is all heavily mortgaged, town house, country house, everything." Morel was all the more ready to believe this lie since M. de Charlus liked to confide in him his relations with hooligans, a race for which the son of a valet, however debauched he may be, professes a feeling of horror as strong as his attachment to Bonapartist principles.

Already, in the cunning mind of Morel, a plan was beginning to take shape similar to what was called in the eighteenth century the reversal of alliances. Determined never to speak to M. de Charlus again, he would return on the following evening to Jupien's niece, and see that everything was made straight with her. Unfortunately for him this plan was doomed to failure, M. de Charlus having made an appointment for that very evening with Jupien, which the ex-tailor dared not fail to keep, in spite of recent events. Other events, as we shall see, having followed upon Morel's action, when Jupien in tears told his tale of woe to the Baron, the latter, no less wretched, assured him that he would adopt the forsaken girl, that she should assume one of the titles that were at his disposal, probably that of Mlle. d'Oléron, that he would see that she received a thorough education, and furnish her with a rich husband. Promises which filled Jupien with joy and left his niece unmoved, for she was still in love with Morel, who, from stupidity or cynicism, used to come into the shop and tease her in Jupien's absence. "What is the matter with you," he would say with a laugh, " with those black marks under your eyes? A broken heart? Gad, the years pass and people change. After all, a man is free to try on a shoe, all the more a woman, and if she doesn't fit him. . . ." He lost his temper once only, because she cried, which he considered cowardly, unworthy of her. People are not always very tolerant of the tears which they themselves have provoked.

But we have looked too far ahead, for all this did not happen until after the Verdurins' party which we have interrupted, and we must go back to the point at which we left off. "I should never have suspected it," Morel groaned, in answer to Mme. Verdurin. "Naturally people do not say it to your face, that does not prevent your being the talk of the Conservatoire," Mme. Verdurin went on wickedly, seeking to make it plain to Morel that it was not only M. de Charlus that was being criticised, but himself also. "I can well believe that you know nothing about it; all the same, people are quite outspoken. Ask Ski what they were saying the other day at Chevillard's within a foot of us when you came into my box. I mean to say, people point you out. As far as I'm concerned, I don't pay the slightest attention, but what I do feel is that it makes a man supremely ridiculous and that he becomes a public laughing-stock for the rest of his life." "I don't know how to thank you," said Charlie in the tone we use to a dentist who has just caused us terrible pain while we tried not to let him see it, or to a too blood-thirsty second who has forced us into a duel on account of some casual remark of which he has said: "You can't swallow that." "I believe that you have plenty of character, that you are a man," replied Mme. Verdurin, "and that you will be capable of speaking out boldly, although he tells everybody that you would never dare, that he holds you fast." Charlie, seeking a borrowed dignity in which to cloak the tatters of his own, found in his memory something that he had read or, more probably, heard quoted, and at once proclaimed: "I was not brought up

to eat that sort of bread. This very evening I will break
with M. de Charlus. The Queen of Naples has gone,
hasn't she? Otherwise, before breaking with him, I
should like to ask him. . . ." "It is not necessary to
break with him altogether," said Mme. Verdurin, anxious
to avoid a disruption of the little nucleus. "There is
no harm in your seeing him here, among our little group,
where you are appreciated, where no one speaks any evil
of you. But insist upon your freedom, and do not let
him drag you about among all those sheep who are
friendly to your face; I wish you could have heard what
they were saying behind your back. Anyhow, you need
feel no regret, not only are you wiping off a stain which
would have marked you for the rest of your life, from the
artistic point of view, even if there had not been this
scandalous presentation by Charlus, I don't mind telling
you that wasting yourself like this in this sham society
will make people suppose that you aren't serious, give
you an amateur reputation, as a little drawing-room performer, which is a terrible thing at your age. I can
understand that to all those fine ladies it is highly convenient to be able to return their friends' hospitality by
making you come and play for nothing, but it is your
future as an artist that would foot the bill. I don't say
that you shouldn't go to one or two of them. You were
speaking of the Queen of Naples—who has left, for she
had to go on to another party—now she is a splendid
woman, and I don't mind saying that I think she has a
poor opinion of Charlus and came here chiefly to please
me. Yes, yes, I know she was longing to meet us, M.
Verdurin and myself. That is a house in which you might
play. And then I may tell you that if I take you—be-

cause the artists all know me, you understand, they have always been most obliging to me, and regard me almost as one of themselves, as their Mistress—that is a very different matter. But whatever you do, you must never go near Mme. de Duras! Don't go and make a stupid blunder like that! I know several artists who have come here and told me all about her. They know they can trust me," she said, in the sweet and simple tone which she knew how to adopt in an instant, imparting an appropriate air of modesty to her features, an appropriate charm to her eyes, "they come here, just like that, to tell me all their little troubles; the ones who are said to be most silent, go on chatting to me sometimes for hours on end and I can't tell you how interesting they are. Poor Chabrier used always to say: 'There's nobody like Mme. Verdurin for getting them to talk.' Very well, don't you know, all of them, without one exception, I have seen them in tears because they had gone to play for Mme. de Duras. It is not only the way she enjoys making her servants humiliate them, they could never get an engagement anywhere else again. The agents would say: 'Oh yes, the fellow who plays at Mme. de Duras's.' That settled it. There is nothing like that for ruining a man's future. You know what society people are like, it's not taken seriously, you may have all the talent in the world, it's a dreadful thing to have to say, but one Mme. de Duras is enough to give you the reputation of an amateur. And among artists, don't you know, well I, you can ask yourself whether I know them, when I have been moving among them for forty years, launching them, taking an interest in them; very well, when they say that somebody is an amateur, that finishes it. And people were beginning to say it of you. Indeed, at times I have been obliged to take up the cudgels, to assure them that you would not play in some absurd drawing-room! Do you know what the answer was: 'But he will be forced to go, Charlus won't even consult him, he never asks him for his opinion.' Somebody thought he would pay him a compliment and said: 'We greatly admire your friend Morel.' Can you guess what answer he made, with that insolent air which you know? 'But what do you mean by calling him my friend, we are not of the same class, say rather that he is my creature, my protégé.'" At this moment there stirred beneath the convex brows of the musical deity the one thing that certain people cannot keep to themselves, a saying which it is not merely abject but imprudent to repeat. But the need to repeat it is stronger than honour, than prudence. It was to this need that, after a few convulsive movements of her spherical and sorrowful brows, the Mistress succumbed: "Some one actually told my husband that he had said 'my servant,' but for that I cannot vouch," she added. It was a similar need that had compelled M. de Charlus, shortly after he had sworn to Morel that nobody should ever know the story of his birth, to say to Mme. Verdurin: "His father was a flunkey." A similar need again, now that the story had been started, would make it circulate from one person to another, each of whom would confide it under the seal of a secrecy which would be promised and not kept by the hearer, as by the informant himself. These stories would end, as in the game called hunt-the-thimble, by being traced back to Mme. Verdurin, bringing down upon her the wrath of the person concerned, who would at last have learned the truth. She knew this, but could not repress the words that were burning her tongue. Anyhow, the word "servant" was bound to annoy Morel. She said "servant" nevertheless, and if she added that she could not vouch for the word, this was so as at once to appear certain of the rest, thanks to this hint of uncertainty, and to shew her impartiality. This impartiality that she shewed, she herself found so touching that she began to speak affectionately to Charlie: "For, don't you see," she went on, "I am not blaming him, he is dragging you down into his abyss, it is true, but it is not his fault, since he wallows in it himself, since he wallows in it," she repeated in a louder tone, having been struck by the aptness of the image which had taken shape so quickly that her attention only now overtook it and was trying to give it prominence. "No, the fault that I do find with him," she said in a melting tone—like a woman drunken with her own success—"is a want of delicacy towards yourself. There are certain things which one does not say in public. Well, this evening, he was betting that he would make you blush with joy, by telling you (stuff and nonsense, of course, for his recommendation would be enough to prevent your getting it) that you were to have the Cross of the Legion of Honour. Even that I could overlook, although I have never quite liked," she went on with a delicate, dignified air, "hearing a person make a fool of his friends, but, don't you know, there are certain little things that one does resent. Such as when he told us, with screams of laughter, that if you want the Cross it's to please your uncle and that your uncle was a footman." "He told you that!" cried Charlie, believing, on the strength of this adroitly interpolated quotation, in the

truth of everything that Mme. Verdurin had said! Mme.
Verdurin was overwhelmed with the joy of an old mistress who, just as her young lover was on the point of
deserting her, has succeeded in breaking off his marriage,
and it is possible that she had not calculated her lie,
that she was not even consciously lying. A sort of sentimental logic, something perhaps more elementary still, a
sort of nervous reflex urging her, in order to brighten her
life and preserve her happiness, to stir up trouble in the
little clan, may have brought impulsively to her lips, without giving her time to check their veracity, these asser-
tions diabolically effective if not rigorously exact. "If
he had only repeated it to us, it wouldn't matter," the
Mistress went on, "we know better than to listen to what
he says, besides, what does a man's origin matter, you
have your own value, you are what you make yourself,
but that he should use it to make Mme. de Portefin
laugh" (Mme. Verdurin named this lady on purpose because she knew that Charlie admired her) "that is what
vexes us: my husband said to me when he heard him: 'I
would sooner he had struck me in the face.' For he is
as fond of you as I am, don't you know, is Gustave"
(from this we learn that M. Verdurin's name was
Gustave). "He is really very sensitive." "But I never
told you I was fond of him," muttered M. Verdurin, acting the kind-hearted curmudgeon. "It is Charlus that
is fond of him." "Oh, no! Now I realise the difference,
I was betrayed by a scoundrel and you, you are good,"
Charlie exclaimed in all sincerity. "No, no," murmured
Mme. Verdurin, seeking to retain her victory, for she felt
that her Wednesdays were safe, but not to abuse it:
"scoundrel is too strong; he does harm, a great deal of

harm, unconsciously; you know that tale about the Legion of Honour was the affair of a moment. And it would be painful to me to repeat all that he said about your family," said Mme. Verdurin, who would have been greatly embarrassed had she been asked to do so. "Oh, even if it only took a moment, it proves that he is a traitor," cried Morel. It was at this moment that we returned to the drawing-room. "Ah!" exclaimed M. de Charlus when he saw that Morel was in the room, advancing upon him with the alacrity of the man who has skilfully organised a whole evening's entertainment with a view to an assignation with a woman, and in his excitement never imagines that he has with his own hands set the snare in which he will presently be caught and publicly thrashed by bravoes stationed in readiness by her husband. "Well, after all it is none too soon; are you satisfied, young glory, and presently young knight of the Legion of Honour? For very soon you will be able to sport your Cross," M. de Charlus said to Morel with a tender and triumphant air, but by the very mention of the decoration endorsed Mme. Verdurin's lies, which appeared to Morel to be indisputable truth. "Leave me alone, I forbid you to come near me," Morel shouted at the Baron. "You know what I mean, all right, I'm not the first young man you've tried to corrupt!" My sole consolation lay in the thought that I was about to see Morel and the Verdurins pulverised by M. de Charlus. For a thousand times less an offence I had been visited with his furious rage, no one was safe from it, a king would not have intimidated him. Instead of which, an extraordinary thing happened. One saw M. de Charlus dumb, stupefied, measuring the depths of his misery without

understanding its cause, finding not a word to utter, raising his eyes to stare at each of the company in turn, with
a questioning, outraged, suppliant air, which seemed to
be asking them not so much what had happened as what
answer he ought to make. And yet M. de Charlus possessed all the resources, not merely of eloquence but of
audacity, when, seized by a rage which had long been
simmering against some one, he reduced him to despera-
tion, with the most outrageous speeches, in front of a
scandalised society which had never imagined that anyone could go so far. M. de Charlus, on these occasions,
burned, convulsed with a sort of epilepsy, which left
everyone trembling. But in these instances he had the
initiative, he launched the attack, he said whatever came
into his mind (just as Bloch was able to make fun of
Jews and blushed if the word Jew was uttered in his
hearing). Perhaps what struck him speechless was—
when he saw that M. and Mme. Verdurin turned their
eyes from him and that no one was coming to his rescue
—his anguish at the moment and, still more, his dread of
greater anguish to come; or else that, not having lost his
temper in advance, in imagination, and forged his thun-
derbolt, not having his rage ready as a weapon in his
hand, he had been seized and dealt a mortal blow at the
moment when he was unarmed (for, sensitive, neurotic,
hysterical, his impulses were genuine, but his courage
was a sham; indeed, as I had always thought, and this
was what made me like him, his malice was a sham also:
the people whom he hated, he hated because he thought
that they looked down upon him; had they been civil to
him, instead of flying into a furious rage with them, he
would have taken them to his bosom, and he did not

shew the normal reactions of a man of honour who has been insulted); or else that, in a sphere which was not his own, he felt himself less at his ease and less courageous than he would have been in the Faubourg. The fact remains that, in this drawing-room which he despised, this great nobleman (in whom his sense of superiority to the middle classes was no less essentially inherent than it had been in any of his ancestors who had stood in the dock before the Revolutionary Tribunal) could do nothing, in a paralysis of all his members, including his tongue, but cast in every direction glances of terror, outraged by the violence that had been done to him, no less suppliant than questioning. In a situation so cruelly unforeseen, this great talker could do no more than stammer: "What does it all mean, what has happened?" His question was not even heard. And the eternal pantomime of panic terror has so little altered, that this elderly gentleman, to whom a disagreeable incident had just occurred in a Parisian drawing-room, unconsciously repeated the various formal attitudes in which the Greek sculptors of the earliest times symbolised the terror of nymphs pursued by the Great Pan.

The ambassador who has been recalled, the undersecretary placed suddenly on the retired list, the man about town whom people begin to cut, the lover who has been shewn the door examine sometimes for months on end the event that has shattered their hopes; they turn it over and over like a projectile fired at them they know not whence or by whom, almost as though it were a meteorite. They would fain know the elements that compose this strange engine which has burst upon them, learn what hostilities may be detected in them. Chemists have at least the power of analysis; sick men suffering from a malady the origin of which they do not know can send for the doctor; criminal mysteries are more or less solved by the examining magistrate. But when it comes to the disconcerting actions of our fellow-men, we rarely discover their motives. Thus M. de Charlus, to anticipate the days that followed this party to which we shall presently return, could see in Charlie's attitude one thing alone that was self-evident. Charlie, who had often threatened the Baron that he would tell people of the passion that he inspired in him, must have seized the opportunity to do so when he considered that he had now sufficiently " arrived " to be able to fly unaided. And he must, out of sheer ingratitude, have told Mme. Verdurin everything. But how had she allowed herself to be taken in (for the Baron, having made up his mind to deny the story, had already persuaded himself that the sentiments for which he was blamed were imaginary)? Some friends of Mme. Verdurin, who themselves perhaps felt a passion for Charlie, must have prepared the ground. Accordingly, M. de Charlus during the next few days wrote terrible letters to a number of the faithful, who were entirely innocent and concluded that he must be mad; then he went to Mme. Verdurin with a long and moving tale, which had not at all the effect that he desired. For in the first place Mme. Verdurin repeated to the Baron: " All you need do is not to bother about him, treat him with scorn, he is a mere boy." Now the Baron longed only for a reconciliation. In the second place, to bring this about, by depriving Charlie of everything of which he had felt himself assured, he asked Mme. Verdurin not to invite him again; a request which she met with a refusal that brought upon her angry and sarcastic letters from M. de Charlus. Flitting from one supposition to another, the Baron never arrived at the truth, which was that the blow had not come from Morel. It is true that he might have learned this by asking him for a few minutes' conversation. But he felt that this would injure his dignity and would be against the interests of his love. He had been insulted, he awaited an explanation. There is, for that matter, almost invariably, attached to the idea of a conversation which might clear up a misunderstanding, another idea which, whatever the reason, prevents us from agreeing to that conversation. The man who is abased and has shewn his weakness on a score of occasions, will furnish proofs of pride on the twenty-first, the only occasion on which it would serve him not to adopt a headstrong and arrogant attitude but to dispel an error which will take root in his adversary failing a contradiction. As for the social side of the incident, the rumour spread abroad that M. de Charlus had been turned out of the Verdurins' house at the moment when he was attempting to rape a young musician. The effect of this rumour was that nobody was surprised when M. de Charlus did not appear again at the Verdurins', and whenever he happened by chance to meet, anywhere else, one of the faithful whom he had suspected and insulted, as this person had a grudge against the Baron who himself abstained from greeting him, people were not surprised, realising that no member of the little clan would ever wish to speak to the Baron again.

While M. de Charlus, rendered speechless by Morel's words and by the attitude of the Mistress, stood there in the pose of the nymph a prey to Panic terror, M. and

Mme. Verdurin had retired to the outer drawing-room, as
a sign of diplomatic rupture, leaving M. de Charlus by
himself, while on the platform Morel was putting his
violin in its case: "Now you must tell us exactly what
happened," Mme. Verdurin appealed avidly to her husband. "I don't know what you can have said to him,
he looked quite upset," said Ski, "there are tears in his
eyes." Pretending not to have understood: "I'm sure,
nothing that I said could make any difference to him,"
said Mme. Verdurin, employing one of those stratagems
which do not deceive everybody, so as to force the sculptor to repeat that Charlie was in tears, tears which filled
the Mistress with too much pride for her to be willing to
run the risk that one or other of the faithful, who might
not have heard what was said, remained in ignorance of
them. "No, it has made a difference, for I saw big tears
glistening in his eyes," said the sculptor in a low tone
with a smile of malicious connivance, and a sidelong
glance to make sure that Morel was still on the platform
and could not overhear the conversation. But there
was somebody who did overhear, and whose presence,
as soon as it was observed, was to restore to Morel
one of the hopes that he had forfeited. This was the
Queen of Naples, who, having left her fan behind, had
thought it more polite, on coming away from another
party to which she had gone on, to call for it in person.
She had entered the room quite quietly, as though she
were ashamed of herself, prepared to make apologies for
her presence, and to pay a little call upon her hostess now
that all the other guests had gone. But no one had
heard her come in, in the heat of the incident the meaning
of which she had at once gathered, and which set her

ablaze with indignation. "Ski says that he had tears in
his eyes, did you notice that? I did not see any tears.
Ah, yes, I remember now," she corrected herself, in the
fear that her denial might not be believed. "As for
Charlus, he's not far off them, he ought to take a chair,
he's tottering on his feet, he'll be on the floor in another
minute," she said with a pitiless laugh. At that moment
Morel hastened towards her: "Isn't that lady the Queen
of Naples?" he asked (albeit he knew quite well that she
was), pointing to Her Majesty who was making her way
towards Charlus. "After what has just happened, I can
no longer, I'm afraid, ask the Baron to present me."
"Wait, I shall take you to her myself," said Mme. Verdurin, and, followed by a few of the faithful, but not by
myself and Brichot who made haste to go and call for
our hats and coats, she advanced upon the Queen who
was talking to M. de Charlus. He had imagined that the
realisation of his great desire that Morel should be presented to the Queen of Naples could be prevented only by
the improbable demise of that lady. But we picture the
future as a reflexion of the present projected into empty
space, whereas it is the result, often almost immediate,
of causes which for the most part escape our notice. Not
an hour had passed, and now M. de Charlus would have
given everything he possessed in order that Morel should
not be presented to the Queen. Mme. Verdurin made the
Queen a curtsey. Seeing that the other appeared not to
recognise her: "I am Mme. Verdurin. Your Majesty
does not remember me." "Quite well," said the Queen
as she continued so naturally to converse with M. de
Charlus and with an air of such complete indifference that
Mme. Verdurin doubted whether it was to herself that

this "Quite well" had been addressed, uttered with a marvellously detached intonation, which wrung from M. de Charlus, despite his broken heart, a smile of expert and delighted appreciation of the art of impertinence. Morel, who had watched from the distance the preparations for his presentation, now approached. The Queen offered her arm to M. de Charlus. With him, too, she was vexed, but only because he did not make a more energetic stand against vile detractors. She was crimson with shame for him whom the Verdurins dared to treat in this fashion. The entirely simple civility which she had shewn them a few hours earlier, and the arrogant pride with which she now stood up to face them, had their source in the same region of her heart. The Queen, as a woman full of good nature, regarded good nature first and foremost in the form of an unshakable attachment to the people whom she liked, to her own family, to all the Princes of her race, among whom was M. de Charlus, and, after them, to all the people of the middle classes or of the humblest populace who knew how to respect those whom she liked and felt well-disposed towards them. It was as to a woman endowed with these sound instincts that she had shewn kindness to Mme. Verdurin. And, no doubt, this is a narrow conception, somewhat Tory, and increasingly obsolete, of good nature. But this does not mean that her good nature was any less genuine or ardent. The ancients were no less strongly attached to the group of humanity to which they devoted themselves because it did not exceed the limits of their city, nor are the men of to-day to their country than will be those who in the future love the United States of the World. In my own immediate surroundings, I have

157

had an example of this in my mother whom Mme. de Cambremer and Mme. de Guermantes could never persuade to take part in any philanthropic undertaking, to join any patriotic workroom, to sell or to be a patroness at any bazaar. I do not go so far as to say that she was right in doing good only when her heart had first spoken, and in reserving for her own family, for her servants, for the unfortunate whom chance brought in her way, her treasures of love and generosity, but I do know that these, like those of my grandmother, were unbounded and exceeded by far anything that Mme. de Guermantes or Mme. de Cambremer ever could have done or did. The case of the Queen of Naples was altogether different, but even here it must be admitted that her conception of deserving people was not at all that set forth in those novels of Dostoievski which Albertine had taken from my shelves and devoured, that is to say in the guise of wheedling parasites, thieves, drunkards, at one moment stupid, at another insolent, debauchees, at a pinch murderers. Extremes, however, meet, since the noble man, the brother, the outraged kinsman whom the Queen sought to defend, was M. de Charlus, that is to say, notwithstanding his birth and all the family ties that bound him to the Queen, a man whose virtue was hedged round by many vices. "You do not look at all well, my dear cousin," she said to M. de Charlus. "Lean upon my arm. Be sure that it will still support you. It is firm enough for that." Then, raising her eyes proudly to face her adversaries (at that moment, Ski told me, there were in front of her Mme. Verdurin and Morel), "You know that, in the past, at Gaeta, it held the mob in defiance. It will be able to serve you as a rampart." And it was thus, taking the Baron on her arm and without having allowed Morel to be presented to her, that the splendid sister of the Empress Elizabeth left the house. It might be supposed, in view of M. de Charlus's terrible nature, the persecutions with which he terrorised even his own family, that he would, after the events of this evening, let loose his fury and practise reprisals upon the Verdurins. We have seen why nothing of this sort occurred at first. Then the Baron, having caught cold shortly afterwards, and contracted the septic pneumonia which was very rife that winter, was for long regarded by his doctors, and regarded himself, as being at the point of death, and lay for many months suspended between it and life. Was there simply a physical change, and the substitution of a different malady for the neurosis that had previously made him lose all control of himself in his outbursts of rage? For it is too obvious to suppose that, having never taken the Verdurins seriously, from the social point of view, but having come at last to understand the part that they had played, he was unable to feel the resentment that he would have felt for any of his equals; too obvious also to remember that neurotics, irritated on the slightest provocation by imaginary and inoffensive enemies, become on the contrary inoffensive as soon as anyone takes the offensive again them, and that we can calm them more easily by flinging cold water in their faces than by attempting to prove to them the inanity of their grievances. It is probably not in a physical change that we ought to seek the explanation of this absence of rancour, but far more in the malady itself. It exhausted the Baron so completely that he had little leisure left in which to think about the Verdurins. He was almost dead. We mentioned offensives; even those which have only a posthumous effect require, if we are to " stage " them properly, the sacrifice of a part of our strength. M. de Charlus had too little strength left for the activity of a preparation. We hear often of mortal enemies who open their eyes to gaze upon one another in the hour of death and close them again, made happy. This must be a rare occurrence, except when death surprises us in the midst of life. It is, on the contrary, at the moment when we have nothing left to lose, that we are not bothered by the risks which, when full of life, we would lightly have undertaken. The spirit of vengeance forms part of life, it abandons us as a rule—notwithstanding certain exceptions which, occurring in the heart of the same person, are, as we shall see, human contradictions,— on the threshold of death. After having thought for a moment about the Verdurins, M. de Charlus felt that he was too weak, turned his face to the wall, and ceased to think about anything. If he often lay silent like this, it was not that he had lost his eloquence. It still flowed from its source, but it had changed. Detached from the violence which it had so often adorned, it was no more now than an almost mystic eloquence decorated with words of meekness, words from the Gospel, an apparent resignation to death. He talked especially on the days when he thought that he would live. A relapse made him silent. This Christian meekness into which his splendid violence was transposed (as is in *Esther* the so different genius of *Andromaque*) provoked the admiration of those who came to his bedside. It would have provoked that of the Verdurins themselves, who could not have helped adoring a man whom his weakness had made them hate. It is true that thoughts which were Christian only in appearance rose to the surface. He implored the Archangel Gabriel to appear and announce to him, as to the Prophet, at what time the Messiah would come to him. And, breaking off with a sweet and sorrowful smile, he would add: "But the Archangel must not ask me, as he asked Daniel, to have patience for 'seven weeks, and threescore and two weeks,' for I should be dead before then." The person whom he awaited thus was Morel. And so he asked the Archangel Raphael to bring him to him, as he had brought the young Tobias. And, introducing more human methods (like sick Popes who, while ordering masses to be said, do not neglect to send for their doctors), he insinuated to his visitors that if Brichot were to bring him without delay his young Tobias, perhaps the Archangel Raphael would consent to restore Brichot's sight, as he had done to the father of Tobias, or as had happened in the sheep-pool of Bethesda. But, notwithstanding these human lapses, the moral purity of M. de Charlus's conversation had none the less become charming. Vanity, slander, the insanity of malice and pride, had alike disappeared. Morally M. de Charlus had been raised far above the level at which he had lived in the past. But this moral perfection, as to the reality of which his oratorical art was for that matter capable of deceiving more than one of his compassionate audience, this perfection vanished with the malady which had laboured on its behalf. M. de Charlus returned along the downward slope with a rapidity which, as we shall see, continued steadily to increase. But the Verdurins' attitude towards him was by that time no more than a somewhat distant memory which more immediate outbursts prevented from reviving.

To turn back to the Verdurins' party, when the host and hostess were by themselves, M. Verdurin said to his wife: "You know where Cottard has gone? He is with Saniette; he has been speculating to put himself straight and has gone smash. When he got home just now after leaving us, and learned that he hadn't a penny in the world and nearly a million francs of debts, Saniette had a stroke." "But then, why did he gamble, it's idiotic, he was the last person in the world to succeed at that game. Cleverer men than he get plucked at it, and he was born to let himself be swindled by every Tom, Dick and Harry." "Why, of course, we have always known that he was an idiot," said M. Verdurin. "Anyhow, this is the result. Here you have a man who will be turned out of house and home to-morrow by his landlord, who is going to find himself utterly penniless; his family don't like him, Forcheville is the last man in the world to do anything for him. And so it occurred to me, I don't wish to do anything that doesn't meet with your approval, but we might perhaps be able to scrape up a small income for him so that he shan't be too conscious of his ruin, so that he can keep a roof over his head." "I entirely agree with you, it is very good of you to have thought of it. But you say 'a roof'; the imbecile has kept on an apartment beyond his means, he can't remain in it, we shall have to find him a couple of rooms somewhere. I understand that at the present moment he is still paying six or seven thousand francs for his apartment." "Six thousand, five hundred. But he is greatly attached to his home. In short, he has had his first stroke, he can scarcely live more than two or three years. Suppose we were to allow him ten thousand francs for three years. It seems to me that we should be able to afford that. We might for instance this year, instead of taking la Raspelière again, get hold of something on a simpler scale. With our income, it seems to me that to sacrifice ten thousand francs a year for three years is not out of the question." "Very well, there's only the nuisance that people will get to know about it, we shall be expected to do it again for others." "Believe me, I have thought about that. I shall do it only upon the express condition that nobody knows anything about it. Thank you, I have no desire that we should become the benefactors of the human race. No philanthropy! What we might do is to tell him that the money has been left to him by Princess Sherbatoff." "But will he believe it? She consulted Cottard about her will." "If the worse comes to the worst, we might take Cottard into our confidence, he is used to professional secrecy, he makes an enormous amount of money, he won't be like one of those busybodies one is obliged to hush up. He may even be willing to say, perhaps, that it was himself that the Princess appointed as her agent. In that way we shouldn't even appear. That would avoid all the nuisance of scenes, and gratitude, and speeches." M. Verdurin added an expression which made quite plain the kind of touching scenes and speeches which they were anxious to avoid. But it cannot have been reported to me correctly, for it was not a French expression, but one of those terms that are to be found in certain families to denote certain things, annoying things especially, probably because people wish to indicate them in the hearing of the persons concerned without being understood! An expression of this sort is generally a survival from an earlier condition of the family. In a Jewish family, for instance, it will be a ritual term diverted from its true meaning, and perhaps the only Hebrew word with which the family, now thoroughly French, is still acquainted. In a family that is strongly provincial, it will be a term in the local dialect, albeit the family no longer speaks or even understands that dialect. In a family that has come from South America and no longer speaks anything but French, it will be a Spanish word. And, in the next generation, the word will no longer exist save as a childish memory. They may remember quite well that their parents at table used to allude to the servants who were waiting, without being understood by them, by employing some such word, but the children cannot tell exactly what the word meant, whether it was Spanish, Hebrew, German, dialect, if indeed it ever belonged to any language and was not a proper name or a word entirely forged. The uncertainty can be cleared up only if they have a great-uncle, a cousin still surviving who must have used the same expression. As I never knew any relative of the Verdurins, I have never been able to reconstruct the word. All I know is that it certainly drew a smile from Mme. Verdurin, for the use of this language less general, more personal, more secret, than their everyday speech inspires in those who use it among themselves a sense of self-importance which is always accompanied by a certain satisfaction. After this moment of mirth: " But if Cottard talks," Mme. Verdurin objected. " He will not talk." He did mention it, to myself at least, for it was from him that I learned of this incident a few years later, actually at the funeral of

Saniette. I was sorry that I had not known of it earlier. For one thing the knowledge would have brought me more rapidly to the idea that we ought never to feel resentment towards other people, ought never to judge them by some memory of an unkind action, for we do not know all the good that, at other moments, their hearts may have sincerely desired and realised; no doubt the evil form which we have established once and for all will recur, but the heart is far more rich than that, has many other forms that will recur, also, to these people, whose kindness we refuse to admit because of the occasion on which they behaved badly. Furthermore, this revelation by Cottard must inevitably have had an effect upon me, because by altering my opinion of the Verdurins, this revelation, had it been made to me earlier, would have dispelled the suspicions that I had formed as to the part that the Verdurins might be playing between Albertine and myself, would have dispelled them, wrongly perhaps as it happened, for if M. Verdurin—whom I supposed, with increasing certainty, to be the most malicious man alive— had certain virtues, he was nevertheless tormenting to the point of the most savage persecution, and so jealous of his domination over the little clan as not to shrink from the basest falsehoods, from the fomentation of the most unjustified hatreds, in order to sever any ties between the faithful which had not as their sole object the strengthening of the little group. He was a man capable of disinterested action, of unostentatious generosity, that does not necessarily mean a man of feeling, nor a pleasant man, nor a scrupulous, nor a truthful, nor always a good man. A partial goodness, in which there persisted, perhaps, a trace of the family whom my great-aunt had

known, existed probably in him in view of this action before I discovered it, as America or the North Pole existed
before Columbus or Peary.   Nevertheless, at the moment
of my discovery, M. Verdurin's nature offered me a new
and unimagined aspect; and so I am brought up against
the difficulty of presenting a permanent image as well
of a character as of societies and passions.   For it changes
no less than they, and if we seek to portray what is rela-
tively unchanging in it, we see it present in succession
different aspects (implying that it cannot remain still but
keeps moving) to the disconcerted artist.

CHAPTER III

Flight of Albertine

SEEING how late it was, and fearing that Albertine might be growing impatient, I asked Brichot, as we left the Verdurins' party, to be so kind as to drop me at my door. My carriage would then take him home. He congratulated me upon going straight home like this (unaware that a girl was waiting for me in the house), and upon ending so early, and so wisely, an evening of which, on the contrary, all that I had done was to postpone the actual beginning. Then he spoke to me about M. de Charlus. The latter would doubtless have been stupefied had he heard the Professor, who was so kind to him, the Professor who always assured him: "I never repeat anything," speaking of him and of his life without the slightest reserve. And Brichot's indignant amazement would perhaps have been no less sincere if M. de Charlus had said to him: "I am told that you have been speaking evil of me." Brichot did indeed feel an affection for M. de Charlus and, if he had had to call to mind some conversation that had turned upon him, would have been far more likely to remember the friendly feeling that he had shewn for the Baron, while he said the same things about him that everyone was saying, than to remember the things that he had said. He would not have thought that he was lying if he had said: "I who speak of you in so friendly a spirit," since he did feel a friendly spirit while he was speaking of M. de Charlus. The Baron had above all for Brichot the charm which the Professor demanded before everything else in his social existence, and which was that of furnishing real examples of what he had long supposed to be an invention of the poets. Brichot, who had often expounded the second Eclogue of Virgil without really knowing whether its fiction had any basis in reality, found later on in conversing with Charlus some of the pleasure which he knew that his masters, M. Mérimée and M. Renan, his colleague M. Maspéro had felt, when travelling in Spain, Palestine, and Egypt, upon recognising in the scenery and the contemporary peoples of Spain, Palestine and Egypt, the setting and the invariable actors of the ancient scenes which they themselves had expounded in their books. "Be it said without offence to that knight of noble lineage," Brichot declared to me in the carriage that was taking us home, "he is simply prodigious when he illustrates his satanic catechism with a distinctly Bedlamite vigour and the persistence, I was going to say the candour, of Spanish whitewash and of a returned *émigré*. I can assure you, if I dare express myself like Mgr. d'Hulst, I am by no means bored upon the days when I receive a visit from that feudal lord who, seeking to defend Adonis against our age of miscreants, has followed the instincts of his race, and, in all sodomist innocence, has gone crusading." I listened to Brichot, and I was not alone with him. As, for that matter, I had never ceased to feel since I left home that evening, I felt myself, in however obscure a fashion, tied fast to the girl who was at that moment in her room. Even when I was talking to some one or other at the Verdurins', I had felt, confusedly, that she was by my side, I had that vague impression of her

168

that we have of our own limbs, and if I happened to think of her it was as we think, with disgust at being bound to it in complete subjection, of our own body. "And what a fund of scandal," Brichot went on, "sufficient to supply all the appendices of the *Causeries du Lundi,* is the conversation of that apostle. Imagine that I have learned from him that the ethical treatise which I had always admired as the most splendid moral composition of our age was inspired in our venerable colleague X by a young telegraph messenger. Let us not hesitate to admit that my eminent friend omitted to give us the name of this ephebe in the course of his demonstrations. He has shewn in so doing more human respect, or, if you prefer, less gratitude than Phidias who inscribed the name of the athlete whom he loved upon the ring of his Olympian Zeus. The Baron had not heard that story. Needless to say, it appealed to his orthodox mind. You can readily imagine that whenever I have to discuss with my colleague a candidate's thesis, I shall find in his dialectic, which for that matter is extremely subtle, the additional savour which spicy revelations added, for Sainte-Beuve, to the insufficiently confidential writings of Chateaubriand. From our colleague, who is a goldmine of wisdom but whose gold is not legal tender, the telegraph-boy passed into the hands of the Baron, 'all perfectly proper, of course,' (you ought to hear his voice when he says it). And as this Satan is the most obliging of men, he has found his protégé a post in the Colonies, from which the young man, who has a sense of gratitude, sends him from time to time the most excellent fruit. The Baron offers these to his distinguished friends; some of the young man's pineapples appeared quite recently on the table at Quai

Conti, drawing from Mme. Verdurin, who at that moment put no malice into her words: 'You must have an uncle or a nephew in America, M. de Charlus, to get pineapples like these!' I admit that if I had known the truth then I should have eaten them with a certain gaiety, repeating to myself *in petto* the opening lines of an Ode of Horace which Diderot loved to recall. In fact, like my colleague Boissier, strolling from the Palatine to Tibur, I derive from the Baron's conversation a singularly more vivid and more savoury idea of the writers of the Augustan age. Let us not even speak of those of the Decadence, nor let us hark back to the Greeks, although I have said to that excellent Baron that in his company I felt like Plato in the house of Aspasia. To tell the truth, I had considerably enlarged the scale of the two characters and, as La Fontaine says, my example was taken 'from lesser animals.' However it be, you do not, I imagine, suppose that the Baron took offence. Never have I seen him so ingenuously delighted. A childish excitement made him depart from his aristocratic phlegm. 'What flatterers all these Sorbonnards are!' he exclaimed with rapture. 'To think that I should have had to wait until my age before being compared to Aspasia! An old image like me! Oh, my youth!' I should like you to have seen him as he said that, outrageously powdered as he always is, and, at his age, scented like a young coxcomb. All the same, beneath his genealogical obsessions, the best fellow in the world. For all these reasons, I should be distressed were this evening's rupture to prove final. What did surprise me was the way in which the young man turned upon him. His manner towards the Baron has been, for some time past, that of a violent partisan, of a feudal vassal,

which scarcely betokened such an insurrection. I hope
that, in any event, even if (*Dii omen avertant*) the Baron
were never to return to Quai Conti, this schism is not
going to involve myself. Each of us derives too much
advantage from the exchange that we make of my feeble
stock of learning with his experience." (We shall see
that if M. de Charlus, after having hoped in vain that
Brichot would bring Morel back to him, shewed no violent
rancour against him, at any rate his affection for the
Professor vanished so completely as to allow him to judge
him without any indulgence.) "And I swear to you
that the exchange is so much in my favour that when the
Baron yields up to me what his life has taught him, I am
unable to endorse the opinion of Sylvestre Bonnard that
a library is still the best place in which to ponder the
dream of life."

We had now reached my door. I got out of the carriage to give the driver Brichot's address. From the
pavement, I could see the window of Albertine's room,
that window, formerly quite black, at night, when she
was not staying in the house, which the electric light inside, dissected by the slats of the shutters, striped from
top to bottom with parallel bars of gold. This magic
scroll, clear as it was to myself, tracing before my tran-
quil mind precise images, near at hand, of which I should
presently be taking possession, was completely invisible
to Brichot who had remained in the carriage, almost
blind, and would moreover have been completely incomprehensible to him could he have seen it, since, like the
friends who called upon me before dinner, when Albertine had returned from her drive, the Professor was
unaware that a girl who was all my own was waiting for

me in a bedroom adjoining mine. The carriage drove
on. I remained for a moment alone upon the pavement.
To be sure, these luminous rays which I could see from
below and which to anyone else would have seemed
merely superficial, I endowed with the utmost consistency,
plenitude, solidity, in view of all the significance that I
placed behind them, in a treasure unsuspected by the
rest of the world which I had concealed there and from
which those horizontal rays emanated, a treasure if you
like, but a treasure in exchange for which I had forfeited
my freedom, my solitude, my thought. If Albertine had
not been there, and indeed if I had merely been in search
of pleasure, I would have gone to demand it of unknown
women, into whose life I should have attempted to pene-
trate, at Venice perhaps, or at least in some corner of noc-
turnal Paris. But now all that I had to do when the
time came for me to receive caresses, was not to set
forth upon a journey, was not even to leave my own
house, but to return there. And to return there not to
find myself alone, and, after taking leave of the friends
who furnished me from outside with food for thought,
to find myself at any rate compelled to seek it in myself,
but to be on the contrary less alone than when I was at
the Verdurins', welcomed as I should be by the person
to whom I abdicated, to whom I handed over most completely my own person, without having for an instant the
leisure to think of myself nor even requiring the effort,
since she would be by my side, to think of her. So that
as I raised my eyes to look for the last time from outside
at the window of the room in which I should presently find
myself, I seemed to behold the luminous gates which were
about to close behind me and of which I myself had

forged, for an eternal slavery, the unyielding bars of gold.

Our engagement had assumed the form of a criminal trial and gave Albertine the timidity of a guilty party. Now she changed the conversation whenever it turned upon people, men or women, who were not of mature years. It was when she had not yet suspected that I was jealous of her that I could have asked her to tell me what I wanted to know. We ought always to take advantage of that period. It is then that our mistress tells us of her pleasures and even of the means by which she conceals them from other people. She would no longer have admitted to me now as she had admitted at Balbec (partly because it was true, partly in order to excuse herself for not making her affection for myself more evident, for I had already begun to weary her even then, and she had gathered from my kindness to her that she need not shew it to me as much as to other men in order to obtain more from me than from them), she would no longer have admitted to me now as she had admitted then: " I think it stupid to let people see that one is in love; I'm just the opposite, as soon as a person appeals to me, I pretend not to take any notice of him. In that way, nobody knows anything about it."

What, it was the same Albertine of to-day, with her pretensions to frankness and indifference to all the world who had told me this! She would never have informed me of such a rule of conduct now! She contented herself when she was talking to me with applying it, by saying of somebody or other who might cause me anxiety: " Oh, I don't know, I never noticed them, they don't count." And from time to time, to anticipate discoveries which I might make, she would proffer those confessions which their accent, before one knows the reality which they are intended to alter, to render innocent, denounces already as being falsehoods.

Albertine had never told me that she suspected me of being jealous of her, preoccupied with everything that she did. The only words—and that, I must add, was long ago—which we had exchanged with regard to jealousy seemed to prove the opposite. I remembered that, on a fine moonlight evening, towards the beginning of our intimacy, on one of the first occasions when I had accompanied her home, and when I would have been just as glad not to do so and to leave her in order to run after other girls, I had said to her: "You know, if I am offering to take you home, it is not from jealousy; if you have anything else to do, I shall slip discreetly away." And she had replied: "Oh, I know quite well that you aren't jealous and that it's all the same to you, but I've nothing else to do except to stay with you." Another occasion was at la Raspelière, when M. de Charlus, not without casting a covert glance at Morel, had made a display of friendly gallantry towards Albertine; I had said to her: "Well, he gave you a good hug, I hope." And as I had added half ironically: "I suffered all the torments of jealousy," Albertine, employing the language proper either to the vulgar class from which she sprang or to that other, more vulgar still, which she frequented, replied: "What a fusspot you are! I know quite well you're not jealous. For one thing, you told me so, and besides, it's perfectly obvious, get along with you!" She had never told me since then that she had changed her mind; but there must all the same have developed in her, upon that subject, a number of fresh ideas, which she concealed from me but which an accident might, in spite of her, betray, for this evening when, having gone indoors, after going to fetch her from her own room and taking her to mine, I had said to her (with a certain awkwardness which I did not myself understand, for I had indeed told Albertine that I was going to pay a call, and had said that I did not know where, perhaps upon Mme. de Villeparisis, perhaps upon Mme. de Guermantes, perhaps upon Mme. de Cambremer; it is true that I had not actually mentioned the Verdurins): "Guess where I have been; at the Verdurins'," I had barely had time to utter the words before Albertine, a look of utter consternation upon her face, had answered me in words which seemed to explode of their own accord with a force which she was unable to contain: "I thought as much." "I didn't know that you would be annoyed by my going to see the Verdurins." It is true that she did not tell me that she was annoyed, but that was obvious; it is true also that I had not said to myself that she would be annoyed. And yet in the face of the explosion of her wrath, as in the face of those events which a sort of retrospective second sight makes us imagine that we have already known in the past, it seemed to me that I could never have expected anything else. "Annoyed? What do you suppose I care, where you've been. It's all the same to me. Wasn't Mlle. Vinteuil there?" Losing all control of myself at these words: "You never told me that you had met her the other day," I said to her, to shew her that I was better informed than she knew. Believing that the person whom I reproached her for having met without telling me was Mme. Verdurin, and not, as I meant to imply, Mlle. Vinteuil: "Did I meet her?" she inquired with a pensive air, addressing at once herself as though she were seeking to collect her fugitive memories and myself as though it were I that ought to have told her of the meeting; and no doubt in order that I might say what I knew, perhaps also in order to gain time before making a difficult response. But I was preoccupied with the thought of Mlle. Vinteuil, and still more with a dread which had already entered my mind but which now gripped me in a violent clutch, the dread that Albertine might be longing for freedom. When I came home I had supposed that Mme. Verdurin had purely and simply invented, to enhance her own renown, the story of her having expected Mlle. Vinteuil and her friend, so that I was quite calm. Albertine, merely by saying: "Wasn't Mlle. Vinteuil there?" had shewn me that I had not been mistaken in my original suspicion; but anyhow my mind was set at rest in that quarter for the future, since by giving up her plan of visiting the Verdurins' and going instead to the Trocadéro, Albertine had sacrificed Mlle. Vinteuil. But, at the Trocadéro, from which, for that matter, she had come away in order to go for a drive with myself, there had been as a reason to make her leave it the presence of Léa. As I thought of this I mentioned Léa by name, and Albertine, distrustful, supposing that I had perhaps heard something more, took the initiative and exclaimed volubly, not without partly concealing her face: "I know her quite well; we went last year, some of my friends and I, to see her act: after the performance we went behind to her dressing-room, she changed in front of us. It was most interesting." Then my mind was compelled to relinquish Mlle. Vinteuil and, in a desperate effort, racing through the abysses of possible reconstructions, attached itself to the actress, to that evening when Albertine had gone behind to her dressing-room. On the other hand, after all the oaths that she had sworn to me, and in so truthful a tone, after the so complete sacrifice of her freedom, how was I to suppose that there was any evil in all this affair? And yet, were not my suspicions feelers pointing in the direction of the truth, since if she had made me a sacrifice of the Verdurins in order to go to the Trocadéro, nevertheless at the Verdurins' Mlle. Vinteuil was expected, and, at the Trocadéro, there had been Léa, who seemed to me to be disturbing me without cause and whom all the same, in that speech which I had not demanded of her, she admitted that she had known upon a larger scale than that of my fears, in circumstances that were indeed shady? For what could have induced her to go behind like that to that dressing-room? If I ceased to suffer because of Mlle. Vinteuil when I suffered because of Léa, those two tormentors of my day, it was either on account of the inability of my mind to picture too many scenes at one time, or on account of the interference of my nervous emotions of which my jealousy was but the echo. I could induce from them only that she had belonged no more to Léa than to Mlle. Vinteuil and that I was thinking of Léa only because the thought of her still caused me pain. But the fact that my twin jealousies were dying down—to revive now and then, alternately—does not, in any way, mean that they did not on the contrary correspond each to some truth of which I had had a foreboding, that of these women I must not say to myself none, but all. I say a foreboding, for I could not project myself to all the points of time and space which I should have had to visit, and besides, what instinct would have given me the coordinate of one with another necessary to enable me to surprise Albertine, here, at one moment, with Léa, or with the Balbec girls, or with that friend of Mme. Bontemps whom she had jostled, or with the girl on the tennis-court who had nudged her with her elbow, or with Mlle. Vinteuil?

I must add that what had appeared to me most serious, and had struck me as most symptomatic, was that she had forestalled my accusation, that she had said to me: "Wasn't Mlle. Vinteuil there?" to which I had replied in the most brutal fashion imaginable: "You never told me that you had met her." Thus as soon as I found Albertine no longer obliging, instead of telling her that I was sorry, I became malicious. There was then a moment in which I felt a sort of hatred of her which only intensified my need to keep her in captivity.

"Besides," I said to her angrily, "there are plenty of other things which you hide from me, even the most trivial things, such as for instance when you went for three days to Balbec, I mention it in passing." I had added the words "I mention it in passing" as a complement to "even the most trivial things" so that if Albertine said to me "What was there wrong about my trip to Balbec?" I might be able to answer: "Why, I've quite forgotten. I get so confused about the things people tell me, I attach so little importance to them." And indeed if I referred to those three days which she had spent in an excursion with the chauffeur to Balbec, from where her postcards had reached me after so long an interval, I referred to them purely at random and regretted that I had chosen so bad an example, for in fact, as they had barely had time to go there and return, it was certainly the one excursion in which there had not even been time for the interpolation of a meeting at all protracted with anybody. But Albertine supposed, from what I had just said, that I was fully aware of the real facts, and had merely concealed my knowledge from her; so she had been convinced, for some time past, that, in one way or another, I was having her followed, or in short was somehow or other, as she had said the week before to Andrée, better informed than herself about her own life. And so she interrupted me with a wholly futile admission, for certainly I suspected nothing of what she now told me, and I was on the other hand appalled, so vast can the disparity be between the truth which a liar has disguised and the idea which, from her lies, the man who is in love with the said liar has formed of the truth. Scarcely had I uttered the words: "When you went for three days to Balbec, I mention it in passing," before Albertine, cutting me short, declared as a thing that was perfectly natural: "You mean to say that I never went to Balbec at all? Of course I didn't! And I have always wondered why you pretended to believe that I had. All the same, there was no harm in it. The driver had some business of his own for three days. He didn't like to mention it to you. And so, out of kindness to him (it was my doing! Besides it is always I that have to bear the brunt), I invented a trip to Balbec. He simply put me down at Auteuil, with my friend in the Rue de l'Assomption, where I spent the three days bored to tears. You see it is not a serious matter, there's nothing broken. I did indeed begin to suppose that you perhaps knew all about it, when I saw how you laughed when the postcards began to arrive, a week late. I quite see that it was absurd, and that it would have been better not to send any cards. But that wasn't my fault. I had bought the cards beforehand and given them to the driver before he dropped me at Auteuil, and then the fathead put them in his pocket and forgot about them instead of sending them on in an envelope to a friend of his near Balbec who was to forward them to you. I kept on supposing that they would turn up. He forgot all about them for five days, and instead of telling me the idiot sent them on at once to Balbec. When he did tell me, I fairly broke it over him, I can tell you! And you go and make a stupid fuss, when it's all the fault of that great fool, as a reward for my shutting myself up for three whole days, so that he might go and look after his family affairs. I didn't even venture to go out into Auteuil for fear of being seen. The only time that I did go out, I was dressed as a man, and that was a funny business. And it was just my luck, which follows me wherever I go, that the first person I came across was your Yid friend Bloch. But I don't believe it was from him that you learned that my trip to Balbec never existed except in my imagination, for he seemed not to recognise me."

I did not know what to say, not wishing to appear astonished, while I was appalled by all these lies. With a sense of horror, which gave me no desire to turn Albertine out of the house, far from it, was combined a strong inclination to burst into tears. This last was caused not by the lie itself and by the annihilation of everything that I had so stoutly believed to be true that I felt as though I were in a town that had been razed to the ground, where not a house remained standing, where the bare soil was merely heaped with rubble—but by the melancholy thought that, during those three days when she had been bored to tears in her friend's house at Auteuil, Albertine had never once felt any desire, the idea had perhaps never occurred to her to come and pay me a visit one day on the quiet, or to send a message asking me to go and see her at Auteuil. But I had not time to give myself up to these reflexions. Whatever happened, I did not wish to appear surprised. I smiled with the air of a man who knows far more than he is going to say: "But that is only one thing out of a thousand. For instance, you knew that Mlle. Vinteuil was expected at Mme. Verdurin's, this afternoon when you went to the Trocadéro." She blushed: "Yes, I knew that." "Can you swear to me that it was not in order to renew your relations with her that you wanted to go to the Verdurins'." "Why, of course I can swear. Why do you say renew, I never had any relations with her, I swear it." I was appalled to hear Albertine lie to me like this, deny the facts which her blush had made all too evident. Her mendacity appalled me. And yet, as it contained a protestation of innocence which, almost unconsciously, I was prepared to accept, it hurt me less than her sincerity when, after I had asked her: "Can you at least swear to me that the pleasure of seeing Mlle. Vinteuil again had nothing to do with your anxiety to go this afternoon to the Verdurins' party?" she replied: "No, that I cannot swear. It would have been a great pleasure to see Mlle. Vinteuil again." A moment earlier, I had been angry with her because she concealed her relations with Mlle. Vinteuil, and now her admission of the pleasure that she would have felt in seeing her again turned my bones to water. For that matter, the mystery in which she had cloaked her intention of going to see the Verdurins ought to have been a sufficient proof. But I had not given the matter enough thought. Although she was now telling me the truth, why did she admit only half, it was even more stupid than it was wicked and wretched. I was so crushed that I had not the courage to insist upon this question, as to which I was not in a strong position, having no damning evidence to produce, and to recover my ascendancy, I hurriedly turned to a subject which would enable me to put Albertine to rout: "Listen, only this evening, at the Verdurins', I learned that what you had told me about Mlle. Vinteuil. . . ." Albertine gazed at me fixedly with a tormented air, seeking to read in my eyes how much I knew. Now, what I knew and what I was about to tell her as to Mlle. Vinteuil's true nature, it was true that it was not at the Verdurins' that I had learned it, but at Montjouvain long ago. Only, as I had always refrained, deliberately, from mentioning it to Albertine, I could now appear to have learned it only this evening. And I could almost feel a joy—after having felt, on the little tram, so keen an anguish—at possessing this memory of Montjouvain, which I postdated, but which would nevertheless be the unanswerable proof, a crushing blow to Albertine. This time at least, I had no need to "seem to know" and to "make Albertine speak"; I did know, I had seen through the lighted window at Montjouvain. It had been all very well for Albertine to tell me that her relations with Mlle. Vinteuil and her friend had been perfectly pure, how could she when I swore to her (and swore without lying) that I knew the habits of these two women, how could she maintain any longer that, having lived in a daily intimacy with them, calling them "my big sisters," she had not been approached by them with suggestions which would have made her break with them, if on the contrary she had not complied? But I had no time to tell her what I knew. Albertine, imagining, as in the case of the pretended excursion to Balbec, that I had learned the truth, either from Mlle. Vinteuil, if she had been at the Verdurins', or simply from Mme. Verdurin herself who might have mentioned her to Mlle. Vinteuil, did not allow me to speak but made a confession, the exact opposite of what I had supposed, which nevertheless, by shewing me that she had never ceased to lie to me, caused me perhaps just as much grief (especially since I was no longer, as I said a moment ago, jealous of Mlle. Vinteuil); in short, taking the words out of my mouth, Albertine proceeded to say: "You mean to tell me that you found out this evening that I lied to you when I pretended that I had been more or less brought up by Mlle. Vinteuil's friend. It is true that I did lie to you a little. But I felt that you despised me so, I saw too that you were so keen upon that man Vinteuil's music that as one of my school friends—this is true, I swear to you—had been a friend of Mlle. Vinteuil's friend, I stupidly thought that I might make myself seem interesting to you by inventing the story that I had known the girls quite well. I felt that I was boring you, that you thought me a goose, I thought that if I told you that those people used to see a lot of me, that I could easily tell you all sorts of things about Vinteuil's work, I should acquire a little importance in your eyes, that it would draw us together. When I lie to you, it is always out of affection for you. And it needed this fatal Verdurin party to open your eyes to the truth, which has been a bit exaggerated besides. I bet, Mlle. Vinteuil's friend told you that she did not know me. She met me at least twice at my friend's house. But of course, I am not smart enough for people like that who have become celebrities. They prefer to say that they have never met me." Poor Albertine, when she imagined that to tell me that she had been so intimate with Mlle. Vinteuil's friend would postpone her own dismissal, would draw her nearer to me, she had, as so often happens, attained the truth by a different road from that which she had intended to take. Her shewing herself better informed about music than I had supposed would never have prevented me from breaking with her that evening, on the little tram; and yet it was indeed that speech, which she had made with that object, which had immediately brought about far more than the impossibility of a rupture. Only she made an error in her interpretation, not of the effect which that speech was to have, but of the cause by virtue of which it was to produce that effect, a cause which was my discovery not of her musical culture, but of her evil associations. What had abruptly drawn me to her, what was more, merged me in her was not the expectation of a pleasure—and pleasure is too strong a word, a slight interest—it was a wringing grief.

Once again I had to be careful not to keep too long a silence which might have led her to suppose that I was surprised. And so, touched by the discovery that she was so modest and had thought herself despised in the Verdurin circle, I said to her tenderly: "But, my darling, I would gladly give you several hundred francs to let you go and play the fashionable lady wherever you please and

invite M. and Mme. Verdurin to a grand dinner." Alas!
Albertine was several persons in one. The most mysterious, most simple, most atrocious revealed herself in the
answer which she made me with an air of disgust and the
exact words to tell the truth I could not quite make out
(even the opening words, for she did not finish her
sentence). I succeeded in establishing them only a little
later when I had guessed what was in her mind. We
hear things retrospectively when we have understood
them. "Thank you for nothing! Fancy spending a cent
upon those old frumps, I'd a great deal rather you left
me alone for once in a way so that I can go and get some
one decent to break my . . . ." As she uttered the
words, her face flushed crimson, a look of terror came to
her eyes, she put her hand over her mouth as though she
could have thrust back the words which she had just
uttered and which I had completely failed to understand.
"What did you say, Albertine?" "No, nothing, I was
half asleep and talking to myself." "Not a bit of it, you
were wide awake." "I was thinking about asking the
Verdurins to dinner, it is very good of you." "No, I mean
what you said just now." She gave me endless versions,
none of which agreed in the least, I do not say with her
words which, being interrupted, remained vague, but with
the interruption itself and the sudden flush that had accompanied it. "Come, my darling, that is not what you
were going to say, otherwise why did you stop short."
"Because I felt that my request was indiscreet." "What
request?" "To be allowed to give a dinner-party."
"No, it is not that, there is no need of discretion between
you and me." "Indeed there is, we ought never to take
advantage of the people we love. In any case, I swear

to you that that was all." On the one hand it was still impossible for me to doubt her sworn word, on the other hand her explanations did not satisfy my critical spirit. I continued to press her. "Anyhow, you might at least have the courage to finish what you were saying, you stopped short at *break*." "No, leave me alone!" "But why?" "Because it is dreadfully vulgar, I should be ashamed to say such a thing in front of you. I don't know what I was thinking of, the words—I don't even know what they mean, I heard them used in the street one day by some very low people—just came to my lips without rhyme or reason. It had nothing to do with me or anybody else, I was simply dreaming aloud." I felt that I should extract nothing more from Albertine. She had lied to me when she had sworn, a moment ago, that what had cut her short had been a social fear of being indiscreet, since it had now become the shame of letting me hear her use a vulgar expression. Now this was certainly another lie. For when we were alone together there was no speech too perverse, no word too coarse for us to utter among our embraces. Anyhow, it was useless to insist at that moment. But my memory remained obsessed by the word "break". Albertine frequently spoke of "breaking sticks" or "breaking sugar" over some one, or would simply say: "Ah! I fairly broke it over him!" meaning "I fairly gave it to him!" But she would say this quite freely in my presence, and if it was this that she had meant to say, why had she suddenly stopped short, why had she blushed so deeply, placed her hands over her mouth, given a fresh turn to her speech, and, when she saw that I had heard the word "break," offered a false explanation. But as soon as I had abandoned the pursuit of an interrogation from which I received no response, the only thing to do was to appear to have lost interest in the matter, and, retracing my thoughts to Albertine's reproaches of me for having gone to the Mistress's, I said to her, very awkwardly, making indeed a sort of stupid excuse for my conduct: " Why, I had been meaning to ask you to come to the Verdurins' party this evening," a speech that was doubly maladroit, for if I meant it, since I had been with her all the day, why should I not have made the suggestion? Furious at my lie and emboldened by my timidity: " You might have gone on asking me for a thousand years," she said, " I would never have consented. They are people who have always been against me, they have done everything they could to upset me. There was nothing I didn't do for Mme. Verdurin at Balbec, and I've been finely rewarded. If she summoned me to her deathbed, I wouldn't go. There are some things which it is impossible to forgive. As for you, it's the first time you've treated me badly. When Françoise told me that you had gone out (she enjoyed telling me that, I don't think), you might have knocked me down with a feather. I tried not to shew any sign, but never in my life have I been so insulted." While she was speaking, there continued in myself, in the thoroughly alive and creative sleep of the unconscious (a sleep in which the things that barely touch us succeed in carving an impression, in which our hands take hold of the key that turns the lock, the key for which we have sought in vain), the quest of what it was that she had meant by that interrupted speech the end of which I was so anxious to know. And all of a sudden an appalling word, of which I had never dreamed, burst upon me: "pot". I cannot say that it came to me in a single flash, as when, in a long passive submission to an incomplete memory, while we try gently, cautiously, to draw it out, we remain fastened, glued to it. No, in contrast to the ordinary process of my memory, there were, I think, two parallel quests; the first took into account not merely Albertine's words, but her look of extreme annoyance when I had offered her a sum of money with which to give a grand dinner, a look which seemed to say: "Thank you, the idea of spending money upon things that bore me, when without money I could do things that I enjoy doing!" And it was perhaps the memory of this look that she had given me which made me alter my method in discovering the end of her unfinished sentence. Until then I had been hypnotised by her last word: "break," she had meant to say break what? Break wood? No. Sugar? No. Break, break, break. And all at once the look that she had given me at the moment of my suggestion that she should give a dinner-party, turned me back to the words that had preceded. And immediately I saw that she had not said "break" but "get some one to break." Horror! It was this that she would have preferred. Twofold horror! For even the vilest of prostitutes, who consents to that sort of thing, or desires it, does not employ to the man who yields to her desires that appalling expression. She would feel the degradation too great. To a woman alone, if she loves women, she says this, as an excuse for giving herself presently to a man. Albertine had not been lying when she told me that she was speaking in a dream. Distracted, impulsive, not realising that she was with me, she had, with a shrug of her shoulders, begun to speak as she would have spoken to one of those women, to one, perhaps, of my young budding girls. And abruptly recalled to reality, crimson with shame, thrusting back between her lips what she was going to say, plunged in despair, she had refused to utter another word. I had not a moment to lose if I was not to let her see how desperate I was. But already, after my sudden burst of rage, the tears came to my eyes. As at Balbec, on the night that followed her revelation of her friendship with the Vinteuil pair, I must immediately invent a plausible excuse for my grief, and one that was at the same time capable of creating so profound an effect upon Albertine as to give me a few days' respite before I came to a decision. And so, at the moment when she told me that she had never received such an insult as that which I had inflicted upon her by going out, that she would rather have died than hear Françoise tell her of my departure, when, as though irritated by her absurd susceptibility, I was on the point of telling her that what I had done was nothing, that there was nothing that could offend her in my going out—as, during these moments, moving on a parallel course, my unconscious quest for what she had meant to say after the word " break " had proved successful, and the despair into which my discovery flung me could not be completely hidden, instead of defending, I accused myself. " My little Albertine," I said to her in a gentle voice which was drowned in my first tears, " I might tell you that you are mistaken, that what I did this evening is nothing, but I should be lying; it is you that are right, you have realised the truth, my poor child, which is that six months ago, three months ago, when I was still so fond of you, never would I have done such a thing. It is a mere nothing, and it is enormous, because of the immense change in my heart of which it is the sign. And since you have detected this change which I hoped to conceal from you, that leads me on to tell you this: My little Albertine " (and here I addressed her with a profound gentleness and melancholy), " don't you see, the life that you are leading here is boring to you, it is better that we should part, and as the best partings are those that are ended at once, I ask you, to cut short the great sorrow that I am bound to feel, to bid me good-bye to-night and to leave in the morning without my seeing you again, while I am asleep." She appeared stupefied, still incredulous and already disconsolate: " To-morrow? You really mean it? " And notwithstanding the anguish that I felt in speaking of our parting as though it were already in the past—partly perhaps because of that very anguish—I began to give Albertine the most precise instructions as to certain things which she would have to do after she left the house. And passing from one request to another, I soon found myself entering into the minutest details. " Be so kind," I said, with infinite melancholy, " as to send me back that book of Bergotte's which is at your aunt's. There is no hurry about it, in three days, in a week, whenever you like, but remember that I don't want to have to write and ask you for it, that would be too painful. We have been happy together, we feel now that we should be unhappy." " Don't say that we feel that we should be unhappy," Albertine interrupted me, " don't say ' we,' it is only you who feel that." " Yes, very well, you or I, as you like, for one reason or another. But it is absurdly late, you must go to bed—we have decided to part to-night." " Pardon me, *you* have decided, and I obey you because I do not wish to cause you any trouble." "Very well, it is I who have decided, but that makes it none the less painful for me. I do not say that it will be painful for long, you know that I have not the faculty of remembering things for long, but for the first few days I shall be so miserable without you. And so I feel that it will be useless to revive the memory with letters, we must end everything at once." "Yes, you are right," she said to me with a crushed air, which was enhanced by the strain of fatigue upon her features due to the lateness of the hour; "rather than have one finger chopped off, then another, I prefer to lay my head on the block at once." "Heavens, I am appalled when I think how late I am keeping you out of bed, it is madness. However, it's the last night! You will have plenty of time to sleep for the rest of your life." And as I suggested to her thus that it was time to say good night I sought to postpone the moment when she would have said it. "Would you like me, as a distraction during the first few days, to tell Bloch to send his cousin Esther to the place where you will be staying, he will do that for me." "I don't know why you say that" (I had said it in an endeavour to wrest a confession from Albertine); "there is only one person for whom I care, which is yourself," Albertine said to me, and her words filled me with comfort. But, the next moment, what a blow she dealt me! "I remember, of course, that I did give Esther my photograph because she kept on asking me for it and I saw that she would like to have it, but as for feeling any liking for her or wishing ever to see her again. . . ." And yet Albertine was of so frivolous a nature that she went on: "If she wants to see me, it is all the same to me, she is very nice, but I don't care in the least either way." And so when I had spoken to her of the photograph of Esther which Bloch had sent me (and which I had not even received when I mentioned it to Albertine) my mistress had gathered that Bloch had shewn me a photograph of herself, given by her to Esther. In my worst suppositions, I had never imagined that any such intimacy could have existed between Albertine and Esther. Albertine had found no words in which to answer me when I spoke of the photograph. And now, supposing me, wrongly, to be in the know, she thought it better to confess. I was appalled. "And, Albertine, let me ask you to do me one more favour, never attempt to see me again. If at any time, as may happen in a year, in two years, in three years, we should find ourselves in the same town, keep away from me." Then, seeing that she did not reply in the affirmative to my prayer: "My Albertine, never see me again in this world. It would hurt me too much. For I was really fond of you, you know. Of course, when I told you the other day that I wanted to see the friend again whom I mentioned to you at Balbec, you thought that it was all settled. Not at all, I assure you, it was quite immaterial to me. You were convinced that I had long made up my mind to leave you, that my affection was all make-believe." "No indeed, you are mad, I never thought so," she said sadly. "You are right, you must never think so, I did genuinely feel for you, not love perhaps, but a great, a very great affection, more than you can imagine." "I can, indeed. And do you suppose that I don't love you!" "It hurts me terribly to have to give you up." "It hurts me a thousand times more," replied

Albertine. A moment earlier I had felt that I could no longer restrain the tears that came welling up in my eyes. And these tears did not spring from at all the same sort of misery which I had felt long ago when I said to Gilberte: "It is better that we should not see one another again, life is dividing us." No doubt when I wrote this to Gilberte, I said to myself that when I should be in love not with her but with another, the excess of my love would diminish that which I might perhaps have been able to inspire, as though two people must inevitably have only a certain quantity of love at their disposal; of which the surplus taken by one is subtracted from the other, and that from her too, as from Gilberte, I should be doomed to part. But the situation was entirely different for several reasons, the first of which (and it had, in its turn, given rise to the others) was that the lack of will-power which my grandmother and mother had observed in me with alarm, at Combray, and before which each of them, so great is the energy with which a sick man imposes his weakness upon others, had capitulated in turn, this lack of will-power had gone on increasing at an ever accelerated pace. When I felt that my company was boring Gilberte, I had still enough strength left to give her up; I had no longer the same strength when I had made a similar discovery with regard to Albertine, and could think only of keeping her at any cost to myself. With the result that, whereas I wrote to Gilberte that I would not see her again, meaning quite sincerely not to see her, I said this to Albertine as a pure falsehood, and in the hope of bringing about a reconciliation. Thus we presented each to the other an appearance which was widely different from the reality. And no doubt it is always so when two people stand face to face, since each of them is ignorant of a part of what exists in the other (even what he knows, he can understand only in part) and since both of them display what is the least personal thing about them, whether because they have not explored themselves and regard as negligible what is most important, or because insignificant advantages which have no place in themselves seem to them more important and more flattering. But in love this misunderstanding is carried to its supreme pitch because, except perhaps when we are children, we endeavour to make the appearance that we assume, rather than reflect exactly what is in our mind, be what our mind considers best adapted to enable us to obtain what we desire, which in my case, since my return to the house, was to be able to keep Albertine as docile as she had been in the past, was that she should not in her irritation ask me for a greater freedom, which I intended to give her one day, but which at this moment, when I was afraid of her cravings for independence, would have made me too jealous. After a certain age, from self-esteem and from sagacity, it is to the things which we most desire that we pretend to attach no importance. But in love, our mere sagacity—which for that matter is probably not the true wisdom—forces us speedily enough to this genius for duplicity. All that I had dreamed, as a boy, to be the sweetest thing in love, what had seemed to me to be the very essence of love, was to pour out freely, before the feet of her whom I loved, my affection, my gratitude for her kindness, my longing for a perpetual life together. But I had become only too well aware, from my own experience and from that of my friends, that the expression of such sentiments is far from being

contagious. Once we have observed this, we no longer
"let ourself go"; I had taken good care in the afternoon
not to tell Albertine how grateful I was to her that she
had not remained at the Trocadéro. And to-night, having been afraid that she might leave me, I had feigned a
desire to part from her, a feint which for that matter was
not suggested to me merely by the enlightenment which
I supposed myself to have received from my former loves
and was seeking to bring to the service of this.

The fear that Albertine was perhaps going to say to
me: "I wish to be allowed to go out by myself at certain
hours, I wish to be able to stay away for a night," in
fact any request of that sort, which I did not attempt to
define, but which alarmed me, this fear had entered my
mind for a moment before and during the Verdurins'
party. But it had been dispelled, contradicted moreover
by the memory of how Albertine assured me incessantly how happy she was with me. The intention to
leave me, if it existed in Albertine, was made manifest
only in an obscure fashion, in certain sorrowful glances,
certain gestures of impatience, speeches which meant
nothing of the sort, but which, if one analysed them (and
there was not even any need of analysis, for we can immediately detect the language of passion, the lower orders
themselves understand these speeches which can be explained only by vanity, rancour, jealousy, unexpressed
as it happens, but revealing itself at once to the listener
by an intuitive faculty which, like the "good sense" of
which Descartes speaks, is the most widespread thing in
the world), revealed the presence in her of a sentiment
which she concealed and which might lead her to form
plans for another life apart from myself. Just as this

intention was not expressed in her speech in a logical fashion, so the presentiment of this intention, which I had felt to-night, remained just as vague in myself. I continued to live by the hypothesis which admitted as true everything that Albertine told me. But it may be that in myself, during this time, a wholly contrary hypothesis, of which I refused to think, never left me; this is all the more probable since, otherwise, I should have felt no hesitation in telling Albertine that I had been to the Verdurins', and, indeed, my want of astonishment at her anger would not have been comprehensible. So that what probably existed in me was the idea of an Albertine entirely opposite to that which my reason formed of her, to that also which her own speech portrayed, an Albertine that all the same was not wholly invented, since she was like a prophetic mirror of certain impulses that occurred in her, such as her ill humour at my having gone to the Verdurins'. Besides, for a long time past, my frequent anguish, my fear of telling Albertine that I loved her, all this corresponded to another hypothesis which explained many things besides, and had also this to be said for it, that, if one adopted the first hypothesis, the second became more probable, for by allowing myself to give way to effusive tenderness for Albertine, I obtained from her nothing but irritation (to which moreover she assigned a different cause).

If I analyse my feelings by this hypothesis, by the invariable system of retorts expressing the exact opposite of what I was feeling, I can be quite certain that if, to-night, I told her that I was going to send her away, it was—at first, quite unconsciously—because I was afraid that she might desire her freedom (I should have been put to it to say what this freedom was that made me tremble, but anyhow some state of freedom in which she would have been able to deceive me, or, at least, I should no longer have been able to be certain that she was not) and wished to shew her, from pride, from cunning, that I was very far from fearing anything of the sort, as I had done already, at Balbec, when I was anxious that she should have a good opinion of me, and later on, when I was anxious that she should not have time to feel bored with me. In short, the objection that might be offered to this second hypothesis—which I did not formulate,—that everything that Albertine said to me indicated on the contrary that the life which she preferred was the life in my house, resting, reading, solitude, a loathing of Sapphic loves, and so forth, need not be considered seriously. For if on her part Albertine had chosen to interpret my feelings from what I said to her, she would have learned the exact opposite of the truth, since I never expressed a desire to part from her except when I was unable to do without her, and at Balbec I had confessed to her that I was in love with another woman, first Andrée, then a mysterious stranger, on the two occasions on which jealousy had revived my love for Albertine. My words, therefore, did not in the least reflect my sentiments. If the reader has no more than a faint impression of these, that is because, as narrator, I reveal my sentiments to him at the same time as I repeat my words. But if I concealed the former and he were acquainted only with the latter, my actions, so little in keeping with my speech, would so often give him the impression of strange revulsions of feeling that he would think me almost mad. A procedure which would not, for that matter, be much more false than that which I have adopted, for the images which prompted me to action, so opposite to those which were portrayed in my speech, were at that moment extremely obscure; I was but imperfectly aware of the nature which guided my actions; at present, I have a clear conception of its subjective truth. As for its objective truth, that is to say whether the inclinations of that nature grasped more exactly than my reason Albertine's true intentions, whether I was right to trust to that nature or on the contrary it did not corrupt Albertine's intentions instead of making them plain, that I find difficult to say. That vague fear which I had felt at the Verdurins' that Albertine might leave me had been at once dispelled. When I returned home, it had been with the feeling that I myself was a captive, not with that of finding a captive in the house. But the dispelled fear had gripped me all the more violently when, at the moment of my informing Albertine that I had been to the Verdurins', I saw her face veiled with a look of enigmatic irritation which moreover was not making itself visible for the first time. I knew quite well that it was only the crystallisation in the flesh of reasoned complaints, of ideas clear to the person who forms and does not express them, a synthesis rendered visible but not therefore rational, which the man who gathers its precious residue from the face of his beloved, endeavours in his turn, so that he may understand what is occurring in her, to reduce by analysis to its intellectual elements. The approximate equation of that unknown quantity which Albertine's thoughts were to me, had given me, more or less: " I knew his suspicions, I was sure that he would attempt to verify them, and so that I might not hinder him, he has worked out his little plan in secret." But if this was the state of mind (and she had never expressed it to me) in which Albertine was living, must she not regard with horror, find the strength fail her to carry on, might she not at any moment decide to terminate an existence in which, if she was, in desire at any rate, guilty, she must feel herself exposed, tracked down, prevented from ever yielding to her instincts, without thereby disarming my jealousy, and if innocent in intention and fact, she had had every right, for some time past, to feel discouraged, seeing that never once, from Balbec, where she had shewn so much perseverance in avoiding the risk of her ever being left alone with Andrée, until this very day when she had agreed not to go to the Verdurins' and not to stay at the Trocadéro, had she succeeded in regaining my confidence. All the more so as I could not say that her behaviour was not exemplary. If at Balbec, when anyone mentioned girls who had a bad style, she used often to copy their laughter, their wrigglings, their general manner, which was a torture to me because of what I supposed that it must mean to her girl friends, now that she knew my opinion on the subject, as soon as anyone made an allusion to things of that sort, she ceased to take part in the conversation, not only in speech but with the expression on her face. Whether it was in order not to contribute her share to the slanders that were being uttered about some woman or other, or for a quite different reason, the only thing that was noticeable then, upon those so mobile features, was that from the moment in which the topic was broached they had made their inattention evident, while preserving exactly the same expression that they had worn a moment earlier. And this immobility of even a light expression was as heavy as a silence; it would have been impossible to say that she blamed, that she approved, that she knew or did not know about these things. None of her features bore any relation to anything save another feature. Her nose, her mouth, her eyes formed a perfect harmony, isolated from everything else; she looked like a pastel, and seemed to have no more heard what had just been said than if it had been uttered in front of a portrait by Latour.

My serfdom, of which I had already been conscious when, as I gave the driver Brichot's address, I caught sight of the light in her window, had ceased to weigh upon me shortly afterwards, when I saw that Albertine appeared so cruelly conscious of her own. And in order that it might seem to her less burdensome, that she might not decide to break her bonds of her own accord, I had felt that the most effective plan was to give her the impression that it would not be permanent and that I myself was looking forward to its termination. Seeing that my feint had proved successful, I might well have thought myself fortunate, in the first place because what I had so greatly dreaded, Albertine's determination (as I supposed) to leave me, was shewn to be non-existent, and secondly, because, quite apart from the object that I had had in mind, the very success of my feint, by proving that I was something more to Albertine than a scorned lover, whose jealousy is flouted, all of his ruses detected in advance, endowed our love afresh with a sort of virginity, revived for it the days in which she could still, at Balbec, so readily believe that I was in love with another woman. For she would probably not have believed that any longer, but she was taking seriously my feigned de-

termination to part from her now and for ever. She
appeared to suspect that the cause of our parting might
be something that had happened at the Verdurins'. Feeling a need to soothe the anxiety into which I was worked
by my pretence of a rupture, I said to her: "Albertine,
can you swear that you have never lied to me?" She
gazed fixedly into the air before replying: "Yes, that is
to say no. I ought not to have told you that Andrée was
greatly taken with Bloch, we never met him." "Then
why did you say so?" "Because I was afraid that you
had believed other stories about her, that's all." I told
her that I had met a dramatist who was a great friend
of Léa, and to whom Léa had told some strange things
(I hoped by telling her this to make her suppose that I
knew a great deal more than I cared to say about Bloch's
cousin's friend. She stared once again into vacancy and
then said: "I ought not, when I spoke to you just now
about Léa, to have kept from you a three weeks' trip
that I took with her once. But I knew you so slightly
in those days!" "It was before Balbec?" "Before the
second time, yes." And that very morning, she had told
me that she did not know Léa, and, only a moment ago,
that she had met her once only in her dressing-room!
I watched a tongue of flame seize and devour in an
instant a romance which I had spent millions of minutes
in writing. To what end? To what end? Of course I
understood that Albertine had revealed these facts to me
because she thought that I had learned them indirectly
from Léa; and that there was no reason why a hundred
similar facts should not exist. I realised thus that Albertine's utterances, when one interrogated her, did not
ever contain an atom of truth, that the truth she allowed

to escape only in spite of herself, as though by a sudden combination in her mind of the facts which she had previously been determined to conceal with the belief that I had been informed of them. "But two things are nothing," I said to Albertine, "let us have as many as four, so that you may leave me some memories of you. What other revelations have you got for me?" Once again she stared into vacancy. To what belief in a future life was she adapting her falsehood, with what Gods less unstable than she had supposed was she seeking to ally herself? This cannot have been an easy matter, for her silence and the fixity of her gaze continued for some time. "No, nothing else," she said at length. And, notwithstanding my persistence, she adhered, easily now, to "nothing else." And what a lie! For, from the moment when she had acquired those tastes until the day when she had been shut up in my house, how many times, in how many places, on how many excursions must she have gratified them! The daughters of Gomorrah are at once so rare and so frequent that, in any crowd of people, one does not pass unperceived by the other. From that moment a meeting becomes easy.

I remembered with horror an evening which at the time had struck me as merely absurd. One of my friends had invited me to dine at a restaurant with his mistress and another of his friends who had also brought his own. The two women were not long in coming to an understanding, but were so impatient to enjoy one another that, with the soup, their feet were searching for one another, often finding mine. Presently their legs were interlaced. My two friends noticed nothing; I was on tenterhooks. One of the women, who could contain herself no longer, stooped under the table, saying that she had dropped something. Then one of them complained of a headache and asked to go upstairs to the lavatory. The other discovered that it was time for her to go and meet a woman friend at the theatre. Finally I was left alone with my two friends who suspected nothing. The lady with the headache reappeared, but begged to be allowed to go home by herself to wait for her lover at his house, so that she might take a dose of antipyrin. They became great friends, used to go about together, one of them, dressed as a man, picking up little girls and taking them to the other, initiating them. One of them had a little boy who, she pretended, was troublesome, and handed him over for punishment to her friend, who set to work with a strong arm. One may say that there was no place, however public, in which they did not do what is most secret.

"But Léa behaved perfectly properly with me all the time," Albertine told me. "She was indeed a great deal more reserved than plenty of society women." "Are there any society women who have shewn a want of reserve with you, Albertine?" "Never." "Then what do you mean?" "Oh, well, she was less free in her speech." "For instance?" "She would never, like many of the women you meet, have used the expression 'rotten,' or say: 'I don't care a damn for anybody.'" It seemed to me that a part of the romance which the flames had so far spared was crumbling at length in ashes.

My discouragement might have persisted. Albertine's words, when I thought of them, made it give place to a furious rage. This succumbed to a sort of tender emotion. I also, when I came home and declared that I wished to break with her, had been lying. And this desire for a parting, which I had feigned with perseverance, gradually affected me with some of the misery which I should have felt if I had really wished to part from Albertine.

Besides, even when I thought in fits and starts, in twinges, as we say of other bodily pains, of that orgiastic life which Albertine had led before she met me, I admired all the more the docility of my captive and ceased to feel any resentment.

No doubt, never, during our life together, had I failed to let Albertine know that such a life would in all probability be merely temporary, so that Albertine might continue to find some charm in it. But to-night I had gone farther, having feared that vague threats of separation were no longer sufficient, contradicted as they would doubtless be, in Albertine's mind, by her idea of a strong and jealous love of her, which must have made me, she seemed to imply, go in quest of information to the Verdurins'.

To-night I thought that, among the other reasons which might have made me decide of a sudden, without even realising except as I went on what I was doing, to enact this scene of rupture, there was above all the fact that, when, in one of those impulses to which my father was liable, I threatened another person in his security, as I had not, like him, the courage to carry a threat into practice, in order not to let it be supposed that it had been but empty words, I would go to a considerable length in pretending to carry out my threat and would recoil only when my adversary, having had a genuine illusion of my sincerity, had begun seriously to tremble. Besides, in these lies, we feel that there is indeed a grain of truth, that, if life does not bring any alteration of our loves, it is ourself who will seek to bring or to feign one, so strongly do we feel that all love, and everything else evolves rapidly towards a farewell. We would like to shed the tears that it will bring long before it comes. No doubt there had been, on this occasion, in the scene that I had enacted, a practical value. I had suddenly determined to keep Albertine because I felt that she was distributed among other people whom I could not prevent her from joining. But had she renounced them all finally for myself, I should have been all the more firmly determined never to let her go, for a parting is, by jealousy, rendered cruel, but, by gratitude, impossible. I felt that in any case I was fighting the decisive battle in which I must conquer or fall. I would have offered Albertine in an hour all that I possessed, because I said to myself: "Everything depends upon this battle, but such battles are less like those of old days which lasted for a few hours than a battle of to-day which does not end on the morrow, nor on the day after, nor in the following week. We give all our strength, because we steadfastly believe that we shall never need any strength again. And more than a year passes without bringing a 'decisive' victory. Perhaps an unconscious reminiscence of lying scenes enacted by M. de Charlus, in whose company I was when the fear of Albertine's leaving me had seized hold of me, was added to the rest. But, later on, I heard my mother say something of which I was then unaware and which leads me to believe that I found all the elements of this scene in myself, in those obscure reserves of heredity which certain emotions, acting in this respect as, upon the residue of our stored-up strength, drugs such as alcohol and coffee act, place at our disposal. When my aunt Léonie learned from Eulalie that Françoise, convinced that her mistress would never again leave the house, had secretly planned some outing of which my aunt was to know nothing, she, the day before, would pretend to have made up her mind that she would attempt an excursion on the morrow. The incredulous Françoise was ordered not only to prepare my aunt's clothes beforehand, to give an airing to those that had been put away for too long, but to order a carriage, to arrange, to within a quarter of an hour, all the details of the day. It was only when Françoise, convinced or at any rate shaken, had been forced to confess to my aunt the plan that she herself had formed, that my aunt would publicly abandon her own, so as not, she said, to interfere with Françoise's arrangements. Similarly, so that Albertine might not believe that I was exaggerating and to make her proceed as far as possible in the idea that we were to part, drawing myself the obvious deductions from the proposal that I had advanced, I had begun to anticipate the time which was to begin on the morrow and was to last for ever, the time in which we should be parted, addressing to Albertine the same requests as if we were not to be reconciled almost immediately. Like a general who considers that if a feint is to succeed in deceiving the enemy it must be pushed to extremes, I had employed in this feint almost as much of my store of sensibility as if it had been genuine. This fictitious parting scene ended by causing me almost as much grief as if it had been real, possibly because one of the actors, Albertine, by believing it to be real, had enhanced the other's illusion. While we were

living, from day to day, in a day which, even if painful,
was still endurable, held down to earth by the ballast
of habit and by that certainty that the morrow, should
it prove a day of torment, would contain the presence of
the person who is all in all, here was I stupidly destroying
all that oppressive life. I was destroying it, it is true,
only in a fictitious fashion, but this was enough to make
me wretched; perhaps because the sad words which we
utter, even when we are lying, carry in themselves their
sorrow and inject it deeply into us; perhaps because we
do not realise that, by feigning farewells, we evoke by
anticipation an hour which must inevitably come later
on; then we cannot be certain that we have not released
the mechanism which will make it strike. In every bluff
there is an element, however small, of uncertainty as to
what the person whom we are deceiving is going to do.
If this make-believe of parting should lead to a parting!
We cannot consider the possibility, however unlikely it
may seem, without a clutching of the heart. We are
doubly anxious, because the parting would then occur at
the moment when it would be intolerable, when we had
been made to suffer by the woman who would be leaving
us before she had healed, or at least appeased us. In
short, we have no longer the solid ground of habit upon
which we rest, even in our sorrow. We have deliberately
deprived ourself of it, we have given the present day an
exceptional importance, have detached it from the days
before and after it; it floats without roots like a day of
departure; our imagination ceasing to be paralysed by
habit has awakened, we have suddenly added to our
everyday love sentimental dreams which enormously enhance it, make indispensable to us a presence upon which,

as a matter of fact, we are no longer certain that we can rely. No doubt it is precisely in order to assure ourself of that presence for the future that we have indulged in the make-believe of being able to dispense with it. But this make-believe, we have ourself been taken in by it, we have begun to suffer afresh because we have created something new, unfamiliar which thus resembles those cures that are destined in time to heal the malady from which we are suffering, but the first effects of which are to aggravate it.

I had tears in my eyes, like the people who, alone in their bedrooms, imagining, in the wayward course of their meditations, the death of some one whom they love, form so detailed a picture of the grief that they would feel that they end by feeling it. And so as I multiplied my advice to Albertine as to the way in which she would have to behave in relation to myself after we had parted, I seemed to be feeling almost as keen a distress as though we had not been on the verge of a reconciliation. Besides, was I so certain that I could bring about this reconciliation, bring Albertine back to the idea of a life shared with myself, and, if I succeeded for the time being, that in her, the state of mind which this scene had dispelled would not revive? I felt myself, but did not believe myself to be master of the future, because I realised that this sensation was due merely to the fact that the future did not yet exist, and that thus I was not crushed by its inevitability. In short, while I lied, I was perhaps putting into my words more truth than I supposed. I had just had an example of this, when I told Albertine that I should quickly forget her; this was what had indeed happened to me in the case of Gilberte, whom I now refrained from going to see in order to escape not a grief but an irksome duty. And certainly I had been grieved when I wrote to Gilberte that I would not come any more, and I had gone to see her only occasionally. Whereas the whole of Albertine's time belonged to me, and in love it is easier to relinquish a sentiment than to lose a habit. But all these painful words about our parting, if the strength to utter them had been given me because I knew them to be untrue, were on the other hand sincere upon Albertine's lips when I heard her exclaim: "Ah! I promise, I will never see you again. Anything sooner than see you cry like that, my darling. I do not wish to cause you any grief. Since it must be, we will never meet again." They were sincere, as they could not have been coming from me, because, for one thing, as Albertine felt nothing stronger for me than friendship, the renunciation that they promised cost her less; because, moreover, in a scene of parting, it is the person who is not genuinely in love that makes the tender speeches, since love does not express itself directly; because, lastly, my tears, which would have been so small a matter in a great love, seemed to her almost extraordinary and overwhelmed her, transposed into the region of that state of friendship in which she dwelt, a friendship greater than mine for her, to judge by what she had just said, which was perhaps not altogether inexact, for the thousand kindnesses of love may end by arousing, in the person who inspires without feeling it, an affection, a gratitude less selfish than the sentiment that provoked them, which, perhaps, after years of separation, when nothing of that sentiment remains in the former lover, will still persist in the beloved.

"My little Albertine," I replied, "it is very good of you to make me this promise. Anyhow, for the first few years at least, I shall avoid the places where I might meet you. You don't know whether you will be going to Balbec this year? Because in that case I should arrange not to go there myself." But now, if I continued to progress thus, anticipating time to come in my lying inventions, it was with a view no less to inspiring fear in Albertine than to making myself wretched. As a man who at first had no serious reason for losing his temper, becomes completely intoxicated by the sound of his own voice, and lets himself be carried away by a fury engendered not by his grievance but by his anger which itself is steadily growing, so I was falling ever faster and faster down the slope of my wretchedness, towards an ever more profound despair, and with the inertia of a man who feels the cold grip him, makes no effort to resist it and even finds a sort of pleasure in shivering. And if I had now at length, as I fully supposed, the strength to control myself, to react and to reverse my engines, far more than from the grief which Albertine had caused me by so unfriendly a greeting on my return, it was from that which I had felt in imagining, so as to pretend to be outlining them, the formalities of an imaginary separation, in foreseeing its consequences, that Albertine's kiss, when the time came for her to bid me good night, would have to console me now. In any case, it must not be she that said this good night of her own accord, for that would have made more difficult the revulsion by which I would propose to her to abandon the idea of our parting. And so I continued to remind her that the time to say good night had long since come and gone, a method which, by leaving the initiative to me, enabled me to put it off for a moment longer. And thus I scattered with allusions to the lateness of the hour, to our exhaustion, the questions with which I was plying Albertine. "I don't know where I shall be going," she replied to the last of these, in a worried tone. "Perhaps I shall go to Touraine, to my aunt's." And this first plan that she suggested froze me as though it were beginning to make definitely effective our final separation. She looked round the room, at the pianola, the blue satin armchairs. "I still cannot make myself realise that I shall not see all this again, to-morrow, or the next day, or ever. Poor little room. It seems to me quite impossible; I cannot get it into my head." "It had to be; you were unhappy here." "No, indeed, I was not unhappy, it is now that I shall be unhappy." "No, I assure you, it is better for you." "For you, perhaps!" I began to stare fixedly into vacancy, as though, worried by an extreme hesitation, I was debating an idea which had occurred to my mind. Then, all of a sudden: "Listen, Albertine, you say that you are happier here, that you are going to be unhappy." "Why, of course." "That appals me; would you like us to try to carry on for a few weeks? Who knows, week by week, we may perhaps go on for a long time; you know that there are temporary arrangements which end by becoming permanent." "Oh, how kind you are!" "Only in that case it is ridiculous of us to have made ourselves wretched like this over nothing for hours on end, it is like making all the preparations for a long journey and then staying at home. I am shattered with grief." I made her sit on my knee, I took Bergotte's manuscript which she so longed to have and wrote on the cover: "To my little

Albertine, in memory of a new lease of life." "Now," I said to her, "go and sleep until to-morrow, my darling, for you must be worn out." "I am very glad, all the same." "Do you love me a little bit?" "A hundred times more than ever."

I should have been wrong in being delighted with this little piece of play-acting, had it not been that I had carried it to the pitch of a real scene on the stage. Had we done no more than quite simply discuss a separation, even that would have been a serious matter. In conversations of this sort, we suppose that we are speaking not merely without sincerity, which is true, but freely. Whereas they are generally, though we know it not, murmured in spite of us; the first murmur of a storm which we do not suspect. In reality, what we express at such times is the opposite of our desire (which is to live for ever with her whom we love), but there is also that impossibility of living together which is the cause of our daily suffering, a suffering preferred by us to that of a parting, which will, however, end, in spite of ourselves, in parting us. Generally speaking, not, however, at once. As a rule, it happens—this was not, as we shall see, my case with Albertine—that, some time after the words in which we did not believe, we put into action a vague attempt at a deliberate separation, not painful, temporary. We ask the woman, so that afterwards she may be happier in our company, so that we on the other hand may momentarily escape from continual worries and fatigues, to go without us, or to let us go without her, for a few days elsewhere, the first days that we have—for a long time past—spent, as would have seemed to us impossible, away from her. Very soon she returns to take her place by our fireside. Only this separation, short, but made real, is not so arbitrarily decided upon, not so certainly the only one that we have in mind. The same sorrows begin afresh, the same difficulty in living together becomes accentuated, only a parting is no longer so difficult as before; we have begun mentioning it, and have then put it into practice in a friendly fashion. But these are only preliminary ventures whose nature we have not recognised. Presently, to the momentary and smiling separation will succeed the terrible and final separation for which we have, without knowing it, paved the way.

"Come to my room in five minutes and let me see something of you, my dearest boy. You are full of kindness. But afterwards I shall fall asleep at once, for I am almost dead." It was indeed a dead woman that I beheld when, presently, I entered her room. She had gone to sleep immediately she lay down, the sheets wrapped like a shroud about her body had assumed, with their stately folds, a stony rigidity. One would have said that, as in certain Last Judgments of the Middle Ages, her head alone was emerging from the tomb, awaiting in its sleep the Archangel's trumpet. This head had been surprised by sleep almost flung back, its hair bristling. And as I saw the expressionless body extended there, I asked myself what logarithmic table it constituted so that all the actions in which it might have been involved, from the nudge of an elbow to the brushing of a skirt, were able to cause me, stretched out to the infinity of all the points that it had occupied in space and time, and from time to time sharply reawakened in my memory, so intense an anguish, albeit I knew those actions to have been determined in her by impulses, desires, which in another person, in herself five years earlier, or five years later, would have left me quite indifferent. All this was a lie, but a lie for which I had not the courage to seek any solution other than my own death. And so I remained, in the fur coat which I had not taken off since my return from the Verdurins', before that bent body, that figure allegorical of what? Of my death? Of my love? Presently I began to hear her regular breathing. I went and sat down on the edge of her bed to take that soothing cure of fresh air and contemplation. Then I withdrew very gently so as not to awaken her.

It was so late that, in the morning, I warned Françoise to tread very softly when she had to pass by the door of Albertine's room. And so Françoise, convinced that we had spent the night in what she used to call orgies, ironically warned the other servants not to "wake the Princess." And this was one of the things that I dreaded, that Françoise might one day be unable to contain herself any longer, might treat Albertine with insolence, and that this might introduce complications into our life. Françoise was now no longer, as at the time when it distressed her to see Eulalie treated generously by my aunt, of an age to endure her jealousy with courage. It distorted, paralysed our old servant's face to such an extent that at times I asked myself whether she had not, after some outburst of rage, had a slight stroke. Having thus asked that Albertine's sleep should be respected, I was unable to sleep myself. I endeavoured to understand the true state of Albertine's mind. By that wretched farce which I had played, was it a real peril that I had averted, and, notwithstanding her assurance that she was so happy living with me, had she really felt at certain moments a longing for freedom, or on the contrary was I to believe what she said?

Which of these two hypotheses was the truth? If it often befell me, if it was in a special case to befall me that I must extend an incident in my past life to the dimensions of history, when I made an attempt to understand some political event; inversely, this morning, I did not cease to identify, in spite of all the differences and in an attempt to understand its bearing, our scene overnight with a diplomatic incident that had just occurred. I had perhaps the right to reason thus. For it was highly probable that, without my knowledge, the example of M. de Charlus had guided me in that lying scene which I had so often seen him enact with such authority; on the other hand, was it in him anything else than an unconscious importation into the domain of his private life of the innate tendency of his Germanic stock, provocative from guile and, from pride, belligerent at need. Certain persons, among them the Prince of Monaco, having suggested the idea to the French Government that, if it did not dispense with M. Delcassé, a menacing Germany would indeed declare war, the Minister for Foreign Affairs had been asked to resign. So that the French Government had admitted the hypothesis of an intention to make war upon us if we did not yield. But others thought that it was all a mere " bluff " and that if France had stood firm Germany would not have drawn the sword. No doubt the scenario was not merely different but almost opposite, since the threat of a rupture had not been put forward by Albertine; but a series of impressions had led me to believe that she was thinking of it, as France had been led to believe about Germany. On the other hand, if Germany desired peace, to have provoked in the French Government the idea that she was anxious for war was a disputable and dangerous trick. Certainly, my conduct had been skilful enough, if it was the thought that I would never make up my mind to break with her that provoked in Albertine sudden longings for independence. And was it not difficult to believe that she did not feel them, to shut one's eyes to a whole secret existence, directed towards the satisfaction of her vice, simply on remarking the anger with which she had learned that I had gone to see the Verdurins, when she exclaimed: " I thought as much," and went on to reveal everything by saying: "Wasn't Mlle. Vinteuil there? " All this was corroborated by Albertine's meeting with Mme. Verdurin of which Andrée had informed me. But perhaps all the same these sudden longings for independence (I told myself, when I tried to go against my own instinct) were caused—supposing them to exist—or would eventually be caused by the opposite theory, to wit that I had never had any intention of marrying her, that it was when I made, as though involuntarily, an allusion to our approaching separation that I was telling the truth, that I would whatever happened part from her one day or another, a belief which the scene that I had made overnight could then only have confirmed and which might end by engendering in her the resolution: " If this is bound to happen one day or another, better to end everything at once." The preparations for war which the most misleading of proverbs lays down as the best way to secure the triumph of peace, create first of all the belief in each of the adversaries that the other desires a rupture, a belief which brings the rupture about, and, when it has occurred, this further belief in each of them that it is the other that has sought it. Even if the threat was not sincere, its success encourages a repetition. But the exact point to which a bluff may succeed is difficult to determine; if one party goes too far, the other which has previously yielded, advances in its turn; the first party, no longer able to change its method, accustomed to the idea that to seem not to fear a rupture is the best way of avoiding one (which is what I had done overnight with Albertine), and moreover driven to prefer, in its pride, to fall rather than yield, perseveres in its threat until the moment when neither can draw back any longer. The bluff may also be blended with sincerity, may alternate with it, and it is possible that what was a game yesterday may become a reality to-morrow. Finally it may also happen that one of the adversaries is really determined upon war, it might be that Albertine, for instance, had the intention of, sooner or later, not continuing this life any longer, or on the contrary that the idea had never even entered her mind and that my imagination had invented the whole thing from start to finish. Such were the different hypotheses which I considered while she lay asleep that morning. And yet as to the last I can say that I never, in the period that followed, threatened Albertine with a rupture unless in response to an idea of an evil freedom on her part, an idea which she did not express to me, but which seemed to me to be implied by certain mysterious dissatisfactions, certain words, certain gestures, of which that idea was the only possible explanation and of which she refused to give me any other. Even then, quite often, I remarked them without making any allusion to a possible separation, hoping that they were due to a fit of ill temper which would end that same day. But it continued at times without intermission for weeks on end, during which Albertine seemed anxious to provoke a conflict, as though there had been at the time, in some region more or less remote, pleasures of which she knew, of which her seclusion in my house was depriving her, and which would continue to influence her until they came to an end, like those atmospheric changes which, even by our own fireside, affect our nerves, even when they are occurring as far away as the Balearic islands.

This morning, while Albertine lay asleep and I was trying to guess what was concealed in her, I received a letter from my mother in which she expressed her anxiety at having heard nothing of what we had decided in this phrase of Mme. de Sévigné: " In my own mind I am convinced that he will not marry; but then, why trouble this girl whom he will never marry? Why risk making her refuse suitors at whom she will never look again save with scorn? Why disturb the mind of a person whom it would be so easy to avoid? " This letter from my mother brought me back to earth. " What am I doing, seeking a mysterious soul, interpreting a face and feeling myself overawed by presentiments which I dare not explore? " I asked myself. " I have been dreaming, the matter is quite simple. I am an undecided young man, and it is a question of one of those marriages as to which it takes time to find out whether they will happen or not. There is nothing in this peculiar to Albertine." This thought gave me an immense but a short relief. Very soon I said to myself: " One can after all reduce everything, if one regards it in its social aspect, to the most commonplace item of newspaper gossip. From outside, it is perhaps thus that I should look at it. But I know well that what is true, what at least is also true, is everything that I have thought, is what I have read in Albertine's eyes, is the fears that torment me, is the problem that I incessantly set myself with regard to Albertine. The story of the hesitating bridegroom and the broken engagement may correspond to this, as the report of a theatrical perform-ance made by an intelligent reporter may give us the subject of one of Ibsen's plays. But there is something beyond those facts which are reported. It is true that this other thing exists perhaps, were we able to discern it, in all hesitating bridegrooms and in all the engagements that drag on, because there is perhaps an element of mystery in our everyday life." It was possible for me to neglect it in the lives of other people, but Albertine's life and my own I was living from within.

Albertine no more said to me after this midnight scene than she had said before it: " I know that you do not trust me, I am going to try to dispel your suspicions." But this idea, which she never expressed in words, might have served as an explanation of even her most trivial actions. Not only did she take care never to be alone for a moment, so that I might not lack information as to what she had been doing, if I did not believe her own statements, but even when she had to telephone to Andrée, or to the garage, or to the livery stable or else-where, she pretended that it was such a bore to stand about by herself waiting to telephone, what with the time the girls took to give you your number, and took care that I should be with her at such times, or, failing myself, Françoise, as though she were afraid that I might imagine reprehensible conversations by telephone in which she would make mysterious assignations. Alas, all this did not set my mind at rest. I had a day of discouragement. Aimé had sent me back Esther's photograph, with a message that she was not the person. And so Albertine had other intimate friends as well as this girl to whom, through her misunderstanding of what I said, I had, when I meant to refer to something quite different, discovered that she had given her photograph. I sent this photograph back to Bloch. What I should have liked to see was the photograph that Albertine had given to Esther. How was she dressed in it? Perhaps with a bare bosom, for all I knew. But I dared not mention it to Albertine (for it would then have appeared that I had not seen the photograph), or to Bloch, since I did not wish him to think that I was interested in Albertine. And this life, which anyone who knew of my suspicions and her bondage would have seen to be agonising to myself and to Albertine, was regarded from without, by Françoise, as a life of unmerited pleasures of which full advantage was cunningly taken by that " trickstress " and (as Françoise said, using the feminine form far more often than the masculine, for she was more envious of women) " charlatante." Indeed, as Françoise, by contact with myself, had enriched her vocabulary with fresh terms, but had adapted them to her own style, she said of Albertine that she had never known a person of such " perfidity," who was so skilful at " drawing my money " by play-acting (which Françoise, who was as prone to mistake the particular for the general as the general for the particular and who had but a very vague idea of the various kinds of dramatic art, called " acting a pantomime ").

Perhaps for this error as to the true nature of the life led by Albertine and myself, I was myself to some extent responsible owing to the vague confirmations of it which, when I was talking to Françoise, I skilfully let fall, from a desire either to tease her or to appear, if not loved, at any rate happy. And yet my jealousy, the watch that I kept over Albertine, which I would have given anything for Françoise not to suspect, she was not long in discovering, guided, like the thought-reader who, groping blindfold, finds the hidden object, by that intuition which she possessed for anything that might be painful to me, which would not allow itself to be turned aside by the lies that I might tell in the hope of distracting her, and also by that clairvoyant hatred which urged her—even more than it urged her to believe her enemies more prosperous, more skilful hypocrites than they really were—to discover the secret that might prove their undoing and to precipitate their downfall. Françoise certainly never made any scenes with Albertine. But I was acquainted with Françoise's art of insinuation, the advantage that she knew how to derive from a significant setting, and I cannot believe that she resisted the temptation to let Albertine know, day by day, what a degraded part she was playing in the household, to madden her by a description, cunningly exaggerated, of the confinement to which my mistress was subjected. On one occasion I found Françoise, armed with a huge pair of spectacles, rummaging through my papers and replacing among them a sheet on which I had jotted down a story about Swann and his utter inability to do without Odette. Had she maliciously left it lying in Albertine's room? Besides, above all Françoise's innuendoes which had merely been, in the bass, the muttering and perfidious orchestration, it is probable that there must have risen, higher, clearer, more pressing, the accusing and calumnious voice of the Verdurins, annoyed to see that Albertine was involuntarily keeping me and that I was voluntarily keeping her away from the little clan. As for the money that I was spending upon Albertine, it was almost impossible for me to conceal it from Françoise, since I was unable to conceal any of my expenditure from her. Françoise had few faults, but those faults had created in her, for their service, positive talents which she often lacked apart from the exercise of those faults. Her chief fault was her curiosity as to all money spent by us upon people other than herself. If I had a bill to pay, a gratuity to give, it was useless my going into a corner, she would find a plate to be put in the right place, a napkin to be picked up, which would give her an excuse for approaching. And however short a time I allowed her, before dismissing her with fury, this woman who had almost lost her sight, who could barely add up a column of figures, guided by the same expert sense which makes a tailor, on catching sight of you, instinctively calculate the price of the stuff of which your coat is made, while he cannot resist fingering it, or makes a painter responsive to a colour effect, Françoise saw by stealth, calculated instantaneously the amount that I was giving. And when, so that she might not tell Albertine that I was corrupting her chauffeur, I took the initiative and, apologising for the tip, said: " I wanted to be generous to the chauffeur, I gave him ten francs "; Françoise, pitiless, to whom a glance, that of an old and almost blind eagle, had been sufficient, replied: " No indeed, Monsieur gave him a tip of 43 francs. He told Monsieur that the charge was 45 francs, Monsieur gave him 100 francs, and he handed back only 12 francs." She had had time to see and to reckon the amount of the gratuity which I myself did not know. I asked myself whether Albertine, feeling herself watched, would not herself put into effect that separation with which I had threatened her, for life in its changing course makes realities of our fables. Whenever I heard a door open, I felt myself shudder as my grandmother used to shudder in her last moments whenever I rang my bell. I did not believe that she would leave the house without telling me, but it was my unconscious self that thought so, as it was my grandmother's unconscious self that throbbed at the sound of the bell, when she was no longer conscious. One morning indeed, I felt a sudden misgiving that she not only had left the house but had gone for good: I had just heard the sound of a door which seemed to me to be that of her room. On tiptoe I crept towards the room, opened the door, stood upon the threshold. In the dim light the bedclothes bulged in a semi-circle, that must be Albertine who, with her body bent, was sleeping with her feet and face to the wall. Only, overflowing the bed, the hair upon that head, abundant and dark, made me realise that it was she, that she had not opened her door, had not stirred, and I felt that this motionless and living semi-circle, in which a whole human life was contained and which was the only thing to which I attached any value, I felt that it was there, in my despotic possession.

If Albertine's object was to restore my peace of mind, she was partly successful; my reason moreover asked nothing better than to prove to me that I had been mistaken as to her crafty plans, as I had perhaps been mistaken as to her vicious instincts. No doubt I added to the value of the arguments with which my reason furnished me my own desire to find them sound. But, if I was to be fair and to have a chance of perceiving the truth, unless we admit that it is never known save by presentiment, by a telepathic emanation, must I not say to myself that if my reason, in seeking to bring about my recovery, let itself be guided by my desire, on the other hand, so far as concerned Mlle. Vinteuil, Albertine's vices, her intention to lead a different life, her plan of separation, which were the corollaries of her vices, my instinct had been capable, in the attempt to make me ill, of being led astray by my jealousy. Besides, her seclusion, which Albertine herself contrived so ingeniously to render absolute, by removing my suffering, removed by degrees my suspicion and I could begin again, when the night brought back my uneasiness, to find in Albertine's presence the consolation of earlier days. Seated beside my bed, she spoke to me of one of those dresses or one of those presents which I never ceased to give her in the effort to enhance the comfort of her life and the beauty of her prison. Albertine had at first thought only of dresses and furniture. Now silver had begun to interest her. And so I had questioned M. de Charlus about old French silver, and had done so because, when we had been planning to have a yacht—a plan which Albertine decided was impracticable, as I did also whenever I had begun to believe in her virtue, with the result that my jealousy, as it declined, no longer held in check other desires in which she had no place and which also needed money for their satisfaction—we had, to be on the safe side, not that she supposed that we should ever have a yacht, asked Elstir

or his advice. Now, just as in matters of women's dress,
he painter was a refined and sensitive critic of the fur-
ishing of yachts. He would allow only English furniture
nd old silver. This had led Albertine, since our return
rom Balbec, to read books upon the silversmith's art,
pon the handiwork of the old chasers. But as our old
ilver was melted twice over, at the time of the Treaty
f Utrecht when the King himself, setting the example to
is great nobles, sacrificed his plate, and again in 1789,
t is now extremely rare. On the other hand, it is true
hat modern silversmiths have managed to copy all this
ld plate from the drawings of Le Pont-aux-Choux, Elstir
onsidered this modern antique unworthy to enter the
ome of a woman of taste, even a floating home. I knew
hat Albertine had read the description of the marvels
hat Roelliers had made for Mme. du Barry. If any of
hese pieces remained, she was dying to see them, and I
o give them to her. She had even begun to form a neat
ollection which she installed with charming taste in a
lass case and at which I could not look without emotion
nd alarm, for the art with which she arranged them was
hat born of patience, ingenuity, home-sickness, the need
o forget, in which prisoners excel. In the matter of
ress, what appealed to her most at this time was every-
hing that was made by Fortuny. These Fortuny gowns,
ne of which I had seen Mme. de Guermantes wearing,
vere those of which Elstir, when he told us about the
nagnificent garments of the women of Carpaccio's and
'itian's day, had prophesied the speedy return, rising
rom their ashes, sumptuous, for everything must return
n time, as it is written beneath the vaults of Saint Mark's,
nd proclaimed, where they drink from the urns of marble

and jasper of the byzantine capitals, by the birds whic
symbolise at once death and resurrection. As soon a
women had begun to wear them, Albertine had remem
bered Elstir's prophecy, she had desired to have one an
we were to go and choose it. Now these gowns, even i
they were not those genuine antiques in which wome
to-day seem a little too much " in fancy dress " and whic
it is preferable to keep as pieces in a collection (I was i
search of these also, as it happens, for Albertine), coul
not be said to have the chilling effect of the artificial, th
sham antique. Like the theatrical designs of Sert, Baks
and Benoist who at that moment were recreating in th
Russian ballet the most cherished periods of art—wit
the aid of works of art impregnated with their spirit an
yet original—these Fortuny gowns, faithfully antique bu
markedly original, brought before the eye like a stag
setting, with an even greater suggestiveness than a set
ting, since the setting was left to the imagination, tha
Venice loaded with the gorgeous East from which the
had been taken, of which they were, even more than
relic in the shrine of Saint Mark suggesting the sun an
a group of turbaned heads, the fragmentary, mysteriou
and complementary colour. Everything of those day
had perished, but everything was born again, evoked t
fill the space between them with the splendour of th
scene and the hum of life, by the reappearance, detaile
and surviving, of the fabrics worn by the Doges' ladie
I had tried once or twice to obtain advice upon this sub
ject from Mme. de Guermantes. But the Duchess care
little for garments which form a " costume ". She her
self, though she possessed several, never looked so we
as in black velvet with diamonds. And with regard t

gowns like Fortuny's, her advice was not of any great value. Besides, I felt a scruple, if I asked for it, lest she might think that I called upon her only when I happened to need her help, whereas for a long time past I had been declining several invitations from her weekly. It was not only from her, moreover, that I received them in such profusion. Certainly, she and many other women had always been extremely kind to me. But my seclusion had undoubtedly multiplied their hospitality tenfold. It seems that in our social life, a minor echo of what occurs in love, the best way for a man to make himself sought-after is to withhold himself. A man calculates everything that he can possibly cite to his credit, in order to find favour with a woman, changes his clothes all day long, pays attention to his appearance, she does not pay him a single one of the attentions which he receives from the other woman to whom, while he betrays her, and in spite of his appearing before her ill-dressed and without any artifice to attract, he has endeared himself for ever. Similarly, if a man were to regret that he was not sufficiently courted in society, I should not advise him to pay more calls, to keep an even finer carriage, I should tell him not to accept any invitation, to live shut up in his room, to admit nobody, and that then there would be a queue outside his door. Or rather I should not tell him so. For it is a certain road to success which succeeds only like the road to love, that is to say if one has not adopted it with that object in view, if, for instance, you confine yourself to your room because you are seriously ill, or are supposed to be, or are keeping a mistress shut up with you whom you prefer to society (or for all these reasons at once), this will justify another person, who is not aware of the woman's existence, and simply because you decline to see him, in preferring you to all the people who offer themselves, and attaching himself to you.

"We shall have to begin to think soon about your Fortuny gowns," I said to Albertine one evening. Surely, to her who had long desired them, who chose them deliberately with me, who had a place reserved for them beforehand not only in her wardrobe but in her imagination, the possession of these gowns, every detail of which, before deciding among so many, she carefully examined, was something more than it would have been to an over-wealthy woman who has more dresses than she knows what to do with and never even looks at them. And yet, notwithstanding the smile with which Albertine thanked me, saying: "You are too kind," I noticed how weary, and even wretched, she was looking.

While we waited for these gowns to be ready, I used to borrow others of the kind, sometimes indeed merely the stuffs, and would dress Albertine in them, drape them over her; she walked about my room with the majesty of a Doge's wife and the grace of a mannequin. Only my captivity in Paris was made more burdensome by the sight of these garments which suggested Venice. True, Albertine was far more of a prisoner than I. And it was curious to remark how, through the walls of her prison, destiny, which transforms people, had contrived to pass, to change her in her very essence, and turn the girl I had known at Balbec into a tedious and docile captive. Yes, the walls of her prison had not prevented that influence from reaching her; perhaps indeed it was they that had produced it. It was no longer the same Albertine, because she was not, as at Balbec, incessantly in flight upon her bicycle, never to be found owing to the number of little watering-places where she would go to spend the night with her girl friends and where moreover her untruths made it more difficult to lay hands upon her; because confined to my house, docile and alone, she was no longer even what at Balbec, when I had succeeded in finding her, she used to be upon the beach, that fugitive, cautious, cunning creature, whose presence was enlarged by the thought of all those assignations which she was skilled in concealing, which made one love her because they made one suffer, in whom, beneath her coldness to other people and her casual answers, one could feel yesterday's assignation and to-morrow's, and for myself a contemptuous, deceitful thought; because the sea breeze no longer buffeted her skirts, because, above all, I had clipped her wings, she had ceased to be a Victory, was a burdensome slave of whom I would fain have been rid.

Then, to change the course of my thoughts, rather than begin a game of cards or draughts with Albertine, I asked her to give me a little music. I remained in bed, and she went and sat down at the end of the room before the pianola, between the two bookcases. She chose pieces which were quite new or which she had played to me only once or twice, for, as she began to know me better, she had learned that I liked to fix my thoughts only upon what was still obscure to me, glad to be able, in the course of these successive renderings, to join together, thanks to the increasing but, alas, distorting and alien light of my intellect, the fragmentary and interrupted lines of the structure which at first had been almost hidden in the mist. She knew and, I think, understood, the joy that my mind derived, at these first hearings, from this task of modelling a still shapeless nebula. She guessed that at the third or four repetition my intellect, having reached, having consequently placed at the same distance, all the parts, and having no longer any activity to spare for them, had reciprocally extended and arrested them upon a uniform plane. She did not, however, proceed at once to a fresh piece, for, without perhaps having any clear idea of the process that was going on in my mind, she knew that at the moment when the effort of my intellect had succeeded in dispelling the mystery of a work, it was very rarely that, in compensation, it did not, in the course of its task of destruction, pick up some profitable reflexion. And when in time Albertine said: "We might give this roll to Françoise and get her to change it for something else," often there was for me a piece of music less in the world, perhaps, but a truth the more. While she was playing, of all Albertine's multiple tresses I could see but a single loop of black hair in the shape of a heart trained at the side of her ear like the riband of a Velasquez Infanta. Just as the substance of that Angel musician was constituted by the multiple journeys between the different points in past time which the memory of her occupied in myself, and its different abodes, from my vision to the most inward sensations of my being, which helped me to descend into the intimacy of hers, so the music that she played had also a volume, produced by the inconstant visibility of the different phrases, accordingly as I had more or less succeeded in throwing a light upon them and in joining together the lines of a structure which at first had seemed to me to be almost completely hidden in the fog.

I was so far convinced that it was absurd to be jealous

of Mlle. Vinteuil and her friend, inasmuch as Albertine
since her confession had made no attempt to see them
and among all the plans for a holiday in the country
which we had formed had herself rejected Combray, so
near to Montjouvain, that, often, what I would ask Albertine to play to me, without its causing me any pain,
would be some music by Vinteuil. Once only this music
had been an indirect cause of my jealousy. This was
when Albertine, who knew that I had heard it performed
at Mme. Verdurin's by Morel, spoke to me one evening
about him, expressing a keen desire to go and hear him
play and to make his acquaintance. This, as it happened,
was shortly after I had learned of the letter, unintention-
ally intercepted by M. de Charlus, from Léa to Morel.
I asked myself whether Léa might not have mentioned
him to Albertine. The words: "You bad woman, you
naughty old girl" came to my horrified mind. But precisely because Vinteuil's music was in this way painfully
associated with Léa—and no longer with Mlle. Vinteuil
and her friend—when the grief that Léa caused me was
soothed, I could then listen to this music without pain;
one malady had made me immune to any possibility of
the others. In this music of Vinteuil, phrases that I had
not noticed at Mme. Verdurin's, obscure phantoms that
were then indistinct, turned into dazzling architectural
structures; and some of them became friends, whom I
had barely made out at first, who at best had appeared
to me to be ugly, so that I could never have supposed
that they were like those people, unattractive at first sight,
whom we discover to be what they really are only after
we have come to know them well. From one state to the
other was a positive transmutation. On the other hand,

phrases that I had distinguished at once in the music that I had heard at Mme. Verdurin's, but had not then recognised, I identified now with phrases from other works, such as that phrase from the Sacred Variation for the Organ which, at Mme. Verdurin's, had passed unperceived by me in the septet, where nevertheless, a saint that had stepped down from the sanctuary, it found itself consorting with the composer's familiar fays. Finally, the phrase that had seemed to me too little melodious, too mechanical in its rhythm, of the swinging joy of bells at noon, had now become my favourite, whether because I had grown accustomed to its ugliness or because I had discovered its beauty. This reaction from the disappointment which great works of art cause at first may in fact be attributed to a weakening of the initial impression or to the effort necessary to lay bare the truth. Two hypotheses which suggest themselves in all important questions, questions of the truth of Art, of the truth of the Immortality of the Soul; we must choose between them; and, in the case of Vinteuil's music, this choice presented itself at every moment under a variety of forms. For instance, this music seemed to me to be something truer than all the books that I knew. Sometimes I thought that this was due to the fact that what we feel in life, not being felt in the form of ideas, its literary (that is to say an intellectual) translation in giving an account of it, explains it, analyses it, but does not recompose it as does music, in which the sounds seem to assume the inflexion of the thing itself, to reproduce that interior and extreme point of our sensation which is the part that gives us that peculiar exhilaration which we recapture from time to time and which when we say: "What a fine day! What glorious sunshine!" we do not in the least communicate to our neighbour, in whom the same sun and the same weather arouse wholly different vibrations. In Vinteuil's music, there were thus some of those visions which it is impossible to express and almost forbidden to record, since, when at the moment of falling asleep we receive the caress of their unreal enchantment, at that very moment in which reason has already deserted us, our eyes are already sealed, and before we have had time to know not merely the ineffable but the invisible, we are asleep. It seemed to me indeed when I abandoned myself to this hypothesis that art might be real, that it was something even more than the simply nervous joy of a fine day or an opiate night that music can give; a more real, more fruitful exhilaration, to judge at least by what I felt. It is not possible that a piece of sculpture, a piece of music which gives us an emotion which we feel to be more exalted, more pure, more true, does not correspond to some definite spiritual reality. It is surely symbolical of one, since it gives that impression of profundity and truth. Thus nothing resembled more closely than some such phrase of Vinteuil the peculiar pleasure which I had felt at certain moments in my life, when gazing, for instance, at the steeples of Martinville, or at certain trees along a road near Balbec, or, more simply, in the first part of this book, when I tasted a certain cup of tea.

Without pressing this comparison farther, I felt that the clear sounds, the blazing colours which Vinteuil sent to us from the world in which he composed, paraded before my imagination with insistence but too rapidly for me to be able to apprehend it, something which I might compare to the perfumed silkiness of a geranium. Only, whereas, in memory, this vagueness may be, if not explored, at any rate fixed precisely, thanks to a guiding line of circumstances which explain why a certain savour has been able to recall to us luminous sensations, the vague sensations given by Vinteuil coming not from a memory but from an impression (like that of the steeples of Martinville), one would have had to find, for the geranium scent of his music, not a material explanation, but the profound equivalent, the unknown and highly coloured festival (of which his works seemed to be the scattered fragments, the scarlet-flashing rifts), the mode in which he " heard " the universe and projected it far beyond himself. This unknown quality of a unique world which no other composer had ever made us see, perhaps it is in this, I said to Albertine, that the most authentic proof of genius consists, even more than in the content of the work itself. " Even in literature? " Albertine inquired. " Even in literature." And thinking again of the monotony of Vinteuil's works, I explained to Albertine that the great men of letters have never created more than a single work, or rather have never done more than refract through various mediums an identical beauty which they bring into the world. " If it were not so late, my child," I said to her, " I would shew you this quality in all the writers whose works you read while I am asleep, I would shew you the same identity as in Vinteuil. These typical phrases, which you are beginning to recognise as I do, my little Albertine, the same in the sonata, in the septet, in the other works, would be for instance, if you like, in Barbey d'Aurevilly, a hidden reality revealed by a material trace, the physiological blush of *l'Ensorcelée*, of *Aimée de Spens*, of *la*

234

Clotte, the hand of the *Rideau Cramoisi,* the old manners and customs, the old words, the ancient and peculiar trades behind which there is the Past, the oral history compiled by the rustics of the manor, the noble Norman cities redolent of England and charming as a Scots village, the cause of curses against which one can do nothing, the Vellini, the Shepherd, a similar sensation of anxiety in a passage, whether it be the wife seeking her husband in *Une Vieille Maîtresse,* or the husband in *l'Ensorcelée* scouring the plain and the 'Ensorcelée' herself coming out from Mass. There are other typical phrases in Vinteuil like that stonemason's geometry in the novels of Thomas Hardy."

Vinteuil's phrases made me think of the "little phrase" and I told Albertine that it had been so to speak the national anthem of the love of Swann and Odette, "the parents of Gilberte whom you know. You told me that she was not a bad girl. But didn't she attempt to have relations with you? She has mentioned you to me." "Yes, you see, her parents used to send a carriage to fetch her from our lessons when the weather was bad, I believe she took me home once and kissed me," she said, after a momentary pause, with a laugh, and as though it were an amusing confession. "She asked me all of a sudden whether I was fond of women." (But if she only believed that she remembered that Gilberte had taken her home, how could she say with such precision that Gilberte had asked her this odd question?) "In fact, I don't know what absurd idea came into my head to make a fool of her, I told her that I was." (One would have said that Albertine was afraid that Gilberte had told me this and did not wish me to come to the conclusion that

235

she was lying.) "But we did nothing at all." (It was strange, if they had exchanged confidences, that they should have done nothing, especially as, before this, they had kissed, according to Albertine.) "She took me home like that four or five times, perhaps more, and that is all." It cost me a great effort not to ply her with further questions, but, mastering myself so as to appear not to be attaching any importance to all this, I returned to Thomas Hardy. "Do you remember the stonemasons in *Jude the Obscure,* in *The Well-Beloved,* the blocks of stone which the father hews out of the island coming in boats to be piled up in the son's studio where they are turned into statues; in *A Pair of Blue Eyes* the parallelism of the tombs, and also the parallel line of the vessel, and the railway coaches containing the lovers and the dead woman; the parallelism between *The Well-Beloved,* where the man is in love with three women, and *A Pair of Blue Eyes* where the woman is in love with three men, and in short all those novels which can be laid one upon another like the vertically piled houses upon the rocky soil of the island. I cannot summarise the greatest writers like this in a moment's talk, but you would see in Stendhal a certain sense of altitude combining with the life of the spirit: the lofty place in which Julien Sorel is imprisoned, the tower on the summit of which Fabrice is confined, the belfry in which the Abbé Blanès pores over his astrology and from which Fabrice has such a magnificent bird's-eye view. You told me that you had seen some of Vermeer's pictures, you must have realised that they are fragments of an identical world, that it is always, however great the genius with which they have been recreated, the same table, the same carpet, the same woman, the same novel and unique beauty, an enigma, at that epoch in which nothing resembles or explains it, if we seek not to find similarities in subjects but to isolate the peculiar impression that is produced by the colour. Well, then, this novel beauty remains identical in all Dostoievski's works, the Dostoievski woman (as distinctive as a Rembrandt woman) with her mysterious face, whose engaging beauty changes abruptly, as though her apparent good nature had been but make-believe, to a terrible insolence (although at heart it seems that she is more good than bad), is she not always the same, whether it be Nastasia Philipovna writing love letters to Aglaé and telling her that she hates her, or in a visit which is wholly identical with this—as also with that in which Nastasia Philipovna insults Vania's family—Grouchenka, as charming in Katherina Ivanovna's house as the other had supposed her to be terrible, then suddenly revealing her malevolence by insulting Katherina Ivanovna (although Grouchenka is good at heart); Grouchenka, Nastasia, figures as original, as mysterious not merely as Carpaccio's courtesans but as Rembrandt's Bathsheba. As, in Vermeer, there is the creation of a certain soul, of a certain colour of fabrics and places, so there is in Dostoievski creation not only of people but of their homes, and the house of the Murder in *Crime and Punishment* with its dvornik, is it not almost as marvellous as the masterpiece of the House of Murder in Dostoievski, that sombre house, so long, and so high, and so huge, of Rogojin in which he kills Nastasia Philipovna. That novel and terrible beauty of a house, that novel beauty blended with a woman's face, that is the unique thing which Dostoievski has given to the world, and the comparisons that literary critics may make, between him and Gogol, or between him and Paul de Kock, are of no interest, being external to this secret beauty. Besides, if I have said to you that it is, from one novel to another, the same scene, it is in the compass of a single novel that the same scenes, the same characters reappear if the novel is at all long. I could illustrate this to you easily in *War and Peace,* and a certain scene in a carriage. . . ." " I didn't want to interrupt you, but now that I see that you are leaving Dostoievski, I am afraid of forgetting. My dear boy, what was it you meant the other day when you said: ' It is, so to speak, the Dostoievski side of Mme. de Sévigné.' I must confess that I did not understand. It seems to me so different." " Come, little girl, let me give you a kiss to thank you for remembering so well what I say, you shall go back to the pianola afterwards. And I must admit that what I said was rather stupid. But I said it for two reasons. The first is a special reason. What I meant was that Mme. de Sévigné, like Elstir, like Dostoievski, instead of presenting things in their logical sequence, that is to say beginning with the cause, shews us first of all the effect, the illusion that strikes us. That is how Dostoievski presents his characters. Their actions seem to us as misleading as those effects in Elstir's pictures where the sea appears to be in the sky. We are quite surprised to find that some sullen person is really the best of men, or vice versa." " Yes, but give me an example in Mme. de Sévigné." " I admit," I answered her with a laugh, " that I am splitting hairs very fine, but still I could find examples." " But did he ever murder anyone, Dostoievski? The novels of his that I know might all be called *The Story of a Crime.* It is an obsession with him, it is not natural that he should always be talking about it." "I don't think so, dear Albertine, I know little about his life. It is certain that, like everyone else, he was acquainted with sin, in one form or another, and probably in a form which the laws condemn. In that sense he must have been more or less criminal, like his heroes (not that they are altogether heroes, for that matter), who are found guilty with attenuating circumstances. And it is not perhaps necessary that he himself should have been a criminal. I am not a novelist; it is possible that creative writers are tempted by certain forms of life of which they have no personal experience. If I come with you to Versailles as we arranged, I shall shew you the portrait of the ultra-respectable man, the best of husbands, Choderlos de Laclos, who wrote the most appallingly corrupt book, and facing it that of Mme. de Genlis who wrote moral tales and was not content with betraying the Duchesse d'Orléans but tormented her by turning her children against her. I admit all the same that in Dostoievski this preoccupation with murder is something extraordinary which makes him very alien to me. I am stupefied enough when I hear Baudelaire say:

> Si le viol, le poison, le poignard, l'incendie
> N'ont pas encor brodé de leurs plaisants dessins
> Le canevas banal de nos piteux destins,
> C'est que notre âme, hélas! n'est pas assez hardie.

But I can at least assume that Baudelaire is not sincere. Whereas Dostoievski. . . . All that sort of thing seems to me as remote from myself as possible, unless there are parts of myself of which I know nothing, for we realise our own nature only in course of time. In Dostoievski

I find the deepest penetration but only into certain isolated regions of the human soul. But he is a great creator. For one thing, the world which he describes does really appear to have been created by him. All those buffoons who keep on reappearing, like Lebedeff, Karamazoff, Ivolghin, Segreff, that incredible procession, are a humanity more fantastic than that which peoples Rembrandt's *Night Watch*. And perhaps it is fantastic only in the same way, by the effect of lighting and costume, and is quite normal really. In any case it is at the same time full of profound and unique truths, which belong only to Dostoievski. They almost suggest, those buffoons, some trade or calling that no longer exists, like certain characters in the old drama, and yet how they reveal true aspects of the human soul! What astonishes me is the solemn manner in which people talk and write about Dostoievski. Have you ever noticed the part that self-respect and pride play in his characters? One would say that, to him, love and the most passionate hatred, goodness and treachery, timidity and insolence are merely two states of a single nature, their self-respect, their pride preventing Aglaé, Nastasia, the Captain whose beard Mitia pulls, Krassotkin, Aliosha's enemy-friend, from shewing themselves in their true colours. But there are many other great passages as well. I know very few of his books. But is it not a sculpturesque and simple theme, worthy of the most classical art, a frieze interrupted and resumed on which the tale of vengeance and expiation is unfolded, the crime of old Karamazoff getting the poor idiot with child, the mysterious, animal, unexplained impulse by which the mother, herself unconsciously the instrument of an avenging destiny, obeying also obscurely her maternal instinct, feeling perhaps a combination of physical resentment and gratitude towards her seducer, comes to bear her child on old Karamazoff's ground. This is the first episode, mysterious, grand, august as a Creation of Woman among the sculptures at Orvieto. And as counterpart, the second episode more than twenty years later, the murder of old Karamazoff, the disgrace brought upon the Karamazoff family by this son of the idiot, Smerdiakoff, followed shortly afterwards by another action, as mysteriously sculpturesque and unexplained, of a beauty as obscure and natural as that of the childbirth in old Karamazoff's garden, Smerdiakoff hanging himself, his crime accomplished. As for Dostoievski, I was not straying so far from him as you thought when I mentioned Tolstoi who has imitated him closely. In Dostoievski there is, concentrated and fretful, a great deal of what was to blossom later on in Tolstoi. There is, in Dostoievski, that proleptic gloom of the primitives which their disciples will brighten and dispel." "My dear boy, what a terrible thing it is that you are so lazy. Just look at your view of literature, so far more interesting than the way we were made to study it; the essays that they used to make us write upon *Esther:* 'Monsieur,'—you remember," she said with a laugh, less from a desire to make fun of her masters and herself than from the pleasure of finding in her memory, in our common memory, a relic that was already almost venerable. But while she was speaking, and I continued to think of Vinteuil, it was the other, the materialist hypothesis, that of there being nothing, that in turn presented itself to my mind. I began to doubt, I said to myself that after all it might be the case that, if

Vinteuil's phrases seemed to be the expression of certain states of the soul analogous to that which I had experienced when I tasted the madeleine that had been dipped in a cup of tea, there was nothing to assure me that the vagueness of such states was a sign of their profundity rather than of our not having learned yet to analyse them, so that there need be nothing more real in them than in other states. And yet that happiness, that sense of certainty in happiness while I was drinking the cup of tea, or when I smelt in the Champs-Elysées a smell of mouldering wood, was not an illusion. In any case, whispered the spirit of doubt, even if these states are more profound than others that occur in life, and defy analysis for the very reason that they bring into play too many forces which we have not yet taken into consideration, the charm of certain phrases of Vinteuil's music makes us think of them because it too defies analysis, but this does not prove that it has the same depth; the beauty of a phrase of pure music can easily appear to be the image of or at least akin to an intellectual impression which we have received, but simply because it is unintellectual. And why then do we suppose to be specially profound those mysterious phrases which haunt certain works, including this septet by Vinteuil?

It was not, however, his music alone that Albertine played me; the pianola was to us at times like a scientific magic lantern (historical and geographical) and on the walls of this room in Paris, supplied with inventions more modern than that of Combray days, I would see, accordingly as Albertine played me Rameau or Borodin, extend before me now an eighteenth century tapestry sprinkled with cupids and roses, now the Eastern steppe in which sounds are muffled by boundless distances and the soft carpet of snow. And these fleeting decorations were as it happened the only ones in my room, for if, at the time of inheriting my aunt Léonie's fortune, I had vowed that I would become a collector like Swann, would buy pictures, statues, all my money went upon securing horses, a motor-car, dresses for Albertine. But did not my room contain a work of art more precious than all these—Albertine herself? I looked at her. It was strange to me to think that it was she, she whom I had for so long thought it impossible even to know, who now, a wild beast tamed, a rosebush to which I had acted as trainer, as the framework, the trellis of its life, was seated thus, day by day, at home, by my side, before the pianola, with her back to my book-case. Her shoulders, which I had seen bowed and resentful when she was carrying her golf-clubs, were leaning against my books. Her shapely legs, which at first I had quite reasonably imagined as having trodden throughout her girlhood the pedals of a bicycle, now rose and fell alternately upon those of the pianola, upon which Albertine who had acquired a distinction which made me feel her more my own, because it was from myself that it came, pressed her shoes of cloth of gold. Her fingers, at one time trained to the handle-bars, now rested upon the keys like those of a Saint Cecilia. Her throat the curve of which, seen from my bed, was strong and full, at that distance and in the lamplight appeared more rosy, less rosy, however, than her face presented in profile, to which my gaze, issuing from the innermost depths of myself, charged with memories and burning with desire, added such a brilliancy, such an intensity of life that its relief seemed to stand out and turn with almost the same magic power as on the day, in the hotel at Balbec, when my vision was clouded by my overpowering desire to kiss her; I prolonged each of its surfaces beyond what I was able to see and beneath what concealed it from me and made me feel all the more strongly—eyelids which half hid her eyes, hair that covered the upper part of her cheeks—the relief of those superimposed planes. Her eyes shone like, in a matrix in which the opal is still embedded, the two facets which alone have as yet been polished, which, become more brilliant than metal, reveal, in the midst of the blind matter that encumbers them, as it were the mauve, silken wings of a butterfly placed under glass. Her dark, curling hair, presenting a different appearance whenever she turned to ask me what she was to play next, now a splendid wing, sharp at the tip, broad at the base, feathered and triangular, now weaving the relief of its curls in a strong and varied chain, a mass of crests, of watersheds, of precipices, with its incisions so rich and so multiple, seemed to exceed the variety that nature normally realises and to correspond rather to the desire of a sculptor who accumulates difficulties in order to bring into greater prominence the suppleness, the fire, the moulding, the life of his execution, and brought out more strongly, by interrupting in order to resume them, the animated curve and, as it were, the rotation of the smooth and rosy face, of the polished dulness of a piece of painted wood. And, in contrast with all this relief, by the harmony also which united them with her, which had adapted her attitude to their form and purpose, the pianola which half concealed her like the keyboard of an organ, the bookcase, the whole of that corner of the room seemed to be reduced to nothing more than the lighted sanctuary, the shrine of this angel musician, a work of art which, presently, by a charming magic, was to detach itself from its niche and offer to my kisses its precious, rosy substance. But no, Albertine was in no way to me a work of art. I knew what it meant to admire a woman in an artistic fashion, I had known Swann. For my own part, moreover, I was, no matter who the woman might be, incapable of doing so, having no sort of power of detached observation, never knowing what it was that I beheld, and I had been amazed when Swann added retrospectively for me an artistic dignity—by comparing her, as he liked to do with gallantry to her face, to some portrait by Luini, by finding in her attire the gown or the jewels of a picture by Giorgione—to a woman who had seemed to me to be devoid of interest. Nothing of that sort with me. The pleasure and the pain that I derived from Albertine never took, in order to reach me, the line of taste and intellect; indeed, to tell the truth, when I began to regard Albertine as an angel musician glazed with a marvellous patina whom I congratulated myself upon possessing, it was not long before I found her uninteresting; I soon became bored in her company, but these moments were of brief duration; we love only that in which we pursue something inaccessible, we love only what we do not possess, and very soon I returned to the conclusion that I did not possess Albertine. In her eyes I saw pass now the hope, now the memory, perhaps the regret of joys which I could not guess, which in that case she preferred to renounce rather than tell me of them, and which, gathering no more of them than certain flashes in her pupils, I no more perceived than does the spectator who has been refused admission to the theatre, and who, his face glued to the glass panes of the door, can take in nothing of what is happening upon the stage. I do not know whether this was the case with her, but it is a strange thing, and so to speak a testimony by the most incredulous to their belief in good, this perseverance in falsehood shewn by all those who deceive us. It is no good our telling them that their lie hurts us more than a confession, it is no good their realising this for themselves, they will start lying again a moment later, to remain consistent with their original statement of how much we meant to them. Similarly an atheist who values his life will let himself be burned alive rather than allow any contradiction of the popular idea of his courage. During these hours, I used sometimes to see hover over her face, in her gaze, in her pout, in her smile, the reflexion of those inward visions the contemplation of which made her on these evenings unlike her usual self, remote from me to whom they were denied. "What are you thinking about, my darling?" "Why, nothing." Sometimes, in answer to this reproach that she told me nothing, she would at one moment tell me things which she was not unaware that I knew as well as anyone (like those statesmen who will never give you the least bit of news, but speak to you instead of what you could read for yourself in the papers the day before), at another would describe without the least precision, in a sort of false confidence, bicycle rides that she had taken at Balbec, the year before our first meeting. And as though I had guessed aright long ago, when I inferred from it that she must be a girl who was allowed a great deal of freedom, who went upon long jaunts, the mention of those rides insinuated between Albertine's lips the same mysterious smile that had captivated me in those first days on the front at Balbec. She spoke to me also of the excursions that she had made with some girl-friends through the Dutch countryside, of returning to Amsterdam in the evening, at a late hour, when a dense and happy crowd of people almost all of whom she knew, thronged the streets, the canal towpaths, of which I felt that I could see reflected in Albertine's brilliant eyes as in the glancing windows of a fast-moving carriage, the innumerable, flickering fires. Since what is called aesthetic curiosity would deserve rather the name of indifference in comparison with the painful, unwearying curiosity that I felt as to the places in which Albertine had stayed, as to what she might have been doing on a particular evening, her smiles, the expressions in her eyes, the words that she had uttered, the kisses that she had received. No, never would the jealousy that I had felt one day of Saint-Loup, if it had persisted, have caused me this immense uneasiness. This love of woman for woman was something too unfamiliar; nothing enabled me to form a certain, an accurate idea of its pleasures, its quality. How many people, how many places (even places which did not concern her directly, vague pleasure resorts where she might have enjoyed some pleasure), how many scenes (wherever there was a crowd, where people could brush against her) Albertine—like a person who, shepherding all her escort, a whole company, past the barrier in front of her, secures their admission to the theatre—from the threshold of my imagination or of my memory, where I paid no attention to them, had introduced into my heart! Now the knowledge that I had of them was internal, immediate, spasmodic, painful. Love, what is it but space and time rendered perceptible by the heart.

And yet perhaps, had I myself been entirely faithful, I should have suffered because of infidelities which I would have been incapable of conceiving, whereas what it tortured me to imagine in Albertine was my own perpetual desire to find favour with fresh ladies, to plan fresh romances, was to suppose her guilty of the glance which I had been unable to resist casting, the other day, even when I was by her side, at the young bicyclists seated at tables in the Bois de Boulogne. As we have no personal knowledge, one might almost say that we can feel no jealousy save of ourself. Observation counts for little. It is only from the pleasure that we ourself have felt that we can derive knowledge and grief.

At moments, in Albertine's eyes, in the sudden inflammation of her cheeks, I felt as it were a gust of warmth pass furtively into regions more inaccessible to me than the sky, in which Albertine's memories, unknown to me, lived and moved. Then this beauty which, when I thought of the various years in which I had known Albertine whether upon the beach at Balbec or in Paris, I found that I had but recently discovered in her, and which consisted in the fact that my mistress was developing upon so many planes and embodied so many past days, this beauty became almost heartrending. Then beneath that blushing face I felt that there yawned like a gulf the inexhaustible expanse of the evenings when I had not known Albertine. I might, if I chose, take Albertine upon my knee, take her head in my hands; I might caress her, pass my hands slowly over her, but, just as if I had been handling a stone which encloses the

salt of immemorial oceans or the light of a star, I felt
that I was touching no more than the sealed envelope of
a person who inwardly reached to infinity. How I suffered from that position to which we are reduced by the
carelessness of nature which, when instituting the divi-
sion of bodies, never thought of making possible the inter-
penetration of souls (for if her body was in the power of
mine, her mind escaped from the grasp of mine). And I
became aware that Albertine was not even for me the
marvellous captive with whom I had thought to enrich
my home, while I concealed her presence there as completely, even from the friends who came to see me and
never suspected that she was at the end of the corridor,
in the room next to my own, as did that man of whom
nobody knew that he kept sealed in a bottle the Princess
of China; urging me with a cruel and fruitless pressure
to the remembrance of the past, she resembled, if anything, a mighty goddess of Time. And if it was necessary that I should lose for her sake years, my fortune—
and provided that I can say to myself, which is by no
means certain, alas, that she herself lost nothing—I have
nothing to regret. No doubt solitude would have been
better, more fruitful, less painful. But if I had led the
life of a collector which Swann counselled (the joys of
which M. de Charlus reproached me with not knowing,
when, with a blend of wit, insolence and good taste, he
said to me: "How ugly your rooms are!") what statues,
what pictures long pursued, at length possessed, or even,
to put it in the best light, contemplated with detachment,
would, like the little wound which healed quickly enough,
but which the unconscious clumsiness of Albertine, of
people generally, or of my own thoughts was never long

in reopening, have given me access beyond my own boundaries, upon that avenue which, private though it be, debouches upon the high road along which passes what we learn to know only from the day on which it has made us suffer, the life of other people?

Sometimes the moon was so bright that, an hour after Albertine had gone to bed, I would go to her bedside to tell her to look at it through the window. I am certain that it was for this reason that I went to her room and not to assure myself that she was really there. What likelihood was there of her being able, had she wished, to escape? That would have required an improbable collusion with Françoise. In the dim room, I could see nothing save on the whiteness of the pillow a slender diadem of dark hair. But I could hear Albertine's breath. Her slumber was so profound that I hesitated at first to go as far as the bed. Then I sat down on the edge of it. Her sleep continued to flow with the same murmur. What I find it impossible to express is how gay her awakenings were. I embraced her, shook her. At once she ceased to sleep, but, without even a moment's interval, broke out in a laugh, saying as she twined her arms about my neck: " I was just beginning to wonder whether you were coming," and she laughed a tender, beautiful laugh. You would have said that her charming head, when she slept, was filled with nothing but gaiety, affection and laughter. And in waking her I had merely, as when we cut a fruit, released the gushing juice which quenches our thirst.

Meanwhile winter was at an end; the fine weather returned, and often when Albertine had just bidden me good night, my room, my curtains, the wall above the curtains being still quite dark, in the nuns' garden next door I could hear, rich and precious in the silence like a harmonium in church, the modulation of an unknown bird which, in the Lydian mode, was already chanting mattins, and into the midst of my darkness flung the rich dazzling note of the sun that it could see. Once indeed, we heard all of a sudden the regular cadence of a plaintive appeal. It was the pigeons beginning to coo. "That proves that day has come already," said Albertine; and, her brows almost knitted, as though she missed, by living with me, the joys of the fine weather, "Spring has begun, if the pigeons have returned." The resemblance between their cooing and the crow of the cock was as profound and as obscure as, in Vinteuil's septet, the resemblance between the theme of the adagio and that of the closing piece, which is based upon the same key-theme as the other but so transformed by differences of tonality, of measure, that the profane outsider if he opens a book upon Vinteuil is astonished to find that they are all three based upon the same four notes, four notes which for that matter he may pick out with one finger upon the piano without recapturing anything of the three fragments. So this melancholy fragment performed by the pigeons was a sort of cockcrow in the minor, which did not soar up into the sky, did not rise vertically, but, regular as the braying of a donkey, enveloped in sweetness, went from one pigeon to another along a single horizontal line, and never raised itself, never changed its lateral plaint into that joyous appeal which had been uttered so often in the allegro of the introduction and in the finale.

Presently the nights grew shorter still and before what had been the hour of daybreak, I could see already stealing above my window-curtains the daily increasing whiteness of the dawn. If I resigned myself to allowing Albertine to continue to lead this life, in which, notwithstanding her denials, I felt that she had the impression of being a prisoner, it was only because I was sure that on the morrow I should be able to set myself, at the same time to work and to leave my bed, to go out of doors, to prepare our departure for some property which we should buy and where Albertine would be able to lead more freely and without anxiety on my account, the life of country or seaside, of boating or hunting, which appealed to her. Only, on the morrow, that past which I loved and detested by turns in Albertine, it would so happen that (as, when it is the present, between himself and us, everyone, from calculation, or courtesy, or pity, sets to work to weave a curtain of falsehood which we mistake for the truth), retrospectively, one of the hours which composed it, and even those which I had supposed myself to know, offered me all of a sudden an aspect which some one no longer made any attempt to conceal from me and which was then quite different from that in which it had previously appeared to me. Behind some look in her eyes, in place of the honest thought which I had formerly supposed that I could read in it, was a desire, unsuspected hitherto, which revealed itself, alienating from me a fresh region of Albertine's heart which I had believed to be assimilated to my own. For instance, when Andrée left Balbec in the month of July, Albertine had never told me that she was to see her again shortly, and I supposed that she had seen her even sooner than she expected, since, in view of the great unhappiness that I had felt at Balbec, on that night of the fourteenth of

September, she had made me the sacrifice of not remaining there and of returning at once to Paris. When she had arrived there on the fifteenth, I had asked her to go and see Andrée and had said to her: "Was she pleased to see you again?" Now one day Mme. Bontemps had called, bringing something for Albertine; I saw her for a moment and told her that Albertine had gone out with Andrée: "They have gone for a drive in the country." "Yes," replied Mme. Bontemps, "Albertine is always ready to go to the country. Three years ago, for instance, she simply had to go, every day, to the Buttes-Chaumont." At the name Buttes-Chaumont, a place where Albertine had told me that she had never been, my breath stopped for a moment. The truth is the most cunning of enemies. It launches its attacks upon the points of our heart at which we were not expecting them, and have prepared no defence. Had Albertine been lying to her aunt, then, when she said that she went every day to the Buttes-Chaumont, or to myself, more recently, when she told me that she did not know the place? "Fortunately," Mme. Bontemps went on, "that poor Andrée will soon be leaving for a more bracing country, for the real country, she needs it badly, she is not looking at all well. It is true that she did not have an opportunity this summer of getting the fresh air she requires. Just think, she left Balbec at the end of July, expecting to go back there in September, and then her brother put his knee out, and she was unable to go back." So Albertine was expecting her at Balbec and had concealed this from me. It is true that it was all the more kind of her to have offered to return to Paris with me. Unless. . . . "Yes, I remember Albertine's mentioning it to me" (this was untrue). "When did the accident occur, again? I am not very clear about it." "Why, to my mind, it occurred in the very nick of time, for a day later the lease of the villa began, and Andrée's grandmother would have had to pay a month's rent for nothing. He hurt his leg on the fourteenth of September, she was in time to telegraph to Albertine on the morning of the fifteenth that she was not coming and Albertine was in time to warn the agent. A day later, the lease would have run on to the middle of October." And so, no doubt, when Albertine, changing her mind, had said to me: "Let us go this evening," what she saw with her mind's eye was an apartment, that of Andrée's grandmother, where, as soon as we returned, she would be able to see the friend whom, without my suspecting it, she had supposed that she would be seeing in a few days at Balbec. Those kind words which she had used, in offering to return to Paris with me, in contrast to her headstrong refusal a little earlier, I had sought to attribute them to a reawakening of her good nature. They were simply and solely the effect of a change that had occurred in a situation which we do not know, and which is the whole secret of the variation of the conduct of the women who are not in love with us. They obstinately refuse to give us an assignation for the morrow, because they are tired, because their grandfather insists upon their dining with him: "But come later," we insist. "He keeps me very late. He may want to see me home." The whole truth is that they have made an appointment with some man whom they like. Suddenly it happens that he is no longer free. And they come to tell us how sorry they are to have disappointed us, that the grandfather can go and hang himself, that there is nothing in the world to keep them from remaining with us. I ought to have recognised these phrases in Albertine's language to me on the day of my departure from Balbec, but to interpret that language I should have needed to remember at the time two special features in Albertine's character which now recurred to my mind, one to console me, the other to make me wretched, for we find a little of everything in our memory; it is a sort of pharmacy, of chemical laboratory, in which our groping hand comes to rest now upon a sedative drug, now upon a dangerous poison. The first, the consoling feature was that habit of making a single action serve the pleasure of several persons, that multiple utilisation of whatever she did, which was typical of Albertine. It was quite in keeping with her character, when she returned to Paris (the fact that Andrée was not coming back might make it inconvenient for her to remain at Balbec, without any implication that she could not exist apart from Andrée), to derive from that single journey an opportunity of touching two people each of whom she genuinely loved, myself, by making me believe that she was coming in order not to let me be alone, so that I should not be unhappy, out of devotion to me, Andrée by persuading her that, as soon as there was no longer any question of her coming to Balbec, she herself did not wish to remain there a moment longer, that she had prolonged her stay there only in the hope of seeing Andrée and was now hurrying back to join her. Now, Albertine's departure with myself was such an immediate sequel, on the one hand to my grief, my desire to return to Paris, on the other hand to Andrée's telegram, that it was quite natural that Andrée and I, unaware, respectively, she of my grief, I of her telegram, should have supposed that Albertine's departure from Balbec was the effect of the one cause that each of us knew, which indeed it followed at so short an interval and so unexpectedly. And in this case, I might still believe that the thought of keeping me company had been Albertine's real object, while she had not chosen to overlook an opportunity of thereby establishing a claim to Andrée's gratitude. But unfortunately I remembered almost at once another of Albertine's characteristics, which was the vivacity with which she was gripped by the irresistible temptation of a pleasure. And so I recalled how, when she had decided to leave, she had been so impatient to get to the tram, how she had pushed past the Manager who, as he tried to detain us, might have made us miss the omnibus, the shrug of connivance that she had given me, by which I had been so touched, when, on the crawler, M. de Cambremer had asked us whether we could not "postpone it by a week." Yes, what she saw before her eyes at that moment, what made her so feverishly anxious to leave, what she was so impatient to see again was that emptied apartment which I had once visited, the home of Andrée's grandmother, left in charge of an old footman, a luxurious apartment, facing south, but so empty, so silent, that the sun appeared to have spread dust-sheets over the sofa, the armchairs of the room in which Albertine and Andrée would ask the respectful caretaker, perhaps unsuspecting, perhaps an accomplice, to allow them to rest for a while. I could always see it now, empty, with a bed or a sofa, that room, to which, whenever Albertine seemed pressed for time and serious, she set off to meet her friend, who had doubtless arrived there before her since her time was more her own. I had never before given a thought to that apartment which now possessed for me a horrible beauty. The unknown element in the lives of other people is like that in nature, which each fresh scientific discovery merely reduces, but does not abolish. A jealous lover exasperates the woman with whom he is in love by depriving her of a thousand unimportant pleasures, but those pleasures which are the keystone of her life she conceals in a place where, in the moments in which he thinks that he is shewing the most intelligent perspicacity and third parties are keeping him most closely informed, he never dreams of looking. Anyhow, Andrée was at least going to leave Paris. But I did not wish that Albertine should be in a position to despise me as having been the dupe of herself and Andrée. One of these days, I would tell her. And thus I should force her perhaps to speak to me more frankly, by shewing her that I was informed, all the same, of the things that she concealed from me. But I did not wish to mention it to her for the moment, first of all because, so soon after her aunt's visit, she would guess from where my information came, would block that source and would not dread other, unknown sources. Also because I did not wish to risk, so long as I was not absolutely certain of keeping Albertine for as long as I chose, arousing in her too frequent irritations which might have the effect of making her decide to leave me. It is true that if I reasoned, sought the truth, prognosticated the future on the basis of her speech, which always approved of all my plans, assuring me how much she loved this life, of how little her seclusion deprived her, I had no doubt that she would remain with me always. I was indeed greatly annoyed by the thought, I felt that I was missing life, the universe, which I had never enjoyed, bartered for a woman in whom I could no longer find anything novel. I could not even go to Venice, where, while I lay in bed, I should be too keenly tormented by the fear of the advances that might be made to her by the gondolier, the people in the hotel, the Venetian women. But if I reasoned, on the other hand, upon the other hypothesis, that which rested not upon Albertine's speech, but upon silences, looks, blushes, sulks, and indeed bursts of anger, which I could quite easily have shewn her to be unfounded and which I preferred to appear not to notice, then I said to myself that she was finding this life insupportable, that all the time she found herself deprived of what she loved, and that inevitably she must one day leave me. All that I wished, if she did so, was that I might choose the moment in which it would not be too painful to me, and also that it might be in a season when she could not go to any of the places in which I imagined her debaucheries, either at Amsterdam, or with Andrée whom she would see again, it was true, a few months later. But in the interval I should have grown calm and their meeting would leave me unmoved. In any case, I must wait before I could think of it until I was cured of the slight relapse that had been caused by my discovery of the reasons by which Albertine, at an interval of a few hours, had been determined not to leave, and then to leave Balbec immediately. I must allow time for the symptoms to disappear which could only go on diminishing if I learned nothing new, but which were still too acute not to render more painful, more difficult, an operation of rupture recognised now as inevitable, but in no sense urgent, and one that would be better performed in "cold blood." Of this choice of the right moment I was the master, for if she decided to leave me before I had made up my mind, at the moment when she informed me that she had had enough of this life, there would always be time for me to think of resisting her arguments, to offer her a larger freedom, to promise her some great pleasure in the near future which she herself would be anxious to await, at worst, if I could find no recourse save to her heart, to assure her of my grief. I was therefore quite at my ease from this point of view, without, however, being very logical with myself. For, in the hypotheses in which I left out of account the things which she said and announced, I supposed that, when it was a question of her leaving me, she would give me her reasons beforehand, would allow me to fight and to conquer them. I felt that my life with Albertine was, on the one hand, when I was not jealous, mere boredom, and on the other hand, when I was jealous, constant suffering. Supposing that there was any happiness in it, it could not last. I possessed the same spirit of wisdom which had inspired me at Balbec, when, on the evening when we had been happy together after Mme. de Cambremer's call, I determined to give her up, because I knew that by prolonging our intimacy I should gain nothing. Only, even now, I imagined that the memory which I should preserve of her would be like a sort of vibration prolonged by a pedal from the last moment of our parting. And so I intended to choose a pleasant moment, so that it might be it which continued to vibrate in me. It must not be too difficult, I must not wait too long, I must be prudent. And yet, having waited so long, it would be madness not to wait a few days longer, until an acceptable moment should offer itself, rather than risk seeing her depart with that same sense of revolt which I had felt in the past when Mamma left my bedside without bidding me good night, or when she said good-bye to me at the station. At all costs I multiplied the favours that I was able to bestow upon her. As for the Fortuny gowns, we had at length decided upon one in blue and gold lined with pink which was just ready. And I had ordered, at the same time, the other five which she had relinquished with regret, out of preference for this last. Yet with the coming of spring, two months after her aunt's conversation with me, I allowed myself to be carried away by anger one evening. It was the very evening on which Albertine had put on for the first time the indoor gown in gold and blue by Fortuny which, by reminding me of Venice, made me feel all the more strongly what I was sacrificing for her, who felt no corresponding gratitude towards me. If I had never seen Venice, I had dreamed of it incessantly since those Easter holidays which, when still a boy, I had been going to spend there, and earlier still, since the Titian prints and Giotto photographs which Swann had given me long ago at Combray. The Fortuny gown which Albertine was wearing that evening seemed to me the tempting phantom of that invisible Venice. It swarmed with Arabic ornaments, like the Venetian palaces hidden like sultanas behind a screen of pierced stone, like the bindings in the Ambrosian library, like the columns from which the Oriental birds that symbolised alternatively life and death were repeated in the mirror of the fabric, of an intense blue which, as my gaze extended over it, was changed into a malleable gold, by those same transmutations which, before the advancing gondolas, change into flaming metal the azure of the Grand Canal. And the sleeves were lined with a cherry pink which is so peculiarly Venetian that it is called Tiepolo pink.

In the course of the day, Françoise had let fall in my hearing that Albertine was satisfied with nothing, that when I sent word to her that I would be going out with her, or that I would not be going out, that the motor-car would come to fetch her, or would not come, she almost shrugged her shoulders and would barely give a polite answer. This evening, when I felt that she was in a bad temper, and when the first heat of summer had wrought upon my nerves, I could not restrain my anger and reproached her with her ingratitude. "Yes, you can ask anybody," I shouted at the top of my voice, quite beyond myself, "you can ask Françoise, it is common knowledge." But immediately I remembered how Albertine had once told me how terrifying she found me when I was angry, and had applied to myself the speech of Esther:

> Jugez combien ce front irrité contre moi
> Dans mon âme troublée a dû jeter d'émoi.
> Hélas sans frissonner quel cœur audacieux
> Soutiendrait les éclairs qui partent de ses yeux.

I felt ashamed of my violence. And, to make reparation for what I had done, without, however, acknowledging a defeat, so that my peace might be an armed and awe-inspiring peace, while at the same time I thought it as well to shew her once again that I was not afraid of a rupture so that she might not feel any temptation to break with me: "Forgive me, my little Albertine, I am ashamed of my violence, I don't know how to apologise. If we are not able to get on together, if we are to be obliged to part, it must not be in this fashion, it would not be worthy of us. We will part, if part we must, but first of all I wish to beg your pardon most humbly and from the bottom of my heart." I decided that, to atone for my rudeness and also to make certain of her intention to remain with me for some time to come, at any rate until Andrée should have left Paris, which would be in three weeks, it would be as well, next day, to think of some pleasure greater than any that she had yet had and fairly slow in its fulfilment; also, since I was going to wipe out the offence that I had given her, perhaps I should do well to take advantage of this moment to shew her that I knew more about her life than she supposed. The resentment that she would feel would be removed on the morrow by my kindness, but the warning would remain in her mind. " Yes, my little Albertine, forgive me if I was violent. I am not quite as much to blame as you think. There are wicked people in the world who are trying to make us quarrel; I have always refrained from mentioning this, as I did not wish to torment you. But sometimes I am driven out of my mind by certain accusations. For instance," I went on, " they are tormenting me at present, they are persecuting me with reports of your relations, but with Andrée." " With Andrée? " she cried, her face ablaze with anger. And astonishment or the desire to appear astonished made her open her eyes wide. " How charming! And may one know who has been telling you these pretty tales, may I be allowed to speak to these persons, to learn from them upon what they are basing their scandals? " " My little Albertine, I do not know, the letters are anonymous, but from people whom you would perhaps have no difficulty in finding" (this to shew her that I did not believe that she would try) " for they must know you quite well. The last one, I must admit (and I mention it because it deals with a trifle, and there is nothing at all unpleasant in it), made me furious all the same. It informed me that if, on the day when we left Balbec, you first of all wished to remain there and then decided to go, that was because in the interval you had received a letter from Andrée telling you that she was not coming." " I know quite well that Andrée wrote to tell me that she wasn't coming, in fact she telegraphed; I can't shew you the telegram because I didn't keep it, but it wasn't that day; what difference do you suppose it could make to me whether Andrée came or not? " The words " what difference do you suppose it could make to me " were a proof of anger and that " it did make " some difference, but were not necessarily a proof that Albertine had returned to Paris solely from a desire to see Andrée. Whenever Albertine saw one of the real or alleged motives of one of her actions discovered by a person to whom she had pleaded a different motive, she became angry, even if the person were he for whose sake she had really performed the action. That Albertine believed that this information as to what she had been doing was not furnished me in anonymous letters against my will but was eagerly demanded by myself, could never have been deduced from the words which she next uttered, in which she appeared to accept my story of the anonymous letters, but rather from her air of anger with myself, an anger which appeared to be merely the explosion of her previous ill humour, just as the espionage in which, by this hypothesis, she must suppose that I had been indulging would have been only the culmination of a supervision of all her actions as to which she had felt no doubt for a long time past. Her anger extended even to Andrée herself, and deciding no doubt that from now onwards I should never be calm again even when she went out with Andrée: "Besides, Andrée makes me wild. She is a deadly bore. I never want to go anywhere with her again. You can tell that to the people who informed you that I came back to Paris for her sake. Suppose I were to tell you that after all the years I've known Andrée, I couldn't even describe her face to you, I've hardly ever looked at it!" Now at Balbec, in that first year, she had said to me: "Andrée is lovely." It is true that this did not mean that she had had amorous relations with her, and indeed I had never heard her speak at that time save with indignation of any relations of that sort. But could she not have changed even without being aware that she had changed, never supposing that her amusements with a girl friend were the same thing as the immoral relations, not clearly defined in her own mind, which she condemned in other women? Was it not possible also that this same change, and this same unconsciousness of change which had occurred in her relations with myself, whose kisses she had repulsed at Balbec with such indignation, kisses which afterwards she was to give me of her own accord every day, which (so, at least, I hoped) she would give me for a long time to come, and which she was going to give me in a moment? "But, my darling, how do you expect me to tell them when I do not know who they are?" This answer was so forceful that it ought to have melted the objections and doubts which I saw crystallised in Albertine's pupils. But it left them intact. I was now silent,

and yet she continued to gaze at me with that persistent
attention which we give to some one who has not finished
speaking. I begged her pardon once more. She replied that she had nothing to forgive me. She had grown
very gentle again. But, beneath her sad and troubled
features, it seemed to me that a secret had taken shape.
I knew quite well that she could not leave me without
warning me, besides she could not either wish to leave
me (it was in a week's time that she was to try on the
new Fortuny gowns), nor decently do so, as my mother
was returning to Paris at the end of the week and her
aunt also. Why, since it was impossible for her to depart, did I repeat to her several times that we should be
going out together next day to look at some Venetian
glass which I wished to give her, and why was I com-
forted when I heard her say that that was settled? When
it was time for her to bid me good night and I kissed her,
she did not behave as usual, but turned aside—it was
barely a minute or two since I had been thinking how
pleasant it was that she now gave me every evening what
she had refused me at Balbec—she did not return my
kiss. One would have said that, having quarrelled with
me, she was not prepared to give me a token of affection
which might later on have appeared to me a treacherous
denial of that quarrel. One would have said that she
was attuning her actions to that quarrel, and yet with
moderation, whether so as not to announce it, or because,
while breaking off her carnal relations with me, she wished
still to remain my friend. I embraced her then a second
time, pressing to my heart the mirroring and gilded azure
of the Grand Canal and the mating birds, symbols of
death and resurrection. But for the second time she drew

away and, instead of returning my kiss, withdrew with the sort of instinctive and fatal obstinacy of animals that feel the hand of death. This presentiment which she seemed to be expressing overpowered me also, and filled me with so anxious an alarm that when she had reached the door I had not the courage to let her go, and called her back. "Albertine," I said to her, "I am not at all sleepy. If you don't want to go to sleep yourself, you might stay here a little longer, if you like, but I don't really mind, and I don't on any account want to tire you." I felt that if I had been able to make her undress, and to have her there in her white nightgown, in which she seemed more rosy, warmer, in which she excited my senses more keenly, the reconciliation would have been more complete. But I hesitated for an instant, for the blue border of her gown added to her face a beauty, an illumination, a sky without which she would have seemed to me more harsh. She came back slowly and said to me very sweetly, and still with the same downcast, sorrowful expression: "I can stay as long as you like, I am not sleepy." Her reply calmed me, for, so long as she was in the room, I felt that I could take thought for the future and that moreover it implied friendship, obedience, but of a certain sort, which seemed to me to be bounded by that secret which I felt to exist behind her sorrowful gaze, her altered manner, partly in spite of herself, partly no doubt to attune them beforehand to something which I did not know. I felt that, all the same, I needed only to have her all in white, with her throat bare, in front of me, as I had seen her at Balbec in bed, to find the courage which would make her obliged to yield. "Since you are so kind as to stay here a moment to console me, you ought to take off your gown, it is too hot, too stiff, I dare not approach you for fear of crumpling that fine stuff and we have those symbolic birds between us. Undress, my darling." "No, I couldn't possibly take off this dress here. I shall undress in my own room presently." "Then you won't even come and sit down on my bed?" "Why, of course." She remained, however, a little way from me, by my feet. We talked. I know that I then uttered the word death, as though Albertine were about to die. It seems that events are larger than the moment in which they occur and cannot confine themselves in it. Certainly they overflow into the future through the memory that we retain of them, but they demand a place also in the time that precedes them. One may say that we do not then see them as they are to be, but in memory are they not modified also?

When I saw that she deliberately refrained from kissing me, realising that I was merely wasting my time, that it was only after the kiss that the soothing, the genuine minutes would begin, I said to her: "Good night, it is too late," because that would make her kiss me and we could then continue. But after saying: "Good night, see you sleep well," exactly as she had done twice already, she contented herself with letting me kiss her on the cheek. This time I dared not call her back, but my heart beat so violently that I could not lie down again. Like a bird that flies from one end of its cage to the other, without stopping I passed from the anxiety lest Albertine should leave the house to a state of comparative calm. This calm was produced by the argument which I kept on repeating several times every minute: "She cannot go without warning me, she never said anything about going," and I was more or less calmed. But at once I reminded myself: "And yet if to-morrow I find that she has gone. My very anxiety must be founded upon something; why did she not kiss me?" At this my heart ached horribly. Then it was slightly soothed by the argument which I advanced once more, but I ended with a headache, so incessant and monotonous was this movement of my thoughts. There are thus certain mental states, and especially anxiety, which, as they offer us only two alternatives, are in a way as atrociously circumscribed as a merely physical pain. I perpetually repeated the argument which justified my anxiety and that which proved it false and reassured me, within as narrow a space as the sick man who explores without ceasing, by an internal movement, the organ that is causing his suffering, and withdraws for an instant from the painful spot to return to it a moment later. Suddenly, in the silence of the night, I was startled by a sound apparently insignificant which, however, filled me with terror, the sound of Albertine's window being violently opened. When I heard no further sound, I asked myself why this had caused me such alarm. In itself there was nothing so extraordinary; but I probably gave it two interpretations which appalled me equally. In the first place it was one of the conventions of our life in common, since I was afraid of draughts, that nobody must ever open a window at night. This had been explained to Albertine when she came to stay in the house, and albeit she was convinced that this was a mania on my part and thoroughly unhealthy, she had promised me that she would never break the rule. And she was so timorous about everything that she knew to be my wish, even if she blamed me for it, that she would have gone to sleep with the stench of a chimney on fire rather than open her window, just as, however important the circumstances, she would not have had me called in the morning. It was only one of the minor conventions of our life, but from the moment when she violated it without having said anything to me, did not that mean that she no longer needed to take precautions, that she would violate them all just as easily? Besides, the sound had been violent, almost ill-bred, as though she had flung the window open crimson with rage, and saying: "This life is stifling me, so that's that, I must have air!" I did not exactly say all this to myself, but I continued to think, as of a presage more mysterious and more funereal than the hoot of an owl, of that sound of the window which Albertine had opened. Filled with an agitation such as I had not felt perhaps since the evening at Combray when Swann had been dining downstairs, I paced the corridor for a long time, hoping, by the noise that I made, to attract Albertine's attention, hoping that she would take pity upon me and would call me to her, but I heard no sound come from her room. Gradually I began to feel that it was too late. She must long have been asleep. I went back to bed. In the morning, as soon as I awoke, since no one ever came to my room, whatever might have happened, without a summons, I rang for Françoise. And at the same time I thought: "I must speak to Albertine about a yacht which I mean to have built for her." As I took my letters I said to Françoise without looking at her: "Presently I shall have something to say to Mlle. Albertine; is she out of bed yet?" "Yes, she got up early." I felt arise in me, as in a sudden gust of wind, a thousand anxieties, which I was unable to keep in suspense in my bosom. The tumult there was so great that I was quite out of breath as though caught in a tempest. "Ah! But where is she just now?" "I expect she's in her room." "Ah! Good! Very well, I shall see her presently." I breathed again, she was still in the house, my agitation subsided. Albertine was there, it was almost immaterial to me whether she was or not. Besides, had it not been absurd to suppose that she could possibly not be there? I fell asleep, but, in spite of my certainty that she would not leave me, into a light sleep and of a lightness relative to her alone. For by the sounds that could be connected only with work in the courtyard, while I heard them vaguely in my sleep, I remained unmoved, whereas the slightest rustle that came from her room, when she left it, or noiselessly returned, pressing the bell so gently, made me start, ran through my whole body, left me with a throbbing heart, albeit I had heard it in a profound slumber, just as my grandmother in the last days before her death, when she was plunged in an immobility which nothing could disturb and which the doctors called coma, would begin, I was told, to tremble for a moment like a leaf when she heard the three rings with which I was in the habit of summoning Françoise, and which, even when I made them softer, during that week, so as not to disturb the silence of the death-chamber, nobody, Françoise assured me, could mistake, because of a way that I had, and was quite unconscious of having, of pressing the bell, for the ring of anyone else. Had I then entered myself into my last agony, was this the approach of death?

That day and the next we went out together, since Albertine refused to go out again with Andrée. I never even mentioned the yacht to her. These excursions had completely restored my peace of mind. But she had continued at night to embrace me in the same novel fashion, which left me furious. I could interpret it now in no other way than as a method of shewing me that she was cross with me, which seemed to me perfectly absurd after my incessant kindness to her. And so, no longer deriving from her even those carnal satisfactions on which I depended, finding her positively ugly in her ill humour, I felt all the more keenly my deprivation of all the women and of the travels for which these first warm days reawakened my desire. Thanks no doubt to the scattered memory of the forgotten assignations that I had had, while still a schoolboy, with women, beneath trees already in full leaf, this springtime region in which the endless round of our dwelling-place travelling through the seasons had halted for the last three days, beneath a clement sky, and from which all the roads pointed towards picnics in the country, boating parties, pleasure trips, seemed to me to be the land of women just as much as it was the land of trees, and the land in which a pleasure that was everywhere offered became permissible to my convalescent strength. Resigning myself to idleness, resigning myself to chastity, to tasting pleasure only with a woman whom I did not love, resigning myself to remaining shut up in my room, to not travelling, all this was possible in the Old World in which we had been only the day before, in the empty world of winter, but was no longer possible in this new universe bursting with green leaves, in which I had awaked like a young Adam faced for the first time with the problem of existence, of happiness, who is not bowed down beneath the weight of the accumulation of previous negative solutions. Albertine's presence weighed upon me, and so I regarded her sullenly, feeling that it was a pity that we had not had a rupture. I wanted to go to Venice, I wanted in the meantime to go to the Louvre to look at Venetian pictures and to the Luxembourg to see the two Elstirs which, as I had just heard, the Duchesse de Guermantes had recently sold to that gallery, those that I had so greatly admired, the *Pleasures of the Dance* and the *Portrait of the X family*. But I was afraid that, in the former, certain lascivious poses might give Albertine a desire, a regretful longing for popular rejoicings, making her say to herself that perhaps a certain life which she had never led, a life of fireworks and country taverns, was not so bad. Already, in anticipation, I was afraid lest, on the Fourteenth of July, she would ask me to take her to a popular ball and I dreamed of some impossible event which would cancel the national holiday. And besides, there were also present, in Elstir's pictures, certain nude female figures in the leafy landscapes of the South which might make Albertine think of certain pleasures, albeit Elstir himself (but would she not lower the standard of his work?) had seen in them nothing more than plastic beauty, or rather the beauty of snowy monuments which is assumed by the bodies of women seated among verdure. And so I resigned myself to abandoning that pleasure and made up my mind to go to Versailles. Albertine had remained in her room, reading, in her Fortuny gown. I asked her if she would like to go with me to Versailles. She had the charming quality of being always ready for anything, perhaps because she had been accustomed in the past to spend half her time as the guest of other people, and, just as she had made up her mind to come to Paris, in two minutes, she said to me: "I can come as I am, we shan't be getting out of the car." She hesitated for a moment between two cloaks in which to conceal her indoor dress—as she might have hesitated between two friends in the choice of an escort—chose one of dark blue, an admirable choice, thrust a pin into a hat. In a minute, she was ready, before I had put on my greatcoat, and we went to Versailles. This very promptitude, this absolute docility left me more reassured, as though indeed, without having any special reason for uneasiness, I had been in need of reassurance. "After all I have nothing to fear, she does everything that I ask, in spite of the noise she made with her window the other night. The moment I spoke of going out, she flung that blue cloak over her gown and out she came, that is not what a rebel would have done, a person who was no longer on friendly terms with me," I said to myself as we went to Versailles. We stayed there a long time. The whole sky was formed of that radiant and almost pale blue which the wayfarer lying down in a field sees at times above his head, but so consistent, so intense, that he feels that the blue of which it is composed has been utilised without any alloy and with such an inexhaustible richness that one might delve more and more deeply into its substance without encountering an atom of anything but that same blue. I thought of my grandmother who—in human art as in nature—loved grandeur, and who used to enjoy watching the steeple of Saint-Hilaire soar into the same blue. Suddenly I felt once again a longing for my lost freedom as I heard a sound which I did not at first identify, a sound which my grandmother would have loved as well. It was like the buzz of a wasp. "Why," said Albertine, "there is an aeroplane, it is high up in the sky, so high." I looked in every direction but could see only, unmarred by any black spot, the unbroken pallor of the serene azure. I continued nevertheless to hear the humming of the wings which suddenly came into my field of vision. Up there a pair of tiny wings, dark and flashing, punctured the continuous blue of the unalterable sky. I had at length been able to attach the buzzing to its cause, to that little insect throbbing up there in the sky, probably quite five thousand feet above me; I could see it hum. Perhaps at a time when distances by land had not yet been habitually shortened by speed as they are to-day, the whistle of a passing train a mile off was endowed with that beauty which now and for some time to come will stir our emotions in the hum of an aeroplane five thousand feet up, with the thought that the distances traversed in this vertical journey are the same as those on the ground, and that in this other direction, where the measurements appeared to us different because it had seemed impossible to make the attempt, an aeroplane at five thousand feet is no farther away than a train a mile off, is indeed nearer, the identical trajectory occurring in a purer medium, with no separation of the traveller from his starting point, just as on the sea or across the plains, in calm weather, the wake of a ship that is already far away or the breath of a single zephyr will furrow the ocean of water or of grain.

" After all neither of us is really hungry, we might have looked in at the Verdurins'," Albertine said to me, " this is their day and their hour." " But I thought you were angry with them? " " Oh! There are all sorts of stories about them, but really they're not so bad as all that. Madame Verdurin has always been very nice to me.

Besides, one can't keep on quarrelling all the time with everybody. They have their faults, but who hasn't?" "You are not dressed, you would have to go home and dress, that would make us very late." I added that I was hungry. "Yes, you are right, let us eat by ourselves," replied Albertine with that marvellous docility which continued to stupefy me. We stopped at a big pastrycook's, situated almost outside the town, which at that time enjoyed a certain reputation. A lady was leaving the place, and asked the girl in charge for her things. And after the lady had gone, Albertine cast repeated glances at the girl as though she wished to attract her attention while the other was putting away cups, plates, cakes, for it was getting late. She came near me only if I asked for something. And what happened then was that as the girl, who moreover was extremely tall, was standing up while she waited upon us and Albertine was seated beside me, each time, Albertine, in an attempt to attract her attention, raised vertically towards her a sunny gaze which compelled her to elevate her pupils to an even higher angle since, the girl being directly in front of us, Albertine had not the remedy of tempering the angle with the obliquity of her gaze. She was obliged, without raising her head unduly, to make her eyes ascend to that disproportionate height at which the girl's eyes were situated. Out of consideration for myself, Albertine lowered her own at once, and, as the girl had paid her no attention, began again. This led to a series of vain imploring elevations before an inaccessible deity. Then the girl had nothing left to do but to put straight a big table, next to ours. Now Albertine's gaze need only be natural. But never once did the girl's eyes rest upon my mistress.

This did not surprise me, for I knew that the woman, with whom I was slightly acquainted, had lovers, although she was married, but managed to conceal her intrigues completely, which astonished me vastly in view of her prodigious stupidity. I studied the woman while we finished eating. Concentrated upon her task, she was almost impolite to Albertine, in the sense that she had not a glance to spare for her, not that Albertine's attitude was not perfectly correct. The other arranged things, went on arranging things, without letting anything distract her. The counting and putting away of the coffee-spoons, the fruit-knives, might have been entrusted not to this large and handsome woman, but, by a "labour-saving" device, to a mere machine, and you would not have seen so complete an isolation from Albertine's attention, and yet she did not lower her eyes, did not let herself become absorbed, allowed her eyes, her charms to shine in an undivided attention to her work. It is true that if this woman had not been a particularly foolish person (not only was this her reputation, but I knew it by experience), this detachment might have been a supreme proof of her cunning. And I know very well that the stupidest person, if his desire or his pocket is involved, can, in that sole instance, emerging from the nullity of his stupid life, adapt himself immediately to the workings of the most complicated machinery; all the same, this would have been too subtle a supposition in the case of a woman as idiotic as this. Her idiocy even assumed the improbable form of impoliteness! Never once did she look at Albertine whom, after all, she could not help seeing. It was not very flattering for my mistress, but, when all was said, I was delighted that Albertine should receive this

little lesson and should see that frequently women paid
no attention to her. We left the pastry-cook's, got into
our carriage and were already on our way home when I
was seized by a sudden regret that I had not taken the
waitress aside and begged her on no account to tell the
lady who had come out of the shop as we were going in
my name and address, which she must know because of
the orders I had constantly left with her. It was indeed
undesirable that the lady should be enabled thus to learn,
indirectly, Albertine's address. But I felt that it would
be a waste of time to turn back for so small a matter, and
that I should appear to be attaching too great an importance to it in the eyes of the idiotic and untruthful waitress. I decided, finally, that I should have to return
there, in a week's time, to make this request, and that
it was a great bore, since one always forgot half the things
that one had to say, to have to do even the simplest
things in instalments. In this connexion, I cannot tell
you how densely, now that I come to think of it, Albertine's life was covered in a network of alternate, fugitive,
often contradictory desires. No doubt falsehood complicated this still further, for, as she retained no accurate
memory of our conversations, when she had said to me:
" Ah! That's a pretty girl, if you like, and a good golfer,"
and I had asked the girl's name, she had answered with
that detached, universal, superior air of which no doubt
there is always enough and to spare, for every liar of this
category borrows it for a moment when he does not wish
to answer a question, and it never fails him: " Ah! That
I don't know" (with regret at her inability to enlighten
me). " I never knew her name, I used to see her on the
golf course, but I didn't know what she was called ";—

if, a month later, I said to her: "Albertine, you remember that pretty girl you mentioned to me, who plays golf so well," "Ah, yes," she would answer without thinking: "Emilie Daltier, I don't know what has become of her." And the lie, like a line of earthworks, was carried back from the defence of the name, now captured, to the possibilities of meeting her again. "Oh, I can't tell you, I never knew her address. I never see anybody who could tell you. Oh, no! Andrée never knew her. She wasn't one of our little band, now so scattered." At other times the lie took the form of a base admission: "Ah! If I had three hundred thousand francs a year. . . ." She bit her lip. "Well? What would you do then?" "I should ask you," she said, kissing me as she spoke, "to allow me to remain with you always. Where else could I be so happy?" But, even when one took her lies into account, it was incredible how spasmodic her life was, how fugitive her strongest desires. She would be mad about a person whom, three days later, she would refuse to see. She could not wait for an hour while I sent out for canvas and colours, for she wished to start painting again. For two whole days she was impatient, almost shed the tears, quickly dried, of an infant that has just been weaned from its nurse. And this instability of her feelings with regard to people, things, occupations, arts, places, was in fact so universal that, if she did love money, which I do not believe, she cannot have loved it for longer than anything else. When she said: "Ah! If I had three hundred thousand francs a year!" or even if she expressed a bad but very transient thought, she could not have attached herself to it any longer than to the idea

of going to Les Rochers, of which she had seen an engraving in my grandmother's edition of Mme. de Sévigné,
of meeting an old friend from the golf course, of going up
in an aeroplane, of going to spend Christmas with her
aunt, or of taking up painting again.

We returned home very late one evening while, here
and there, by the roadside, a pair of red breeches pressed
against a skirt revealed an amorous couple.   Our carriage
passed in through the Porte Maillot.   For the monuments
of Paris had been substituted, pure, linear, without depth,
a drawing of the monuments of Paris, as though in an
attempt to recall the appearance of a city that had been
destroyed.   But, round about this picture, there stood
out so delicately the pale-blue mounting in which it was
framed that one's greedy eyes sought everywhere for
a further trace of that delicious shade which was too
sparingly measured out to them: the moon was shining.
Albertine admired the moonlight.   I dared not tell her
that I would have admired it more if I had been alone,
or in quest of a strange woman.   I repeated to her poetry
or passages of prose about moonlight, pointing out to her
how from " silvery " which it had been at one time, it had
turned " blue " in Chateaubriand, in the Victor Hugo of
Eviradnus and *La Fête chez Thérèse,* to become in turn
yellow and metallic in Baudelaire and Leconte de Lisle.
Then, reminding her of the image that is used for the
crescent moon at the end of *Booz endormi,* I repeated the
whole of that poem to her.   And so we came to the house.
The fine weather that night made a leap forwards as the
mercury in the thermometer darts upward.   In the early-
rising mornings of spring that followed, I could hear the
tramcars moving, through a cloud of perfumes, in an air

with which the prevailing warmth became more and more blended until it reached the solidification and density of noon. When the unctuous air had succeeded in varnishing with it and isolating in it the scent of the wash-stand, the scent of the wardrobe, the scent of the sofa, simply by the sharpness with which, vertical and erect, they stood out in adjacent but distinct slices, in a pearly chiaroscuro which added a softer glaze to the shimmer of the curtains and the blue satin armchairs, I saw myself, not by a mere caprice of my imagination, but because it was physically possible, following in some new quarter of the suburbs, like that in which Bloch's house at Balbec was situated, the streets blinded by the sun, and finding in them not the dull butchers' shops and the white freestone facings, but the country dining-room which I could reach in no time, and the scents that I would find there on my arrival, that of the bowl of cherries and apricots, the scent of cider, that of gruyère cheese, held in suspense in the luminous congelation of shadow which they delicately vein like the heart of an agate, while the knife-rests of prismatic glass scatter rainbows athwart the room or paint the waxcloth here and there with peacock-eyes. Like a wind that swells in a regular progression, I heard with joy a motor-car beneath the window. I smelt its odour of petrol. It may seem regrettable to the oversensitive (who are always materialists) for whom it spoils the country, and to certain thinkers (materialists after their own fashion also) who, believing in the importance of facts, imagine that man would be happier, capable of higher flights of poetry, if his eyes were able to perceive more colours, his nostrils to distinguish more scents, a philosophical adaptation of the simple thought of those who believe that life was finer when men wore, instead of the black coats of to-day, sumptuous costumes. But to me (just as an aroma, unpleasant perhaps in itself, of naphthaline and flowering grasses would have thrilled me by giving me back the blue purity of the sea on the day of my arrival at Balbec), this smell of petrol which, with the smoke from the exhaust of the car, had so often melted into the pale azure, on those scorching days when I used to drive from Saint-Jean de la Haise to Gourville, as it had accompanied me on my excursions during those summer afternoons when I had left Albertine painting, called into blossom now on either side of me, for all that I was lying in my darkened bedroom, cornflowers, poppies and red clover, intoxicated me like a country scent, not circumscribed and fixed, like that which is spread before the hawthorns and, retained in its unctuous and dense elements, floats with a certain stability before the hedge, but like a scent before which the roads took flight, the sun's face changed, castles came hurrying to meet me, the sky turned pale, force was increased tenfold, a scent which was like a symbol of elastic motion and power, and which revived the desire that I had felt at Balbec, to enter the cage of steel and crystal, but this time not to go any longer on visits to familiar houses with a woman whom I knew too well, but to make love in new places with a woman unknown. A scent that was accompanied at every moment by the horns of passing motors, which I set to words like a military call: "Parisian, get up, get up, come out and picnic in the country, and take a boat on the river, under the trees, with a pretty girl; get up, get up!" And all these musings were so agreeable that I congratulated myself upon the "stern decree" which prescribed that until I should have rung my bell, no "timid mortal", whether Françoise or Albertine, should dream of coming in to disturb me "within this palace" where

> ". . . a terrible
> Majesty makes me all invisible
> To my subjects."

But all of a sudden the scene changed; it was the memory, no longer of old impressions, but of an old desire, quite recently reawakened by the Fortuny gown in blue and gold, that spread itself before me, another spring, a spring not leafy at all but suddenly stripped, on the contrary, of its trees and flowers by the name that I had just uttered to myself: "Venice", a decanted spring, which is reduced to its essential qualities, and expresses the lengthening, the warming, the gradual maturing of its days by the progressive fermentation, not (this time) of an impure soil, but of a blue and virgin water, springlike without bud or blossom, which could answer the call of May only by gleaming facets, carved by that month, harmonising exactly with it in the radiant, unaltering nakedness of its dusky sapphire. And so, no more than the seasons to its unflowering inlets of the sea, do modern years bring any change to the gothic city; I knew it, I could not imagine it, but this was what I longed to contemplate with the same desire which long ago, when I was a boy, in the very ardour of my departure had shattered the strength necessary for the journey; I wished to find myself face to face with my Venetian imaginings, to behold how that divided sea enclosed in its meanderings, like the streams of Ocean, an urbane and refined civilisation, but one that, isolated by their azure belt, had developed by itself, had had its own schools of painting and architecture, to admire that fabulous garden of fruits and birds in coloured stone, flowering in the midst of the sea which kept it refreshed, splashed with its tide against the base of the columns and, on the bold relief of the capitals, like a dark blue eye watching in the shadows, laid patches, which it kept perpetually moving, of light. Yes, I must go, the time had come. Now that Albertine no longer appeared to be cross with me, the possession of her no longer seemed to me a treasure in exchange for which we are prepared to sacrifice every other. For we should have done so only to rid ourself of a grief, an anxiety which were now appeased. We have succeeded in jumping through the calico hoop through which we thought for a moment that we should never be able to pass. We have lightened the storm, brought back the serenity of the smile. The agonising mystery of a hatred without any known cause, and perhaps without end, is dispelled. Henceforward we find ourself once more face to face with the problem, momentarily thrust aside, of a happiness which we know to be impossible. Now that life with Albertine had become possible once again, I felt that I could derive nothing from it but misery, since she did not love me; better to part from her in the pleasant moment of her consent which I should prolong in memory. Yes, this was the moment; I must make quite certain of the date on which Andrée was leaving Paris, use all my influence with Mme. Bontemps to make sure that at that moment Albertine should not be able to go either to Holland or to Montjouvain. It would fall to our lot, were we better able to analyse our loves, to see that often women rise in our estimation only because of the dead

283

weight of men with whom we have to compete for them, although we can hardly bear the thought of that competition; the counterpoise removed, the charm of the woman declines. We have a painful and salutary example of this in the predilection that men feel for the women who, before coming to know them, have gone astray, for those women whom they feel to be sinking in perilous quicksands and whom they must spend the whole period of their love in rescuing; a posthumous example, on the other hand, and one that is not at all dramatic, in the man who, conscious of a decline in his affection for the woman whom he loves, spontaneously applies the rules that he has deduced, and, to make sure of his not ceasing to love the woman, places her in a dangerous environment from which he is obliged to protect her daily. (The opposite of the men who insist upon a woman's retiring from the stage even when it was because of her being upon the stage that they fell in love with her.)

When in this way there could be no objection to Albertine's departure, I should have to choose a fine day like this—and there would be plenty of them before long —one on which she would have ceased to matter to me, on which I should be tempted by countless desires, I should have to let her leave the house without my seeing her, then, rising from my bed, making all my preparations in haste, leave a note for her, taking advantage of the fact that as she could not for the time being go to any place the thought of which would upset me, I might be spared, during my travels, from imagining the wicked things that she was perhaps doing—which for that matter seemed to me at the moment to be quite unimportant—and, without seeing her again, might leave for Venice.

I rang for Françoise to ask her to buy me a guide-book and a time-table, as I had done as a boy, when I wished to prepare in advance a journey to Venice, the realisation of a desire as violent as that which I felt at this moment; I forgot that, in the interval, there was a desire which I had attained, without any satisfaction, the desire for Balbec, and that Venice, being also a visible phenomenon, was probably no more able than Balbec to realise an ineffable dream, that of the gothic age, made actual by a springtime sea, and coming at moments to stir my soul with an enchanted, caressing, unseizable, mysterious, confused image. Françoise having heard my ring came into the room, in considerable uneasiness as to how I would receive what she had to say and what she had done. "It has been most awkward," she said to me, "that Monsieur is so late in ringing this morning. I didn't know what I ought to do. This morning at eight o'clock Mademoiselle Albertine asked me for her trunks, I dared not refuse her, I was afraid of Monsieur's scolding me if I came and waked him. It was no use my putting her through her catechism, telling her to wait an hour because I expected all the time that Monsieur would ring; she wouldn't have it, she left this letter with me for Monsieur, and at nine o'clock off she went." Then—so ignorant may we be of what we have within us, since I was convinced of my own indifference to Albertine—my breath was cut short, I gripped my heart in my hands suddenly moistened by a perspiration which I had not known since the revelation that my mistress had made on the little tram with regard to Mlle. Vinteuil's friend, without my being able to say anything else than: "Ah! Very good, you did quite right not to wake me, leave me now for a little, I shall ring for you presently."

Printed in Great Britain by R. & R CLARK LIMITED, *Edinburgh.*